Bitsey Gagne

EVANGELINE

SHORES OF FOREVER

EVANGELINE

SHORES OF FOREVER

BITSEY GAGNE

This book is a work of fiction. The characters, incidents, and dialogue are drawn from the author's imagination. They are not real. Any resemblance to actual events or persons, living or dead, is entirely coincidental.

Evangeline Shores of Forever.

Self-Published by Kindle Direct Publishing.

Edited by Mary Dempsey

Illustrations by Katie Ferree

ISBN #979-8-988-5007-0-4

This book is fondly dedicated to Terri Domenici, my childhood friend and a fellow writer who has stood by me through all the trials and tribulations of rewriting this novel. I will always think of our cozy afternoons brainstorming on how to make this a better book. You have supported me by always offering helpful solutions, and you told me to never give up on my dream of creating my book.

We've been to writer's conferences together and a whole lot more, growing up together in our quaint neighborhood of Ripley, Maryland. Our childhood is much like my character's childhood. From the day we met, we became lifelong friends, and I am grateful for your friendship and help with writing this book.

Thank you so much.

Fairy dust filters

through the sunbeams

and leaves magical prisms

of light.

Everything mystical

becomes lost in a

Cluster of Spellbinding Allusions.

—Bitsey Gagne

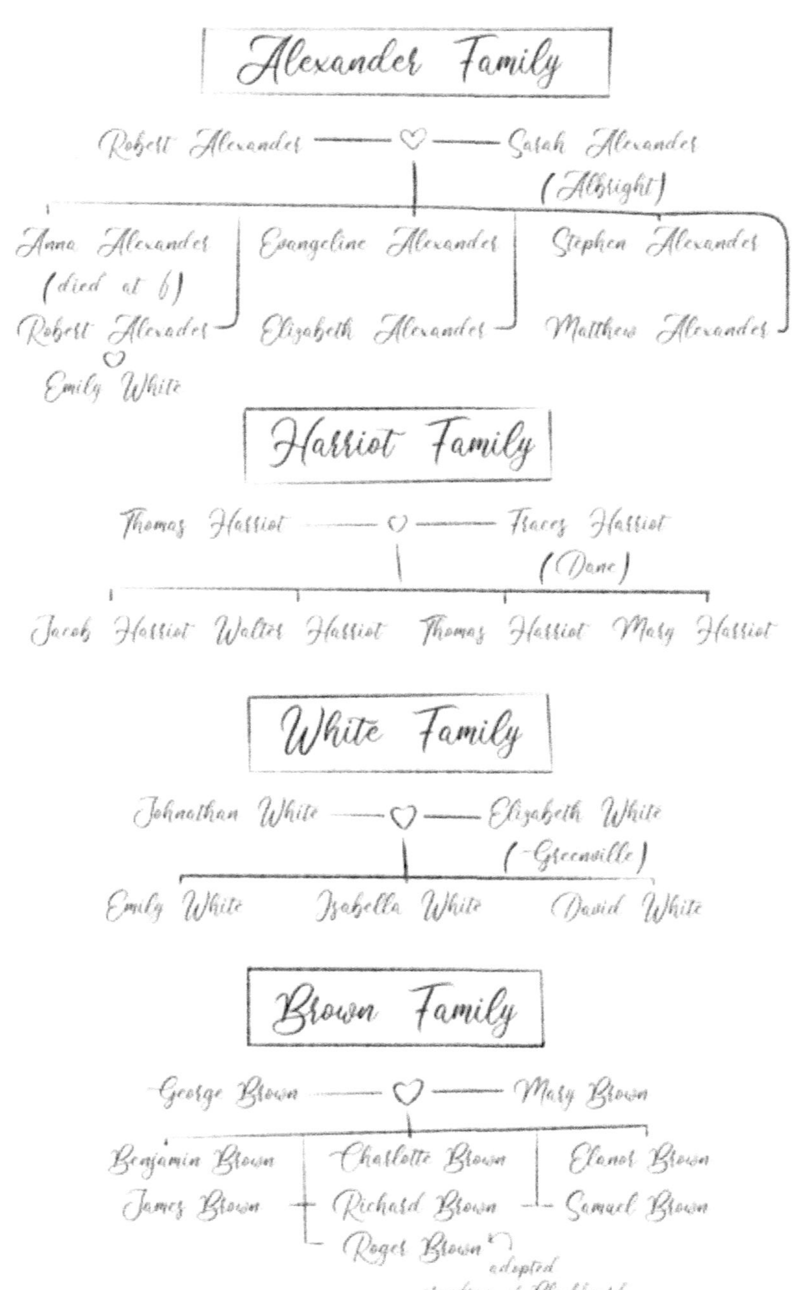
Alexander Family
Robert Alexander
Sarah Alexander
(Albright)
Anna Alexander
(died at 6)
Evangeline Alexander
Stephen Alexander
Robert Alexader
Elizabeth Alexander
Matthew Alexander
Emily White
Harriot Family
Thomas Harriot
Tracey Harriot
(Dane)
Jacob Harriot
Walter Harriot
Thomas Harriot
Mary Harriot
White Family
Johnathan White
Elizabeth White
(Greenville)
Emily White
Isabella White
David White
Brown Family
George Brown
Mary Brown
Benjamin Brown
Charlotte Brown
Elanor Brown
James Brown
Richard Brown
Samuel Brown
Roger Brown*
adopted
grandson of Blackbeard

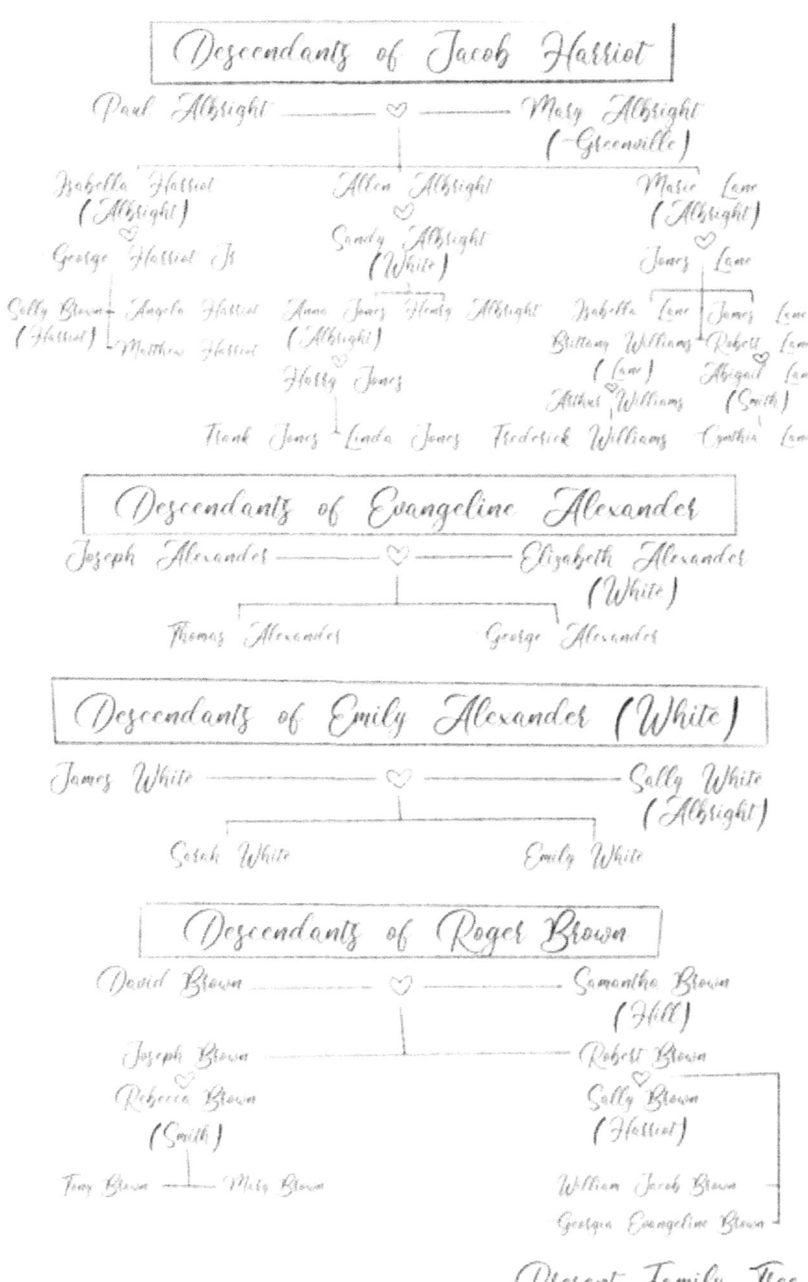

Present Family Tree

TABLE OF CONTENTS

Chapter 1

Coming Home Again

After a long drive down Highway 168, I merge onto Highway 12, but I still have quite a distance left to go. Coquina Beach is ahead on my left. In the distance on my right, I see Bodie Island Lighthouse, the beacon for all who enter Pamlico Sound. It beckons us home.

I open the windows of my forest green Mustang and breathe. The crisp aroma of the sea breeze—fresh and briny—revitalizes me as I drive down the winding road. The seagrass is blowing wildly on the sandy shore. The smell of fresh pines hits me as I slide past the cedars that line the somewhat lonely highway. I am anxious to reach Ocracoke Island, my destination.

Like a glass of Chardonnay, the salty bouquet of the Atlantic always calms me. I can't believe this day is happening. I have always dreamed of making Ocracoke Island my home, even if just for the summer.

I feel giddy with excitement about returning to the Oxford Pub to play my music. The metal clasps of my guitar case sparkle gold as the dwindling sunlight flashes over them, and my fingers tingle at the thought of playing for the locals and the visitors. The visitors love the island almost as much as I do.

I have always called this place the Shores of Forever. Why? Because the island is loaded with rich history. Because its banks hold mystical and magical mysteries.

My grandfather, Paul Albright, used tell us how there were three Bodie lighthouses built. The first two went up on Pea Island. One had to be abandoned after it started to tilt, like the Leaning Tower of Pisa. That was in 1859. The second lighthouse was blown up by the Confederates during the Civil War. The third lighthouse stands near the Oregon Inlet. There are over 200 steps to reach its top. When we were children, we counted the steps as we climbed them on one of our annual family trips.

The islands of the Outer Banks possess so much history—and so many secrets. Blackbeard's treasures. The Lost Colonists of Roanoke Island and the First Flight of the Wright Brothers. When my siblings, our friends, and I were younger, we sat for hours next to a roaring bonfire on the quiet beach of Ocracoke Island, mesmerized by tales of buried pirate treasure and ghosts searching for lost loves.

Today, as I pass the Oregon Inlet Fishing Dock on my right, I see that most of the boats are out. The fishing charters with their weary anglers should be returning to the graying docks soon with crazy stories about the one that got away.

My car starts over the Bonner Bridge. Wait. That's right, they changed the name, but I can't remember what they call it now. The metal grates rattle and my tires vibrate as I rumble over the grilles. On either side of the picturesque bridge, powerful dredgers are operating at full force, carving out placid canals. Whitecaps splash over the slippery rocks along the roaring oceanside while gentle water laps the peaceful shore on the sound side. I sigh. A calmness washes over me. My tense shoulders relax. I eat up the views.

Instinctively, I feel like I should duck my head when white and gray seagulls fly in front of my car. I leave the windows down, and the cool ocean breeze ripples through my long black hair as I cross the arched bridge that leads to Hatteras Island. Waves, Rodanthe, and Salvo are the popular beaches for both tourists and anglers on Hatteras Island. Visitors mob these pristine areas in the summer to enjoy the idyllic ocean and estuarine shorelines. In spring and fall, the same magnificent beaches are practically empty, despite the year-round natural beauty of the sandy shores.

This is an area where majestic sunrises shine over the ocean and the ripples off powerful incoming waves twinkle like gold coins. On the other side, sunsets melt into the Pamlico Sound in a riot of glorious colors—orange, tangerine, lavender, and copper. No two sunrises or sunsets are ever the same. Photographers, locals, and tourists throng to the shores to try to capture the glory of a perfect shot. I am one of them.

No one knows how many priceless sunken treasures have been lost in these treacherous waters. Outer Banks coastlines have caused over six hundred now-unseen shipwrecks, maybe more. Many careless vessels have been lost in the shallow shoals and dangerous waterways, giving this unusually disastrous coastline its nickname: the Graveyard of the Atlantic.

Pirates used to roam freely on these islands, nearly three hundred years ago. Blackbeard being one of them, and there are people who believe the mighty shipwrecks still safeguard hidden treasures. Zealous scuba divers poke around the wreckages in search of forgotten bounty. My friends and family love speculating on the treasures we might find one day.

On my right, I am passing Pamlico Sound, a beautiful tidal sound with grassy marshland surrounded by succulent reedy shores and brackish water. White egrets fly over the windswept marsh and feed in the boundless sand, devouring tiny coquina clams, small fish, and sand fleas. For birdwatchers, this wild and untamed land is a tropical paradise populated by flocks of geese, seagulls, egrets, herons, and osprey.

I think of the many days I've spent kayaking in the peaceful waterways with my family and friends as parasailers soar over the humble tributary and cheerful sound. Kayakers row out into the marshy estuary to enjoy the peaceful surroundings. In my head, I hear the birdsong of past visits.

Pea Island is coming up ahead of me. I can still remember fishing on the shoreline with my parents, older sister, and my younger brother. Those were such happy times. We loaded up the family van with all our fishing gear and a scrumptious picnic lunch. We spent the day frolicking in the briny surf, fishing, and searching for shells, sea glass, and buried treasure. At night, we feasted on freshly grilled blues, pompano, and puppy drum. The mouthwatering aromas of smoky grilled fish and early summer vegetables fill my memory.

My heart tugs when I think about my father—and his absence this year. His sudden death makes me ache. Without warning, grief reaches out and grabs me. How many more times will it leave me crippled and raw?

The next stretch of coastal road leading to Waves, Rodanthe, and Salvo feels wide open, spanning forever. Loose powdery sand blows over the road near Pea Island. At times, the over wash floods Highway 12. During bad storms, hurricanes, and nor'easters, it can be impassable. There are plans for a new bridge to bypass this area.

It's June and Hatteras Island is still fairly quiet. The tourists haven't invaded the isolated island yet. I have always loved this time of year. The air is crisp, and everything is green. Seagulls squeal over my head. It feels like a new beginning.

Oh, the memories I have of eating at Lisa's Pizzeria in Rodanthe! My mouth waters just thinking about the delicious, mind-numbing pizza. I imagine the buttery mozzarella sticks—a total comfort food—dipped in their signature marinara sauce.

Cars line the crowded parking lot at the Blue Whale. Folks come by this local mom-and-pop store to pick up ice, groceries, and drinks—or to gas up for their daily beach adventures.

There is another winding length of highway ahead of me that leads to Avon. I am becoming impatient. I can't wait to reach Ocracoke Island. I had planned to stop in Avon for supplies, but I think I'll wait until I get to Cape Hatteras. I can go to Conners in Buxton. I love to shop at the local businesses. As I drive by, I see that one of my favorite restaurants, Diamond Shoals, is already packed for an early dinner.

I pull into the parking lot of Conners Grocery Store and, as I get out of my car, I stretch my pale arms over my windblown head. It's warm today. It must be at least 75 degrees. I look up at a blue sky; the sun feels so good on my face. I take a quick trip into the quaint country store to gather up a few much-needed items. My supply of my favorite coconut-scented sunscreen needs replenishing, and I need to pick up some razors so I can have baby smooth legs, not that I am planning to attract anyone. The air conditioner leaves goosebumps on my legs as I race down the aisles.

Sheila is working the register. She hugs me.

"I spoke to Sarah, and Emily," she says, grinning as she gives me a thumbs up. "I heard you are going to be playing your music at the Oxford Pub this summer. For sure, I'll be down there to watch you play.

"Angie, I just can't wait," she adds. "It's always so much fun listening to you sing."

Shelia grew up on Ocracoke Island but comes to the mainland to work in the store. In her shorts and navy-blue uniform smock, her long legs—tanned and muscular—are on show. She swims and surfs on the beach, keeping active.

"Did you get your invitation to Sally's surprise baby shower, yet? I'll be playing after the shower that night," I say as she bags my groceries. "And I don't know if you heard, but Sally is throwing a surprise 30th birthday party for her husband, Robert. Neither knows that they are planning surprises for each other. It should be great fun."

Shelia pulls a folded invitation from the worn pocket of her smock. "That's so funny. I just got the invitation in the mail yesterday. I was planning to RSVP today. I've known Robert and Sally since we were teenagers. I wouldn't miss it for the world."

Passing Buxton Village Bookstore reminds me of many a summer day with my sister, Sally, combing through the store. One day when I finish my novel, I hope the owner, Gigi, will let do a book signing and sell my novel from her shop, which is jammed with books, a reader's treasure trove. Gigi is great —friendly and always ready with a smile—but before I talk about *my* book with her, I guess I need to get started on the writing!

I finally reach the ferry entrance. There is a line, but it is a short one because the morning rush is over. The smell of diesel fuel brings back fond and distant memories. It amazes me how certain scents will carry me back to earlier times. My family and I always enjoyed riding the ferry to our summer beach home on Ocracoke Island. Most day trippers have already gone over to Ocracoke and will be heading back on the returning ferry shortly. I remember one time my sister and I almost missed the ferry back to the island because we lost track of time.

The broad bargelike ferry chugs into the sunbaked port and I drive aboard. The attendants guide me into a cramped parking spot at the front. That's lucky—it means I won't have to crawl past everyone else to get out of my car. Sturdy blocks are placed in front of my tires to make sure my Mustang doesn't fall into the surf.

This is the last leg of my trip. I am so looking forward to seeing my friends.

Out of the car, I stretch my legs. I'm achy from sitting for so long. It's splendid to feel the sun on my face and warm summer breezes brush through my long wavy hair. The tug horn deafens me as we pull away from the dock. We slide over a fresh wake from another passing ferry, and saltwater splashes up on me. The cool spray feels refreshing. Seagulls squawk overhead, wanting to be thrown morsels of food, while porpoises dance in and out of the waves, chasing our ferry.

I think about all the good things happening in my life right now. My agent has been urging me to go on tour. I don't really want to do that. I just want to write my songs and sing in my friend's small pub.

One of my truest dreams is to write a novel. I hope I can get started on it while I am here this summer. I think back to the story about one of our ancestors, Evangeline Alexander. She lost her love when she was captured by a pirate over 250 years ago. My story will be about her escapades.

It takes me about 45 minutes to get across the hypnotic, melodic Pamlico Sound. My stomach growls—I remember I haven't eaten since breakfast and that was around 5 a.m. I will have to stop at SmacNally's before I meet Emily and Sarah at their home at Shepard's Head B&B. I can already imagine the raw bar at SmacNally's, the mellow wooden restaurant at the Silver Lake dock. Sometimes bits of history just pop into my head. The original name for Silver Lake was Cockle Creek. It was changed in 1931 when the town was renamed.

All the seating at SmacNally's is outside on a deck of graying timber. The quiet coastal water here sparkles like silver coins when the sunlight hits the spectacular estuary. You can see majestic sailboats glide across the brackish water, leaving a gentle wake. Yes, I think I will stop at SmacNally's before I meet up with my friends. The restaurant starts serving lunch around 11 a.m. so I should be right on time.

Every summer since I was born, my family has spent a month on Ocracoke Island. My parents own a beach home that local lore claims belonged to a pirate back in the 1700s. I'm not sure how true that is, but my dad used to tell us that story when we were growing up. Emily and Sarah White, my sister Sally, and

I use to play on the beach, diving into the mighty tidal waves and running along the hot, sandy dunes—little freckled girls with the wind pulling at our pigtails. Even now when we get together, the beach is our magnet.

This year's stay on the island will carry sadness. As I think about my dad, a lonesome tear slips down my cheek. I swipe it away. He wouldn't want us to be heavyhearted. I grasp the heart- shaped pendant necklace that my father gave to me last summer after we arrived home from our vacation on Ocracoke Island. I remember him telling me that he had a dream that our ancestor Evangeline told him that the time was right to give me this trinket. I really didn't know what he meant by the time being right.

My father died suddenly last year, in October, and I am still haunted by the shrill ring of my phone that foggy autumn day. My mother was on the other end of the line. In a trembling voice, she told me that my father had died from a massive heart attack. The shearing pain comes back, and I feel again as if my heart has been ripped out. I haven't been able to process the loss yet. I'm counting on this trip to help me say goodbye to him.

I fight back the tears, shake away the sadness in my heart, and take a deep breath. Sometimes I think I can feel his presence. I don't know, it's just a feeling I get.

My father's death made me reevaluate my dismal life with my now ex-boyfriend, Larry. My mom never liked the way Larry spoke to me. Although he was never physically abusive, I couldn't do anything right in his eyes. He never offered me support, even when I won my songwriting award. I realized that the life I had with him over the last six years—with Larry so critical of me, even verbally abusive at times—was one I didn't want to continue.

My father's death led me to realize that I deserved more in my life. What better place than beautiful Ocracoke Island to do some soul searching?

Back in Washington, D.C., where I live, it was a fluke that I entered and won a contest for new songwriters. My cousin, Pam, told me about the contest and, on a whim, I sent a recording of one of my original songs about Ocracoke Island. It is a breezy beach tune I wrote while sitting on the seashore last summer. The contest launched my songwriting and singing career.

A couple of my songs have even reached No. 1. I still can't believe my good fortune. Some people ask why I don't go on tour. I tell them that I don't like the limelight. I just want to write and play my songs, much to my agent's disappointment. I can live comfortably on the royalties for a long while. The generous royalties are another reason I decided to move to Ocracoke Island for the summer. Emily offered me a gig singing my songs in her pub in exchange for room and board. I have played my music in clubs most of my life.

Songwriting is just part of my dream. I've always wanted to become a book author, too. Ever since I was a little girl running around the beach, I have dreamed of becoming an author of romance novels, like Nora Roberts. Maybe my first novel—about Evangeline and her boyfriend, Jacob—will make that aspiration real. I know my father would have enjoyed a book built around the stories that he and my grandfather told us. Maybe I'll dedicate the book to my father.

This island, so rich in history, feels like the right place to research my characters. I originally thought of writing a book focused on the Lost Colonists of Roanoke Island. There are so many stories in my head that long to spill out onto the page. But it's the story about Evangeline and Jacob that I love the most.

Our family is related to Evangeline and Jacob. She was a young girl who traveled across the sea with her family to this island in the 1700s. She fell in love with Jacob, one of the boys who came to America on the same ocean voyage. But theirs was a love that was never fully realized, a love that never came to fruition.

Instead, Evangeline was abducted by Daniel Teach, a pirate thought to be Blackbeard's grandson, and taken to a faraway tropical island. When she disappeared, her family thought she was dead, drowned in the surf along Ocracoke Island. Some islanders even thought she had succumbed to despair and grief at missing her dear love, Jacob.

No one realized that she had been captured.

It is rumored that she knew where Blackbeard's treasure is buried, or that she even brought some of the treasure back with her when she unexpectedly returned.

My mind snaps back to the present as the ferry heaves up to the bayside docks. Boy, I have become quite a daydreamer lately. The ferry chugs when it pulls into the barnacle-ridden cement port, and the gears grind as we arrive at the ferry landing.

My pulse picks up as we approach the docks. I am both excited and fearful. Have I made the right decision to move here for the summer? I quit a steady job playing my music and sometimes bartending at the little pub I worked for in Washington, D.C. I know I don't have to stay on the island forever, but moving here has always been my dream.

I get back into my car as they lower the orange fencing, and the attendants remove the blocks from under my tires. My tires crunch over the gravel on the pier. As I drive, I see that the parking lot is full at Ramp 72, the access point for the public beach. I pass by Springers Point and the pony stables. According to local lore, Springers Point was a local hangout for pirates back in the 1700s. The pony stables are where some of the Banker ponies—a feral breed—are kept. It is said that the wild ponies are descended from horses brought over by the Spaniards almost three hundred years ago. It is also said that Blackbeard might have buried his treasures right here on Springers Point.

The air smells of fish as I drive into the parking lot of the Ocracoke Island Visitor Center. I leave my car and take the short jaunt down the sidewalk, past the docked fishing boats, to SmacNally's Raw Bar. I'm smiling. This place has always been a favorite spot when I visit the island. Several locals I haven't seen for years are already at the pub. They greet me with open arms.

"Angie, great see you. I heard from Emily that you are moving here for the summer," says Frank, the bartender. "So, you're going to play at the Oxford Pub? I can't wait to hear you."

He pulls out my favorite beer. "Your usual? Blue Moon with an orange slice?"

I nod and he pours the frosty golden ale into a plastic pint cup then adds a juicy slice of orange. I savor that first sip. It tastes so good that I almost down the whole glass at once.

"Hey Frank," I say, as I wipe the ale from my lips, "how are the fish tacos, today? I've been thinking about them the whole way over on the ferry. I haven't eaten since breakfast and I'm starving."

"They're good as usual. Bobby brought in some fresh mahi-mahi this morning," the bartender replies. "I'll have Sandy make some for you right away. They'll be out in a second."

SmacNally's is famous for its fresh fish tacos. And rightly so, I think when I bite into a delicious taco. I grab a paper napkin to catch the juice that drips down my chin, then munch on a couple of the bar's equally famous fries.

"Oh, my heavens, Frank. This is good. I'm so glad I stopped by for lunch."

Joe, one of the other bartenders who has just arrived for his shift, gives me a hug from across the bar.

"Hey Angie. How are you doing? Emily said you're moving to the island," Joe says. "On my way to work, I heard your new song about the island on the radio. I can't wait to hear you play."

I nod. "Joe, it's great to see you, too. Yes, I'm playing every night the pub is open this summer. I'm really excited. And, yes, that song is part of my regular playlist.

"Will you and June be able to stop by sometime?" I continue.

"We'll be there Wednesday night," Joe says, grinning.

He moves away for a minute to pass a Bloody Mary to one of the locals, Bill, sitting beside me. I hear him mention a planning party by the Ocracoke Historical Society next weekend for the Blackbeard Festival in the fall. I make a mental note of it before Joe turns back to me.

"So how are you doing, Joe? I heard you and June got married," I said.

"Yeah, this past spring. It's awesome."

It is great to seeing old friends and there are lots of goodbyes as I get ready to continue on to the Shepard's Head B&B. Heading back to my car, I sprint down the gray wooden deck stairs of SmacNally's, breath in the salty air, and stop for a minute to gaze out at the sparkling water.

As I walk away from the water, I see the golf cart rental sign and, beside it, the bike rental stand. Everyone walks, bikes, or drives golf carts in the summer. It is a simple, laid-back life here on the island.

Up ahead, I catch a glimpse of the Ocracoke Lighthouse as its old lamp catches the evening sunlight. When I pass by the Ocracoke Preservation Museum on the right, I make a mental note to talk to the local curator, Mr. … Ugh. I can't remember his name.

Back in the car, it's just a short distance to Emily and Sarah's family home. My tires crunch over the oyster shell driveway leading to the Shepard's Head B&B—and my new life.

My friend Emily, her sister Sarah, my sister Sally, and I were inseparable in the summers when we were kids. We played on the shore, built sandcastles, splashed in the waves on the beach, and played dress up in Emily and Sarah's old family attic. Emily started managing the Oxford Pub a couple of years ago when her parents retired and moved to Florida. Her dad told us the pub was a local drinking hole for pirates more than two centuries ago.

Emily is the tomboy in our group. When she isn't working, she can be found on the sandy shore, surfing on her bright purple surfboard, her strawberry blonde hair in a French braid down her back. Her long-sleeved neon orange beach top makes her stand out as she waits for the next big wave. Up close, you immediately notice her bright green eyes and the freckles across her cheeks and nose. Even though she spends her days on the beach, her skin is pale.

George, her trustworthy friend, has been in the picture for years and is always by Emily's side. His blue eyes light up whenever he sees her. Everyone can see that he is in love with her, and that she is in love with him, but George and Emily have not allowed anything romantic to happen between them. Years ago, Emily told me she doubted she would ever marry. "I think I'm too picky. It will have to be a very strong person to put up with my moods," she explained.

She is a perfect bar owner, excelling at the gift of gab and making everyone who enters her pub feel at ease. Emily can be found in the pub most nights, chatting with the locals and telling stories about the legends of the island.

Sarah, meanwhile, is the romantic in her family. The older of the two sisters, she spends her days as innkeeper at Shepard's Head B&B. The friendly island business has been in the White family for over 200 years. It is said that Evangeline moved back there when she returned from being a pirate's captive. At night, Sarah lounges in the pub with Emily.

Sarah is a girly girl. In the summer, her wispy blonde hair looks the color of corn silk. Her eyes, a bright jade green, dazzle when she laughs.

Emily, Sarah, my sister Sally, my brother Matt, and I have known one another since we were babies. My parents and Emily's parents, Jim and Sally White, met before I was born. My sister is named after Sally White. Emily and Sarah's grandparents also have a vacation home on the beach.

Oh, the teenage memories I have with Sarah and Emily! We would sit on the beach around a crackling fire. If I close my eyes, I can smell the musky smoke and hear the sizzling pops of the pine needle sparks flashing against the darkness. I used to love the aroma of my t-shirt the next morning when I tossed it into the clothes hamper. I can still hear the crickets in the background as we sang love songs and beach music. I miss those days and look forward to forging many more memories this summer.

With SmacNally's in my rearview mirror, I look ahead, then round the corner of the dirt road. There before me, is the Shepard's Head B&B. I can't wait to see the girls.

Chapter 2

The Never-Ending Romance

My grandfather, Paul Albright, is a local historian who loves researching the rich history of Outer Banks. I think back to the story he would tell as we sat around beach bonfires, the story about us being descendants of the Lost Colonists. It is a mystery that long has fascinated our family: an entire settlement where everyone vanished, leaving behind only cryptic clues.

I know, how can we be descendants of people who were never found? It turns out that our ancestors are linked to the Albright family that came over on the infamous voyage in the 1500s.

One of my father's other favorite stories focused on another family story—of how Evangeline Alexander and Jacob Harriott traveled across the Atlantic Ocean, falling in love with one another. They planned to marry one day and promised their undying love to each other. Each wore a pendant necklace bearing half of a heart etched with initials. Jacob's silver pendant carried the initials EA, for his sweetheart, and Evangeline's bore a JH. The necklaces were made from a spoon Jacob got from his family's silver. He had the local silversmith shape it into the two halves of a heart. My own heart breaks for them each time I think of their love-crossed story.

I reach up to grasp the tiny half-heart pendant hanging around my neck on a silver chain. It once belonged to Jacob. It was passed down in our family, and I recall the day my dad gave it to me. He said he felt that Evangeline wanted me to have it. It makes me think again how much we will miss my father this year. Tears well up as I remember the last time we were on the island together. I take a deep breath.

Both Evangeline and Jacob were devoted to their families, and they planned to help them establish a settlement on Ocracoke Island before they got married. But their new life was hard, and both families had a difficult time adjusting to the island. Jacob's father decided his family's best chance for survival would be further inland at an existing settlement, so they packed up and moved to what is now Richmond, Virginia. Evangeline stayed on Ocracoke to help her parents set up their home and to care for the family when melancholy left her mother unable to.

Although Evangeline planned to reunite later with her love, she was distraught by Jacob's absence. When his father passed away from malaria, Jacob, as the eldest son, became the head of his household. He had no choice: He had to stay and help take care of his family.

Evangeline waited anxiously for his return. Days turned into weeks and weeks turned into months. She began to fear that he would never return for her. In her grief, she wandered the beaches of Ocracoke Island. It is said that she would sit on the beach and sing—in her beautiful, heartfelt voice—into the strong Carolina breeze. Even now, some people say they can hear her tender, woeful songs drifting through the air.

During Jacob's absence, Evangeline's mother died. Now the matriarch of the family, the young woman dedicated her life to taking care of her younger siblings. One day while walking on the beach, daydreaming about Jacob's return, Evangeline was kidnapped by pirates from the ship of Daniel Teach, said to have been Blackbeard's grandson. When they dragged her down the beach, her silver necklace was ripped from her neck. It fell onto the dunes, along with a letter she was writing to Jacob and a letter he had sent to her.

Once on the pirate vessel, Evangeline became Daniel Teach's wench. She was one of many women violently abducted on the shores by vicious pirates—except that in this case, Daniel fell in love with Evangeline. In his weakness, he wrote her love letters that carried clues about the location of Blackbeard's treasure map. Evangeline was not only beautiful, she was intelligent, and she became the most valuable captive on Daniel's ship. Because of her upbringing, she was able to teach other women on the vessel to read and write. She also served as a midwife, helping to deliver many of the babies born on Daniel Teach's vessel and, later, on the beautiful Caribbean island where she was kept.

Evangeline became a beloved member of the crew, and the islanders came to love her, too, but Daniel Teach refused to free her. She was his possession. He eventually allowed her to roam at will on the pirates' island, even as she longed for her home, family, and her beloved Jacob. She vowed to escape.

Evangeline's family and friends, meanwhile, did not realize she had been kidnapped. They believed that she had cast herself into the sea in despair over Jacob's absence. The letter and necklace they found in the dunes fed that misbelief. "Jacob, my heart is breaking. I miss you dearly. I fear I can no longer live without you," the note had said. As for the necklace, they knew it was her most valued possession and she would never just abandon it. Her death seemed the only explanation. Her family and friends mourned her.

Many years after Evangeline's capture, one of Daniel's closest companions and most-valued crew members, Roger Brown—said to be another of Blackbeard's grandsons and a distant cousin of Daniel Teach—returned from a pirating trip with the news that Daniel had drowned at sea. Before Roger Brown became a pirate, he and his adopted family had crossed the Atlantic on the same journey that brought Evangeline and her family to the Americas.

Roger knew that Teach's death meant other buccaneers would inevitably come to the pirates' island in search of Daniel's treasure. Roger had to get himself—and Evangeline—away quickly. Their lives were in danger. So, he put Evangeline aboard Daniel's ship and returned her to Ocracoke Island.

Back with her family, she moved into one of the cottages close to the Shepard's Head B&B. She brought back treasures from her days with the pirates. It is rumored that she also brought Daniel's love letters containing clues to the location of a treasure map on Ocracoke Island. The letters were said to refer to an area called Springers Point, a pirate hangout back in the day.

Evangeline brought something else with her: a beautiful, blond son named William Jacob Alexander. Locals assumed he was Daniel Teach's child. Only Evangeline and Roger knew the truth. Not even Jacob was aware that he had a son. William grew up to be a handsome man with bright green eyes like Evangeline's beloved Jacob.

Evangeline never married—her heart belonged forever to Jacob—but Roger Brown remained by her side, ever faithful to her and her son.

A lot of people tell me I am the spitting image of Evangeline. She had raven hair and blue eyes that changed like the colors of the sea. I have only seen pencil sketches of her, but I notice a slight resemblance. After returning to the island, according to the story, Evangeline resumed her role as her family's caregiver. She helped to nurture her younger siblings and new nieces and nephews.

Months after Evangeline's capture, Jacob had come back to the island to make her his wife. His heart broke when he was told that she perished in the briny sea. He returned to his home in Richmond and mourned her for years. As he waited for his heart to heal, Jacob became a woodworker for Frederick Knight and a friend of Mr. Knight's daughter, Anna. Jacob's heart would always belong to Evangeline, but he knew he could never be with her. Jacob and Anna married and raised five children together.

Jacob never learned that Evangeline had returned, alive, nor that she had given birth to his son, William.

In her later years, Evangeline moved from her cottage into the Shepard's Head B&B with her dear friend and sister-in-law, Emily White Alexander. Emily had married Evangeline's brother, Robert, and they had raised four children. My friend, Emily, is named after Emily White Alexander, her ancestor. It is said that the two Emilys, across centuries, resemble each other greatly.

Emily, Sarah, Sally, and I still love to speak of the tragic romance of Evangeline and Jacob and how Evangeline's spirit wanders the shores and the inn looking for her lost love. People on Ocracoke Island believe Evangeline hid her letters from Daniel Teach in the inn, along with the precious necklace Jacob had given her. Neither the treasures nor the letters have been found to this day.

I amuse myself with a thought: Maybe I'll do some treasure hunting this summer.

Chapter 3
Long Ago Memories

The old inn stands as it has for over three hundred years, staring out toward Silver Lake. Its glistening white windows have seen so much. You can almost feel the weight of the memories. The lower-level windows watch me as I pull into the circular oyster-shell driveway.

Sixteen years ago, when I was 10 years old, Emily, Sally, Sarah, and I had one of our many slumber parties in a second-story room at the inn. That same room, Sarah's and Emily's father told us, had once been Evangeline's. As she got older, Evangeline disliked living alone in her cottage. She moved into the inn once her son grew up and moved on. That night, at the slumber party, we could sense Evangeline's presence.

Emily, a tomboy, she did not like to play with dolls, but we all loved playing dress-up. So, we had great fun the time Emily came back from the local thrift store with a pirate's costume. She even found an eye patch. Despite the costume, she was a ridiculous pirate, calling out, "Ahoy, matey!" at intervals.

We fell onto our sleeping bags laughing hysterically that day. Then I heard something.

"Hey, I just heard a lady laughing," I remember saying.

The four of us examined the room, checking all the corners and opening the door to the hallway to see if someone was playing a trick on us. My brother, Matt, was famous for teasing us. But no one was there.

"Angie, do you think that was Evangeline?" Sarah asked. "How come you can always hear her, and we can't?"

It was just one of the many times I've heard the tinkling of Evangeline's laughter. Sometimes I even think I catch a momentary glimpse of her. But I never am afraid. I feel linked to Evangeline, like part of her soul is part of my soul. It makes no sense, but it's a feeling I get whenever I am on the island.

Now, as I look up at the B&B, I feel that same second-story window watching me. Or maybe it is Evangeline. Who knows?

I snap back to reality. The Oxford Pub sits behind the Shepard's Head B&B. The tavern was of the first drinking holes on the island, established more than three-hundred years ago. I will be able to walk from my cedar-shingled cottage, my new home, to my summer gig along the stone pathway of gray and tan pavers that links to the B&B and the pub.

I plan to stay for the summer in the same cottage that Evangeline and her son, William, shared after Roger Brown rescued her. The little cottage is as old as the pub and the inn. My small cottage is dilapidated, the screens on the porch ripped and flapping in the wind. This place truly needs work before I can move in. No one has lived in the cottage since Evangeline, although Emily's family has kept the roof shingled so the inside will not be ruined.

Emily lives in one of the other recently renovated houses attached to the pub. She and Sarah have hired a local architect, Thomas Alexander, to do the upgrade on my cottage. Strangely enough, I have never met him, even though I have been vacationing on Ocracoke Island all my life. Our paths just never crossed.

The girls tell me that he always went to soccer camp for a month in the summers, and then he moved away to the nation's capital to study architecture at Georgetown University. I probably passed him on the streets of D.C. or even rode the Metro train with him. Maybe he came into the D.C. pub when I sang. Who knows?

Emily said Thomas's idea of refurbishing the old homes and cottages has been a passion of his ever since he was a young boy running along the shores of Ocracoke Island with his younger brother, George Alexander. His dream came true when he moved back to the Island.

On one of our recent phone calls Emily teased me, "He is a real looker and quite handsome." She and Sarah tell me that Thomas is a burly six-feet four, with long blond hair that he wears in a braid most days. They describe his eyes as the color of the forest and say the hue changes from the bright green of newly buffed leaves to the color of moss that grows on stones. They claim his eyes reveal his moods and, whenever he laughs, they sparkle with golden flecks. They also tell me he is unattached.

"He said he has given up on women because he prefers the company of his golden retriever, Max," Emily explains. Boy, do I understand totally how he feels, especially since my breakup with Larry.

Thomas is working with his brother George, who has never left the island. I've known George all my life from my family's summer visits. He takes care of all the heating, air-conditioning, and plumbing jobs on Ocracoke and Hatteras islands. George also has been in the picture for years because of Emily. The two of them grew up in a tightknit community with the ocean as their playground, and they're frequently together.

George is a vibrant, muscular fellow, with bright red hair and brilliant blue eyes that light up whenever he sees Emily. He can be found most evenings at the Oxford Pub flirting with Emily, and everyone can see that he is in love with her, and that she is in love with him. But they have not allowed anything romantic to happen between them. George and his brother Thomas are partnered in a new business, In-Time Renovations and Air. My brother, Matt, is working with them. Evangeline's cottage will be their first job.

Looking away from the cottage, I stare up at the grand old home that forms the B&B. Massive white pillars support the wraparound porch with its white rocking chairs. A swing hangs from the rafters above and swivels in a gentle sea breeze. This butter cream mansion will be where I lay my head each night until my cottage is ready. I feel like I have come home.

Before I can get out of my car, the elaborate wooden door to the house swings open and Emily and Sarah bounce down the steps to greet me. Our laughter blows through the warm summer air as we hug. The flower beds are overflowing with glorious pink and white blossoms, and the fragrance of the lilac bushes and the blooming roses that border the porch hits me. The scent is heavenly.

As I embrace Emily and Sarah, I feel a weight lift from my shoulders and neck. My heart swells with love for these girls I have known my entire life.

The breakup with Larry has made the last few months rough on me. The end of our relationship had been coming for years, but it is still such a relief to be away from him. He dampened my spirit with his never-ending criticism and complaints. I hadn't realized how anxious I have been until I reached the island and the tension melted away.

Emily, Sarah, and I walk through the massive entryway of the country inn. My heart does a little flip flop and I feel goosebumps run down the back of my neck and my legs. Deja-vu. Past moments in this welcoming place rush at me. Even as a child, whenever I walked into the inn I would be overcome by this same sensation. I sometimes caught images of people from a faraway time or heard the sound of their laughter.

I realize as I stand in the inn how close I am to my father's grave. The island's little cemetery, where he is buried, is only a ten-minute walk. From the second-story of the inn, I will be able to see the cemetery in the distance.

I can't believe it has been over eight months since he has passed away on that dreary October morning. My mother, Isabella, is still struggling with the loss. She told me just a few days ago that she sometimes forgets he is gone. When she returns home from an outing, she calls out his name to tell him about her day—then she remembers. I think of how much she must miss him.

My mom keeps busy with church and the local chapter of the Ladies of the Red Hats. She has adopted Skippy and Ace, two rescue dogs she fostered, and they help her feel less lonely. The white-and-black cocker spaniels were abandoned by their previous owners. Mom takes them for walks every morning and night. She talks to my father on these walks, even though she knows there will be no answer. "Talking to him makes me feel closer to him," she explains.

I still haven't been able to properly say goodbye to my father. His death left a hole in my heart that remains. I wonder if that void will ever be filled again. I can't imagine how my mother must feel. My parents had been together since they were teenagers. They met here on the Outer Banks while vacationing with their parents. My grandfather, Paul Albright, introduced them. They were married at the Ocracoke United Methodist Church, and their wedding reception was held at the Shepard's Head Inn. They bought their island summer house long before I was born.

My grandfather and father used to spend hours theorizing about what has happened to the Lost Colonists and Blackbeard's treasure. The amount of time that they would spend researching was crazy.

This summer, my family plans to stay at the Shepard's Head B&B for a couple weeks while waiting for George to repair the air conditioner in our beach home. My parents bought the old house from my dad's family over twenty-eight years ago. My mother's siblings—Aunt Marie and Uncle Allan—and their families will be vacationing here, too, like they have every summer.

Our vacations are spent lounging on the beach and surfing in crisp waves under a brilliant sun. On rainy days, we play cards and put puzzles together. And in the evenings, we feast on freshly grilled fish that we catch in the Carolina surf. The smoky, mouthwatering flavor rushes back. Every night, we take turns cooking dinner. Scrumptious shrimp and spicy seasoned steak are some of my favorites.

We always have a great time together, and the love and laughter of the days spent with my loved ones will be forever special to me.

Sometimes our camaraderie spills over into the Oxford Pub, another of my favorite places. Last year, after a long day on the beach, my family and I pulled up to the tavern at four o'clock in the afternoon to meet the girls. We had spent the whole day body surfing in the turbulent waves. I love to body surf but have never mastered the art of standing on a surfboard. I am too clumsy. That day the ocean had been particularly rough, and we were tired and hungry. I looked forward to eating some local seafood and pub grub. My guitar was strapped to my back.

"Hey, Angie, will you play 'Sitting on the Dock of the Bay' for us?" Emily had asked, as she slid a shot of tequila across the bar to me. I guess she'd forgotten that I prefer the vodka cocktail, Lemon Drop. But I was game. I licked my hand, sprinkled salt on it, and threw back the shot with an "Up yours, ladies"—our version of "Cheers." The lime was sour, but the icy shot tasted good.

This summer my guitar and I have a more formal commitment to Oxford Pub, and I look forward to it. There will also be several special celebrations, including the surprise baby shower for my older sister Sally and her husband Robert. Mom is overjoyed awaiting the arrival of her first grandchild.

In truth, the gathering for Sally and Robert will be a surprise inside of a surprise. Robert has planned a surprise baby shower for Sally. Sally, in turn, has planned a surprise thirtieth birthday party for Robert.

Sally has had an easy pregnancy and wants to be on Ocracoke with everyone. Her doctor gave his approval for the long trek to the island, and Sarah asked the local midwife, Georgia, to be on standby in case she is needed. Georgia is an old family friend. We have known her all our lives. She has delivered many of the babies on the island, including Emily and Sarah. Believe it or not, she is also a direct descendant of Evangeline. Georgia once confided that there are times she feels Evangeline's presence, just like I do. She even channels Evangeline's midwifery knowledge. She says she can feel Evangeline's force helping her, especially during a difficult delivery.

I am looking forward to moving into my new cottage. I think it will make me feel closer to Evangeline and enable me to write my new novel. Who knows, maybe I'll even find Blackbeard's treasure!

Chapter 4

Reunion of Two Souls

Jim and Sally White, Emily, and Sarah's parents, come into the parlor and greet me with open arms. There are like second parents to me, and they have always offered their support. They were there for my family when my father died. Hugs and kisses flow freely as I say hello to my second set of parents. My heart floods with love for them.

Still hugging me, Sally White smiles. "Angie, why don't you take your things on up to your old room and get settled." She gently pats me on the cheek. "The girls will help you."

She brings back memories of when I was a little girl, of Emily and Sarah helping me drag my belongings up the ornate spiral staircase.

Giggling, laughing, and talking—all at the same time—Emily, Sarah, and I manage to lug my luggage up the beautiful white stairs. When I was young, I often pictured myself waltzing down this staircase in an ivory-colored gown on my wedding day. Oh, the dreams of a young girl. Me and marriage? That won't be happening anytime soon.

My room faces Silver Lake, and I can see the sun as it sparkles off the crystal blue water, like slivers of silver. "This is the best room in the inn. I just love the view," I tell my friends. "Sarah, I adore the quaint little touches that y'all have added."

Sarah works hard to make her guests feel welcome, and you can tell from the preparation of the rooms. She places delightful decorations that make guests special. In my room, she has arranged yellow roses and placed them in a crystal vase on the beautifully crafted wooden mantel over the old fireplace.

I catch the delicate floral scent in the air when I walk into the room. She touches one of the flowers. "I'm so glad you like it. I remembered how much you loved yellow roses."

We are animated by our reunion, and we all talk at the same time. They tell me what they have been doing since last summer. Then they turn their attention to me.

"So, what's the scoop with Larry and you?" Emily asks, patting me on the back. "Not that I'm surprised. He is such a jerk. I never liked him."

"I know you guys didn't like the way he treated me," I respond. "I guess it just took me a while to see what everyone had been trying to tell me all these years. The final straw happened when my dad died. You know, he didn't even come to the funeral with me.

"I knew then it was over between us," I added. "But, enough of that. What's been happening in town?"

Emily bounces down on the bed, twirling her long strawberry-blonde hair. "Same old, same old," she says. "The biggest thing is you agreeing to sing in the pub. The whole island has been talking about it." She winks at me. "We have a celebrity on the island. It's so cool that your songs went all the way up to Top 10 this week."

I laugh. "I don't feel any different. My agent wants me to go on tour but I'm not really into that. I'm more into playing in your family's pub." I think of how I can't wait until Sally gets here so we can all catch up.

"We're really going to have fun once Sally gets here," I tell them. "She looks so cute with her big 'ole belly. You should see her."

Sarah rearranges the flowers on the mantel. "It will be great to have the four of us back together again. When we're together, it's like we've never been apart. You two are like our sisters."

"I wonder if we'll see anyone else," I say as I rub the goosebumps on my arms. "You know, when I stay in this room, I sometimes catch a glimpse of a raven-haired woman. I guess it's Evangeline. She is always sitting over there on the window seat, gazing out, as if she is searching for something or someone.

"I feel her presence now. It's as if she wants to tell me something," I add.

Sarah touches my arm. "I can tell when it happens to you. You go into a trance for a second and drift away from us."

"Don't you guys ever see her?" I ask them with surprise.

"Sometimes, I think I see her out of the corner of my eye," Emily answers. "I can feel her and, sometimes, I can hear her singing when I am walking alone on the dunes."

Sarah hugs me. "Angie, I wish I could stay to talk to you more about your apparitions, but I've got to get downstairs. I need to take care of some things for the rest of our guests."

As Sarah walks toward the door, she turns. "We're going to have a full house this summer. I'm hiring extra staff because it is going to be so busy. A few of the locals have come to work for me.

"We'll have even more guests once Thomas and George finish the renovations on the other cottages," she continues. I am reminded that I only intend to stay in the inn until the renovation work on my cottage is finished.

Lying back on the bed, Emily crosses her hands under her head. "Dad's been helping me out in the pub, too. He said to me he really missed being here.

"He said that he and Mom might decide to stay on the island for good."

She sits up, rubbing her freckled face. "And on that note, I need to get down to the pub. We open in an hour. I have a bar to set up."

Emily reaches into the pocket of her faded jean shorts. "Angie, here's the key to your cottage. You should go check on the progress. You might even get to meet Thomas." Emily lifts her eyebrows and winks at me.

"Oh, knock it off, Emily!" I blush. She is already trying to set me up with someone.

Emily jumps up. "Will I see you at the pub for dinner?"

I shake my head, yes. "Definitely. I'm ready for some of your yummy pub food. And I definitely want to go see the cottage. See you girls in a little while."

We hug each other goodbye. 'What a wonderful world,' one of my most favorite songs, springs into my head. How lucky I am to be staying in this room, which is just as I remember with its pale yellow walls and elaborate, white crown molding. The golden oak four-poster with a feather mattress is covered in a charming patchwork quilt of cream, pale yellow, and gray. Evangeline slept in this bed. This is the room where she grew old after her son began his own life and she moved in with her sister-in-law, Emily.

When Evangeline returned to the island, Emily became her support. Local folklore has it that the two friends were so deeply linked that they could read each other's minds and feel what the other was feeling. When Evangeline disappeared, everyone believed she had drowned—except Emily. Emily always believed Evangeline was still alive. She could feel her presence.

I turn, glancing toward the window facing Silver Lake. Suddenly, a vibration runs through me. The air becomes cool, and hairs stand up on the back of my neck. I feel a presence in the room.

Startled, I look around the room. Evangeline appears before me. She is pointing toward the cottage that once belonged to her. "Angie, you must go now," she says. "The time is right. Someone there is waiting for you."

Then she vanishes. I wonder if I am going crazy. She has never spoken to me before. I grab the keys to the cottage and run down the stairs of the inn and through its massive oak door. I race across the gravel driveway. The cottage sits in front of me. The broken screen door slams behind me as I cross the small summer porch to the main wooden door into my cottage.

I turn the doorknob and energetically push the door open.

A tanned, well-built man is leaning over the old, weathered stone fireplace. As he stands up and turns toward me, I see in his muscular hand a silver chain with half a silver heart dangling from it. I reach up, grasping its twin—the fragile necklace around my neck. My beloved silver necklace exactly matches the one in his hand.

I rush across the room and reach out to touch the necklace. My fingertips graze his, and time seems to freeze as the translucent forms of a man and a woman appear. The sight makes us both gasp.

We are cast back into a bygone era, some two-hundred-and-fifty years ago. In awe, we watch as the young man bends down on one knee. He vows: "Evangeline, I will return to make you, my wife." He then pulls the two silver heart pendant necklaces from his pocket and places one around her neck. "Evangeline, my love. Wear this necklace until I can bring a ring to wed thee." He keeps the other necklace in his hand.

Evangeline drops down on her knees beside the young man and clasps his hands in hers. "Jacob, I will always be yours," she replies.

"These will remind us of our undying love for each other while I am away," Jacob replies. "I engraved my initials, JH, on your heart. EA is etched onto mine. I will wear you on my heart so that we will forever be close to one other."

We watch the interaction unfolding between the beautiful raven-haired girl and the young man with long, wavy blonde hair. Tears stream down the faces of the two young lovers as they say goodbye to each other.

Jacob wraps his arms around Evangeline and kisses her lips. The two lovers' passion is so strong that we can feel it, like a force in the room. They whisper their goodbyes, not knowing that this would be the last time they would see each other.

Suddenly, they vanish.

My hand falls and I release my hold on the necklace entwined in the muscular man's hand. I lift my eyes to meet his stormy green ones. I am unable to pull away from his gaze. Strong emotions and sparks fly between us. I have a feeling of déjà-vu, like I've been with him before.

"Wow, that was incredible. Can you believe that really happened?" I gasp. Then I hold out my hand and stutter. "Hi, I'm Angie. You must be Thomas."

Thomas stares at me as he takes my hand and squeezes it. "What was that? It was unbelievable!" After a pause, he adds, "Your eyes are so crystal blue!"

Suddenly I am a little bit embarrassed "Thank you?" I answer tentatively. Emily and Sarah are right. He is a hunk. Whoo! I feel the heat rise in my chest, up my neck, and into my face.

Thomas continues to gaze at me. "Never in a million years would I have thought that I would witness anything like that," he says.

He pauses before continuing. "I have heard the stories of Evangeline and Jacob all my life. I could feel their passion when they said goodbye to each other."

I realize that I feel a connection to Thomas that I have never felt to anyone before.

"Evangeline sent me here to you," I say. Then I realize that I am still holding his hand in mine. I let go, self-consciously. "She told me that I must go to the cottage, that there was someone there I needed to meet.

"She said the time is right," I added "I didn't know what she meant by that."

"I wasn't planning to come here today but something kept drawing me here," Thomas says. "Crazy, huh?"

"I can't wait to tell Sarah and Emily. They will be blown away. Where did you find that necklace? People have been wondering where it has been hiding for centuries." I realize in my excitement that I am babbling.

Thomas says he was working on the old fireplace in the cottage, removing one of the stones, when he spotted something shiny. He says he even chuckled to himself, wondering it was part of Blackbeard's treasure that Evangeline allegedly had hidden so many years ago.

Thomas is standing over the decaying stone fireplace. He bends down, pointing to where he found the necklace. He holds a gray stone in his hand. "I pulled this loose stone out of all the crumbling mortar. There is a small hidden chamber that opens in the floor of the fireplace. It must have been a hiding place of Evangeline's. I was just getting ready to see if there is anything else in it when you came in.

"And then… well, you know. God, I feel like I was in a dream. It's so weird," he says. He falls silent for a minute, points toward my neck, and asks, "Where did you get *your* necklace?"

I explain how my father gave me the silver necklace last summer before he died. "He told me that Evangeline came to him in a dream and said it was the right time for me to have it."

"Are you sure we have never met before?" Thomas asks, abruptly. "I feel some sort of existing connection with you."

"I feel the same," I answer. "Maybe it's just the necklaces that are linking us together. Anyway, it sure feels like something out of a movie."

Thomas runs his muscular hand through his wavy blond hair. "Well," he says, pointing toward the fireplace, "let's look and see if there are any other treasures in here."

He reaches into the little niche and pulls out a small wooden box with a delicately carved heart on the lid. On the heart are the initials EA and JH. He hands me the box. "You open it." Then he shakes his head in wonder. "Wow, you know, you look like all the pictures that I have seen of Evangeline. I feel like this should belong to you."

I open the tiny cedar coffer. We both peer inside to find an old piece of parchment paper. I take the paper out and hold it up. "This paper looks really ancient," I say, as I try to read the script. "Oh look, it's an old letter. It's signed, 'All my Love, Daniel.'"

Thomas stares at the letter in disbelief. "Oh man. Do you think this is one of the legendary love letters that Evangeline brought back with her from her kidnapping by Daniel Teach?"

Excitedly I whisper, "Do you know what this might mean? We may have found a way to find Blackbeard's treasure!" I am so excited by our find, jumping up and down, that I grab Thomas by the shoulders and—not thinking—kiss him boldly on the lips.

Lights flash before my eyes and all my senses are exploding. My skin is smoldering and I turn bright red, "I'm so sorry! I got carried away."

Our arms remain locked together for several more moments, as if we are frozen in time. Both of us are left dumbstruck. He teases me, "Whoa, that was some kiss. I saw stars flashes before my eyes."

"Sorry about that." I push back my shiny black hair. "I just got so excited."

Now I am not sure what I am more excited about, the letter or the kiss. I try to focus on the box.

"Hey, look that isn't all that's in here. There's a little book, too."

Thomas lifts the book and examines it. "This book probably belonged to Evangeline," he says. "It looks like it could be her diary."

I take the journal. It has Evangeline's name on the cover. I open it.

"It's dated, 1754–1756. I can't wait to read it. Let's go show the others what we've found. Boy, are they going to be amazed!"

Before we can make our way outside, the bedroom door pushes open and a happy—and exuberant—Golden Retriever puppy bounces into the room, knocking me over. The pup lands wet kisses on my face and wags his tail.

It makes me laugh when he rolls over and exposes his fat belly. I rub his tummy and laugh, "Down boy. And who might you be? You're a beauty."

Thomas is embarrassed, grabbing his oversized puppy by the collar. "I'm so sorry. This is Max. He's usually very timid. He doesn't normally act this way unless he knows you. He must sense that you like animals. I got him as a foster and ended up adopting him. He's so lovable." He rubs Max's ears.

Max whines, wanting to be let loose. He nudges his rope toy into my hand, wanting me to play with him. I pet him on the head. "I promise I'll play later, Max. Right now, we need to show the girls the things that we have found."

Thomas reaches down for my hand and pulls me up from the floor. I am ready to rush out the door.

"Come on! Emily has to be in the pub at 2 o'clock. We have to hurry."

We race out the door, across the gravel-and-oyster-shell driveway. When we reach the big white manor, we run up the steps. Pushing open the door, we hear the tinkling of laughter. At the top of the stairwell is a vision of Evangeline.

With her is the same blond-haired man we saw in our misty vision, Jacob. His arms are wrapped around her.

Thomas and I both stop short, out of breath and astonished yet again.

We start to race again and almost knock over Sarah and Emily inside the B&B. I grab them both, pull them toward the staircase, and point to the top of the stairs. They look up to see the brawny man with his arms wrapped around Evangeline.

Emily and Sarah look shocked. Emily finally speaks. “Guys, do you see what I’m seeing?”

Both Thomas and I start talking at once trying to tell them about what happened in the cottage. Thomas stops and points to me, “Go ahead, Angie. You tell them. They aren’t going to believe it.”

Hearing all the commotion, Emily and Sarah’s parents rush over to see what is going on. My grandparents, Paul and Mary Albright, are with them. They all look up to witness the heavenly vision of Evangeline and Jacob at the top of the stairwell.

I rush into my grandparents’ arms and hug them. Thomas looks at me, adoringly.

Emily, seeing Thomas’ reaction, pats him on the back. “Ooh, steady boy!” she laughs. Thomas is blushing and shrugging his shoulders.

Excitedly I tell them what has happened.

“Emily, after you left, Evangeline appeared. She sent me to the cottage. She told me I had to meet someone and that the time was right. I went, and when I opened the door, Thomas had just found Evangeline’s necklace.”

I paused to catch my breath. “I touched my necklace and the necklace in Thomas’ hand at the same time. A vision appeared before us of Evangeline and Jacob saying their last goodbye. It was as if we were transported back in time when Jacob vowed his love to Evangeline.”

Thomas reaches out to show the others the necklace in his hand. I look at Thomas, reaching up to touch my necklace. “I wonder if it will happen again?”

I reach over to touch the necklace in Thomas' hand, and we all stare in wonderment as the past collides with the present. We see Evangeline and Jacob's passionate goodbye, so many years ago. No one breathes or makes a sound until the vision vanishes. It leaves us all amazed and awestruck.

A thought strikes me. "You know, in the past, I have only seen Evangeline. Do you think that Jacob and Evangeline's souls have been reunited in the afterlife because we reunited the necklaces?" I ask.

"Who knows," Thomas replies. "This is all crazy to me." Then he adds, "But the necklace isn't all we found."

He opens the tiny wooden cedar box he has been holding in his hands. He lifts up the parchment. "Look at this," he says, as he hands it to my grandfather, "It's a love letter from Daniel to Evangeline. And we found Evangeline's diary.

"The stories we heard growing up are all true. Evangeline really did bring home love letters from Daniel!"

My grandfather takes the letter and stares at it in utter amazement. He rubs a hand over his thin graying hair. "I can't believe these have stayed hidden for so long. All the stories we've heard over the years. I wonder if there are really clues in the letter that will lead us to Blackbeard's treasure."

I make a suggestion. "Maybe that's what Evangeline means by 'the time is right.' Maybe she means the time is right to find the treasure, and that's why it has stayed hidden for so long."

Before I can continue, the big front door of the B&B swings open. In comes my mother Isabella, my sister Sally, and her husband Robert. We pull them into the parlor. Momentarily, the excitement of our findings is set aside. We hug and kiss the newcomers. Sally's pregnant belly is making quite an entrance. "Watch out. Whale in the building," she laughs as she rubs her hands over her big belly.

Everyone congratulates Robert and Sally on their soon-to-arrive baby. "Oh, you look so cute, Sally. Pregnancy really agrees with you," Sarah says. "You're glowing. And you don't look like a whale at all."

My mom tries to remain animated, but I can feel a quiet sadness in her. It is a bittersweet reunion, and the unmentioned absence of my father, George, is evident.

Sarah has a plan that puts everyone in the inn this year for a few weeks. Thomas's brother, George, is still waiting for a part to come in to repair the broken air-conditioning unit in our family beach home. So the consensus is that the family, especially Sally, will be more comfortable—and cooler—staying at the inn.

Before we can continue, my brother, Matt, waltzes into the inn, making his traditional dramatic appearance. This year, he arrives alone. Normally, he has a woman on his arm, a new one every year. He tells me that he can't find the right one, but he keeps trying. Sarah blushes furiously when Matt swings her up in an embrace and plants a wet kiss on her cheek. Emily and I burst out laughing.

We tease Sarah and she squeals, turning crimson red. "Stop it. You're embarrassing me." We howl as our laughter echoes out in the parlor.

I'm suddenly conscious of Thomas. I turn in his direction and catch his eye. He's been watching me. "Are you sure we have never met before?" he asks again.

Chapter 5

The Letter

"I can't wait any longer."

My grandfather, Paul, holds the letter up in his hand as he makes this announcement. He has brought everyone up-to-date on the discovery of the necklace and the box with the letter and journal. "I have to examine this antiquated letter," he says as he unfolds the crumbling parchment paper and starts to read aloud.

Dear Evangeline, My Love,

My heart stays with you, though I am far away. Should I ever leave this world, remember this. There is a huge treasure waiting to be found. I give to you a treasure map of where to find my grandfather Blackbeard's treasure.

Do not keep the map pieces together but separate them into sections. This will protect it from being found by others.

All my Love,

Daniel

Attached to the letter is a clue from Evangeline. It reads:

"If you have found this letter, you will need to find the next. To find the next, you must go to where the Tiger meets the Inlet on the land where the Bankers roam free and where the Yaupon meets the Pines."

Emily shouts out, "I think I know!"

"We need to check where Sir Richard Greenville's Ship, Tiger, ran aground trying to reach Ocracoke Inlet," she says, excitedly.

Paul scratches his chin in thought. "I think you might be right, Emily," he responds. "In 1585, the story goes that when Sir Richard Greenville tried to enter Ocracoke Inlet, his ship ran aground on the shoals. The Spanish mustangs escaped from the shipwreck." We all know that those horses, which continue to roam this island freely, are called Bankers.

"There are Yaupon holly trees growing wild in that area," Paul continues. "According to the stories, the Native Americans on the island taught the earlier White settlers how to brew Yaupon leaves into a tea called Ersatz tea."

Sally throws her arms up in the air. "How are we supposed to find the next letter? There are over 200 acres to search! Plus, the Ocracoke beaches have been eroding and narrowing for years."

Paul laughs. "We'll have to think like a pirate."

After a pause, Paul says, "The next letter has to be hiding under something that existed over 200 years ago. If I remember correctly, there is a statue placed as a memorial to Greenville's shipwrecked vessel."

Matt shrugs his shoulders. "That seems way too easy. How is it possible that someone has not found the letter before now? That is, if it has even survived all these years."

"Well, you just never know, what we will find," Paul says, still staring at the long-forgotten letter. Mom hugs him. "Dad," she says, "I think that's enough of treasure hunting for now. We have a lot of visiting and catching up to do."

I hold up Evangeline's journal. "Okay, that's sounds good, but I really want to read Evangeline's journal. Anyone want to hear what's in it?"

Sarah points to the parlor. "I've set up snacks and sandwiches in the sunroom. Let's all go in there, sit down, and listen to Evangeline's story."

Chapter 6
Evangeline

I open the long-forgotten journal. We all step back in time as I read Evangeline's diary, which begins with her journey across the Atlantic so many years ago.

April 27, 1754—*My name is Evangeline Alexander. I am but fifteen years old. My family and I have left Newcastle, England, today to embark upon a journey to a faraway land. I am excited and in fear, all at the same time. I do not know what my future holds. My father has decided to book us passage with a merchant passenger ship, as this will allow us to travel to the New World at a decreased cost. Our final destination is Ocracoke Island, where we have purchased land with a house on it. Our first stop will be Portugal, where our captain will deliver supplies and pick up provisions. I do not even know if we will survive this adventure.*

My papa's name is Robert Alexander. My momma's name is Sarah Albright Alexander. I have four brothers and two sisters. My oldest brother's name is Robert. He is quite fond of my best friend Emily. I am the eldest girl. The baby is Anna, and she is only six months old. Elizabeth, whom we call Lizzie, is only fourteen years old and quite a beauty. She has wavy black hair and sparkling blue eyes. My two younger brothers are Stephen and Matthew.

I try to help my mama as much as I can. I help take care of the younger ones.

We are all very close in age. Luckily, we all get along well, as we are staying in the same cabin aboard The Sheffield, a large ship with impressive sails. There are nine of us in one room, including the babe. I fear that some days it will be so stifling having all of us in the one room. The weather has been quite pretty for this time of the year, although it is still very cold in the evenings.

***May 7, 1754**—I have never been on a ship before this journey. The rocking motion of the sloop sometimes makes my head swim. My little brothers have not fared very well so far as the motion makes them vomit. I try to keep them to the top of the vessel to ease their seasickness. It seems to help. The weather has improved. The days are balmy, but the nights are brisk.*

My friend, Emily, and I keep busy helping all the children with their studies. We have story time every day in the afternoon. It helps us pass the time. We have been telling the children the stories from the Canterbury Tales. The babes sit transfixed listening to the stories of the thirty-one pilgrims who embarked upon a journey from Southwark to the Canterbury Cathedral. The older boys will sometimes join us for story time. I'm sure it helps them pass the hours, too. It has been a very long journey.

I have my eye on a boy named Jacob Harriott. He is several years older than I am. I feel my heart race each time he comes close to me. Jacob has green eyes. They are the color of newly budded leaves, with golden flecks that sparkle when he laughs. Jacob and my brother, Robert, are grand friends. Robert and Roger Brown, who is another boy on the boat, have all become such great comrades. Roger Brown is also quite a handsome fella. It is rumored that he is Blackbeard's grandson. He is being raised by his aunt and the Brown family. The three boys enjoy teasing us girls at every chance they get.

The boys came by today to tell us about the furniture they are making. Emily fawns over my brother, Robert. They make quite a striking couple. Emily is a petite yellow-haired girl with eyes the color of jade. My brother is a tall, dark-haired boy with baby blue eyes that match the color of the sky.

Our deckhand, Jim Davis, is teaching the boys to work with wood. Jim—we called him Mr. Davis when we first came aboard but he has become a friend and he said we could use his first name—has been on this sloop for many years. He wears tan-colored breeches all of the time. He has sandy blond hair and warm brown eyes. He can be found on deck helping the other members of his crew. Jim plans to settle on the new land with his wife, Lucy. She is abundant with child. She thinks she is about nine months into her confinement. She rarely gets sickness now but, when she does, it occurs mostly in the morning hours.

Other than her belly, she's a petite lady. She is only a couple years older than I. She tells me that she is quite lonely and misses her family. We have included her into our little circle. Emily and I have been teaching her and the others how to read, write, and do mathematics.

Lucy is truly timid but quite pretty. Jim adores her. She is related to Sandra Hall, the wives of one of the servants brought on board by a family. Lucy and Sandra are cousins. They are quite fun to be around. In the evenings, after our supper, we sometimes gather to play music and dance. The deckhands bring out their own flutes and lutes and play for us. I love to sing and dance along with them when they're playing. Papa says I sing like a songbird.

We have become quite close with the deckhands. Some of them are very rough and rugged. Most of them are very kind and helpful. They are good to me and tell me that I am a beauty and that I will break many a heart. Some of the men, though, Emily and I try to avoid at all costs. Papa tells Emily and me never to be alone with them because they are sea rovers. Sea rovers are sea rovers, and they can't be trusted. They can be quite dangerous he told us. Some of them make my hair prickle in fear when I pass by them. I can feel their eyes follow me.

But Jim is a good man, and he is teaching the boys to work with wood. Robert, Roger, and Jacob took us to see the cradle that they made. Jacob has carved a little heart in the arch of the cradle. This work helps them to pass the time and the boys are becoming quite good at it. The three boys are very proud of their accomplishment. They made sure to show it to us when story time was finished.

May 14, 1754—*We reached Portugal today. The captain said that we will be picking up spices to take to the Canary Islands for trade. Papa said this should be a good learning experience for us, being able to travel to the different cities. The language is foreign to me, but the city is beautiful.*

The captain lets me smell some of the aromatic spices. The name of one of the spices was cinnamon. Cook told me that it was what he used to make apple tarts and that he would make me some for my birthday next. It smelled sweet and spicy. There are other spices that we will pick up this journey. Salt, pepper, cumin, and something called paprika are among the spices that we will transport to the islands and to the New World. Captain said some of the spices are very expensive and worth their price in gold.

It's so hot today that I can barely breathe. There is only a tiny breeze outside. Sweat trickles down the back of my shift. We have been holding our studies top side. We hope for a draft of air from the sea. It never ceases to amaze me how the sun will barrel down on you and make you blaze. Emily and I must be careful so that we do not scorch the children and burn their skin. We have to sit in the shade of the ship's sails. There are some days when I think this journey will never end, and yet it has only just begun. I wonder if we will ever reach our final destination. We should set sail for a place called the Canary Islands by next week.

Mama won't allow us to just wear just our petticoats for fear of the deckhands and our modesty. I say pooh-pooh to this. Emily and I have found a hiding place on top of the sloop to get a little air without our shifts. It would cause such a scandal and commotion if we were caught. It makes it such fun.

Oh, another exciting bit of news. Our friend Lucy had her babe the other day. He is a perfect child. We went to visit her and Jim. Their bairn was resting in the cradle that the boys made for him. He is quite bonny and has pretty blue eyes that peeked up at us.

September 7, 1754—*We have reached the Canary Islands. It is quite tropical, and there are beautiful flowers that smell divine. There are huge, leafed trees that are shaped like umbrellas that they call palm trees. We are permitted to leave the boat to walk around the island, but Papa says the boys must accompany us at all times. With the boys, we are even permitted to float around the reef in the clear, aqua-colored water. It was heavenly but I had to swim in my flannel bathing gown. It was quite cumbersome. Jacob told me my eyes are the color of the sea and that he could float in them forever. It was a paradise, almost what I think heaven would be like.*

Today is my birthday. I reached my sixteenth year. Cook, whose Christian name is Robert Williams, made me a pastry for my special day. He is quite a rugged looking fella with no teeth and a large barrel sized belly. He has graying red hair and his whiskers are white. He wears baggy breeches that are the color of the sand. His smudged white apron covers his big round belly. He's quite a jolly fella but sometimes he scares our wee ones with his loud boisterous voice. We girls have become quite fond of him over the last five months. Our mothers have insisted that we learn how to cook. They feel it will be a great skill for us. I don't mind as it helps the day not be so endless. He is a great teacher, and he makes cooking fun to learn.

He made for me a birthday tart with dried apples that he brought on board the sloop. He teases me frequently and he reminds me of my uncle. It warms my heart every time he makes me treats. The tart he made is delicious and the apples are a combination of sweet and tangy. He used the cinnamon spice that we picked up when we were in Portugal. He let me taste the apple filling before he added the spice and it truly added to its wonderful smoky flavor. The crust melts in my mouth like butter.

It has come to my attention that there is one on the sloop that might have a crush on me. It is Roger Brown, the grand friend of my brother Robert and Jacob. But my heart lies elsewhere. I feel Jacob is the love of my life. I just know one day that he and I will be married.

Roger tells us a tale of how his mother died in childbirth. She was one of the many women claimed by Blackbeard's son. Roger brags about being Blackbeard's grandson, but he has never met his own father. The story goes that when Roger's father, Thomas Teach, who was named after Blackbeard's half-brother, was in a port, he had his way with Roger's mother, Abigail. Abigail was a mousey brown-haired girl, petite in size, and very naïve. Thomas swept Abigail off her feet, but he was a seafarer, not always in port. He promised to come back, to make her his wife, but never did. Roger's mother died in childbirth and Roger never met his father, Thomas.

Roger is quite tall, tanned, and brawny with glorious black hair. His eyes glow like warm chocolate. Roger gave me a birthday gift. He told me it was because I was turning sixteen and that was such a special birthday. I am of the opinion that he is enamored with me. Oh, but I am not in love with him. It is Jacob who has my heart.

Jacob just shrugs his shoulders and winks at me. He gave me one of his drawings. It was a charcoal sketch from our ship and a sunset from one of the islands we passed. It was so lifelike. The sun looks to melt into the never-ending sea. He even framed the picture. The frame has a hidden panel for parchment or letters. It is quite clever. It comes in useful as I can hide my precious journal from prying eyes.

When I look at Jacob, I am pulled slowly into his bright green eyes that sparkle when he laughs. My heart does pitter patter and my cheeks grow hot and flame bright red whenever he is around me. He says we will marry me one day, after we reach the new land. He's becoming a great woodcarver and furniture maker. He has made for me three tiny coffers that each have the wood carving of a heart in the lid. They are quite beautiful.

In the wooden boxes, he has carved our initials inside each heart. The insides are lined with purple and pearl-colored oyster shells. He said that he crushed oyster shells into the linings. He used the sap from a gum tree to help it set the shells in the bottom. There is a hidden compartment in each box to hide our love letters.

Around the bonfire, under the stars, we danced the night away. I was able to dance with Jacob. His hand in mine made my palms perspire, as well did his. Emily's parents and my parents attempted to teach us the latest English country dances. I thought poor Emily would swoon when Robert took her hand for the first time. She has told me that she has fallen desperately in love with him. He is also in love with her.

We didn't get back on our sloop until very late. Jacob was so charming. We sneaked away and hid in our secret alcove, where he kissed me on my cheek and we held hands. I wished that the night would never end. It was well past ten when the festivities were over. Papa said, looking at his time piece, "I can't believe how late it has become." It was a glorious night filled with fun and laughter. I will always remember it.

October 13, 1754—*A lot has happened. I have become a woman. Thank heavens for mama being there. I thought I was dying when my time came. I have never been more terrified for my life.*

We are still in the Canary Islands and the captain says we must remain here to await the arrival of more provisions. They will come in within the next couple of weeks. There is a sadness in our little group. Some of us have caught a fever. They call it malaria. They say it comes from mosquitoes. Some of the others say that it is caused by the swamp air. They call it swamp fever.

My little babe of a sister caught the fever. My mama has been frantic with fear. Some of the ill have perished. One of the ship's doctors tried to give little Anna a tea made from the bark of the Cinchona tree. My baby sister wailed and screamed with fever. I felt her little body would surely burst into flames. Her breathing became very rugged. I watched her gasp for air as my mama trembled. Mama was beside herself.

Papa lifted my baby sister's tiny body and placed her in a tepid bath. All that we had was our ceramic wash basin. She screamed louder. Emily's mother, Elizabeth, heard the screams and rushed to our room to help. It was too late. Anna took one last gasp. She was gone.

My mama gripped little Anna tightly against her chest and rocked her frantically. She was saying, "Here, here my little one. All is alright." My mama had such a wild look in her eyes. I think at that moment she must have lost her mind. We all cried hysterically. Papa tried to calm Mama and us. But he was very distraught himself. I could see tears dripping down his nose.

Emily's mother, Elizabeth gathered all of us children and took us back to their room on the ship. Emily met us at the door. She hugged me tightly. Tears rolled down my face. Elizabeth wrapped her arms around all of us, trying to offer some comfort. It was of no use. We are all devastated.

The little ones finally fell asleep on the old, feathered mattress with the rest of the other children. My younger sister Lizzy, Emily, and Emily's sister Isabella fell asleep wrapped in each other's arms.

Jonathan, Emily's father, went to help my papa with Mama. I heard Papa tell Emily's parents that Mama is inconsolable. "I fear she is broken," I heard him say. My heart is also broken for my little sister. We stayed with the Whites that night and for several other nights after poor Anna passed away.

Her loss has been felt by all. We buried her tiny little body on the island. We buried her by a beautiful waterfall. It was so serene. Papa said he wanted her to be buried on land and not tossed out into the big sea. Papa held a very nice, burial service for Anna. We prayed over her to go to Heaven. He said these words:

"My wee beautiful child, you were the light of your mama's eyes. We loved you in your short time here on this earth. It breaks our hearts to lose you but know that you rest in the hands of our Lord. May we find peace in knowing that you are in heaven and will always be our little angel."

There was not a dry eye at her burial. We all felt her loss especially my mama. She had not spoken since Anna's death and is but a cocoon of her previous self.

November 15, 1754—*We arrived in the island of Barbados only eight days ago. I'm afraid of the different languages. I am so anxious about what lies ahead of us. The children and I have fallen into a daily routine. They have been helping me with the chores. We have all had to grow up very quickly. Mama is still lost within herself.*

Barbados is truly like a paradise. We are told that the island got its name from a Portuguese sea captain who was on his way to Brazil. He called the island "Los Barbados" because the fig trees had a bearded appearance. However, other people say it has its name because the ones that live on the island are all bearded.

Some days, I wish we could just stay here. I dread getting back on that sloop. We are free to roam here as much as we want, as long as we have the boys with us. Some days we even get to swim off the shore. The teal-colored water rolls gently on to the shore. The silky sand feels good between my toes when we walk on the beach.

There is also a fear of some savages on the island. We are told that there is a tribe called the Kalinago and they are cannibals. They eat human flesh. The thought terrifies me, but my papa says we are safe and well protected by her crew.

Cook is still teaching Emily and me how to prepare meals. We are learning all the essential kitchen skills that Papa says I will need. My mama used to say, "It's very important for girls to learn culinary techniques."

In the mornings after everyone is washed and dressed, I go with Emily and we school all the little ones. Emily and I have set up a little room in one of the alcoves of the ship to use when it is cold. If the weather is good, we go top side. The fresh air lifts all our spirits.

I don't see how anyone can bear to make their living at sea. I find the boat and sailing too confining. I feel trapped, especially when we have to stay in the cabin.

Jacob, Robert, and Roger stop by sometimes to watch our class. Roger has been learning how to read and write. He's getting very good at it. He is a fast learner. He is very quick with his numbers, too. He tells me that one day he plans to become a pirate, just like his grandfather, Blackbeard. I sometimes catch him looking at me when he doesn't realize it.

Jacob tells me that Roger has a crush on me. I laugh and I tell Jacob that I only have eyes for him. My love for him sometimes makes me feel that I might burst. My feelings for Jacob are so strong. My body tingles whenever he's around. I long to feel the touch of his lips on mine. He tells me that we will marry when we get to the new land. I cannot wait to be his wife.

November 25, 1754—*Papa hopes the continued warm weather will help Mama's spirits return, but I am not sure. Mama sits and stares into space with her arms wrapped tightly around herself. Our room aboard the sloop smells of death and body odor.*

It is as if Mama does not see us when we enter the sloop's cabin. I, being the eldest, have taken on the responsibility of caring for the children. Robert helps me when he can. Lizzie and Robert have been a wondrous support, but they are grief stricken, too. Little did I know that my fate had changed forever the day little Anna left this world. My life is no longer my own.

December 14, 1754—*Today, Emily turned sixteen. Robert asked her papa if he can have her hand in marriage. It was so exciting. Even my mama smiled when she heard the news. My papa gave Robert a very pretty, ornate gold band to give to Emily.*

Emily shed tears of joy when Robert went down on one knee to ask for her hand. There was a lot of laughing and crying this evening. Cook outdid himself with another roasted pig. There were fresh fruits and vegetables. We danced all night to the music that our crew played on their flutes and lutes.

December 25, 1754—*Today is Christmas Day. We are still on the island of Barbados waiting for our latest shipment to arrive from Cape Verde. Papa and the Whites are* *trying to make it a special Christmas for us. We all gathered in prayer to celebrate the birth of Jesus. Yesterday, Emily and all of us girls helped Cook make sweets for everyone. We helped the little ones make gifts for their families. Then today we all gathered together for a feast of pig roasted on a spit. The tasty island vegetables were grilled over the firepit. Emily and I took turns reading to everyone the story of the birth of Jesus.*

There is happiness mixed with the sadness remembering the death of my little sister, Anna, and the other poor souls that were lost to that horrid illness. It has been about two months since we buried Anna's tiny little body on the island. Jacob's father fell ill to the dreadful disease. Luckily he has survived but he continues to feel weak.

Despite the sadness, we have been able to enjoy our Christmas. There was dancing as music floated in the air. We had fresh fruit in abundance from the island. Cook showed us how to dry tropical fruit for our upcoming trip. We are scheduled to set sail for Pascole, Florida, at year's end.

Jacob, my love, has been here for me, supporting me through this sad time. I am forever busy, taking over the role of caring for my little brothers and sisters. Papa tries his best, but Mama just sits, staring out into the unknown.

Jacob has brought me another heartfelt gift for Christmas. It is a beautifully carved wooden comb set for my hair. It is such a thoughtful gift. He amazes me with his talent.

Robert, Emily, Jacob, and I sneaked away after dinner to our secret hiding place on the bow of the sloop. Jacob held my hand as we gazed up at the brilliant stars. My heart is filled with a love that knows no end. Robert and Emily told us their dream of becoming man and wife once we reach Ocracoke Island, our destination. We were able to steal only a few moments of time together because I needed to return to get the little ones ready for slumber, but we had a heavenly breeze blowing up to the front of the boat. I only wish that we could have stayed there forever. I miss the happy days when I was not responsible for everyone. I want my mama to come back to us. I fear we have lost her forever.

January 5, 1755—*We set sail two weeks ago. The sea is quite rough. The children have suffered from a sickness of the sea, again. My brothers Steven and Matthew have tried to stay brave, after losing our little Anna. Mama still sits most days staring, with her arms wrapped around herself, rocking in her chair. As we have been unable to get her involved in life, I have taken upon myself a new role as my siblings' nanny. Elizabeth and Robert have been helping me with the chores. I miss my mama. I wonder if she'll ever come back to us. I start my days getting the family up and ready for the day. The days are long and warm, but the nights can chill you to the bone. It is such a damp cold.*

***September 7, 1755**—I turned seventeen years old today. My papa teased me, that he cannot believe his baby girl is growing up so swiftly. He also says he does not know what he would do without me. Cook spoiled me, again. He has made me a scrumptious apple cake with something he calls apple frappe icing. It melts in your mouth.*

He made us a special feast and even grilled a hog that he got from one of the locals. We are now on an island called the Bahamas. There is a fruit—pineapple—with juice that trickles down my chin and tastes so sweet. It tastes like liquid sunshine. The whole colony gathered together for a feast to celebrate my birthday. I feel so special. We even had a fire on the beach.

It is a beautiful tranquil day on the island. We plan to set sail in another couple weeks for America. This island has a strange mystifying history with many foreign tongues. There's a brown fruit that is called a fig. Papa says it also grows in some places in England but we have never seen it before. Cook has made us a special treat called figgy pudding. He also made us a biscuit with mashed figs in the middle. It is quite delicious.

There is also something here they call sugarcane. They have enslaved many people on the island. It is so foreign to me. Papa says to keep my distance from the masters of the slaves. They can be unkind. Cook says that they use the sugarcane to make a very sweet powder and use it to make spirits. Sometimes I can hear the drunken howling of our crew after they have partaken of this special brew.

Jacob traded some of his furniture to the locals for one of my birthday gifts. It is a pretty ruby necklace. He says one day that he will get me a broach to match it. He put the pretty necklace around my neck. He nuzzled my ear, making goosebumps on my body. We manage to sneak away for a quick kiss. Our passion is smoldering, and he tells me he cannot wait to make me his bride.

Emily has been given a pearl necklace by Robert, who managed to get it by also selling some of his furniture to the locals. Robert and Jacob have gotten so good at making furniture.

We are learning to make baskets out of the reed from the island. Today it is quite warm, so we are all allowed to float in the aqua water at the beautiful coral reef nearby. The reef is colorful with numerous tropical fish swimming in its midst.

Jacob kissed me on my lips tonight. I felt tingly all over. Our kiss deepened until I thought I would be swallowed with passion. I felt his male hardness against my groin. I told him I could not wait to be his wife. The evening ended and I lay awake that night dreaming of the day he would be mine. I think I cannot be happier than I am today.

***July 24, 1755**—Today I saw the shoreline come into view. I am told that this is America. The Spaniards called it Pascoe, Florida. It means festival of flowers. It is good to be on land again. I can see how this land got its name. There are so many beautiful, tropical flowers. There are orange groves. The fragrance is a tangy, heavenly scent as is the taste. The nectar from the fruit drips down my chin. A sweetness of pure delight.*

My papa says we will be staying here for several months. We have docked in a port in Saint Augustine, Florida. It is a bustling harbor where many foreign tongues are spoken. Jacob says that there is much unrest with the Spaniards. Papa says there are a lot of pirates in this port and we must be wary.

Our friend, Roger Brown, met his cousin Daniel Teach today. Roger said he plans to join his cousin on Teach's next adventure at sea. Like Roger, Daniel Teach is said to be Blackbeard's grandson. He is a striking man. He is ruggedly handsome with a large, muscular body. His skin is tanned and his threadbare shirt, open to the waist, reveals his bare, muscled chest. His wavy dark brown hair is braided down his back. His beard is scruffy.

I watch him from a distance from my hiding place behind the pier, but I barely breath when he walks straight past where am hidden. I saw him one day from the sloop and he saw me through his coal-black eyes. I feel that he is drawn to me. Luckily, I am under the protection of our crew.

He has made lewd comments about my beautiful raven hair and sapphire eyes, making me blush furiously. I hid behind Papa and Jim, the deckhand. My skin crawls at the sight of Daniel Teach. I can tell he is quite a dangerous man. Roger plans to join Daniel's crew to become a deckhand. I fear for Roger. He has a gentle and generous heart. I cannot bear to see him becoming a pirate.

Lucy Davis is again abundant with child. She and Jim are excitedly awaiting the babe's arrival. Because Lucy is such a petite thing, her cousin Sandra thinks she might have another difficult delivery. Jim seems more preoccupied with the thought of having a second bonny baby boy, but Lucy hopes for a girl.

I have been helping, Sandra, one of the servants on the ship, with the care of the injured and the ill. She has asked me to help her deliver Lucy's child. Sandra tells me that the last time she assisted Lucy's childbirth, she had to pull the little one from the womb. She fears that this could happen again and she wants my assistance if need be. I am anxious but I am also fascinated by the idea of bringing a new life into this world.

***July 27, 1755**—Although the days seem to last forever, time has flown since our arrival in Florida earlier this year. The weather has broken. The sky is crystal blue. Where we are anchored looks out at such a vast open sea. The sun shines brightly and burns one's skin red if one is not careful.*

Mama spends most days staring at the sea or sitting in our cabin. Papa moved her chair to the top deck so that she can get some fresh air. He is hoping that the sunlight and fresh breezes will bring her spirit back to life. I started giving her our socks to darn, to try to make her come back to us. Papa is beside himself. He blames himself for bringing us on this journey.

Sandra woke me in the middle of the night to help her with the delivery and birthing of Lucy and Jim's baby. I rushed to assist her. I saw Lucy writhing in pain. She whimpered and sweated profusely when her large belly hardened like a rock. Sandra says the spasm is called a contraction and it helps the babe be born.

Sandra had me help Lucy breathe through her pain after she had been having contractions for six hours. Suddenly there was a large gush of fluid and Lucy screamed in pain. Things were happening so quickly. I saw a little head with curly brown hair appear between Lucy's legs. Sandra told me to have Lucy push with all her might. The babe's shoulders, arms, legs, and body popped out as Sandra caught the little one. She placed the screaming baby on Lucy's belly. Sandra asked me to go help cut the cord but first told me I must tie it off. She gave me a cutlass to cut the cord. The birth was messy but beautiful. The baby nuzzled and latched onto Lucy's bosom. I was in utter amazement.

Sandra told me it was not over yet and asked me to massage Lucy's belly. She said to me, "We must deliver the afterbirth. It's very important so that the Lucy does not get 'child sick.' One day you will be able to deliver ladies' bairns all on your own."

The sun beamed through the tiny porthole as the new day began. I have witnessed a birth, a miracle. I helped Sandra finish cleaning up. Then the proud papa, Jim, came rushing in to see his new babe. It was a little girl. Her velvety hair was dark as coal. She had perfect little lips, delicate fingers, and toes. Jim held his tiny daughter. He asked me, "Is it alright if we name her after your baby sister, Anna."

I felt the tears prick at my eyes. "That would be so special. My papa and mama will love that," I told him.

Sandra hugged me and thanked me for my help, then she and I went back to our cabins to start our day. Later my papa asked me, "What do you think about babies being born?

It is a gift from God." I grinned and nodded. I told him that they had decided to name their little girl Anna, after our precious Anna.

He smiled, but a lone tear escaped and rolled down his cheek. He wiped his eyes with his old worn handkerchief. He turned away from me, blew his nose, and shrugged his shoulders.

August 14, 1755—*Jacob turned nineteen years old today. He has grown from a boy into a man on this journey. His muscles are ripping out of his tight clothes. He has filled them out over the last year. The other day, I whispered in his ear that I could not wait to be his in body and spirit.*

We sneaked away with Emily and Robert to hold hands. We found a hidden lake inland from the port. Spanish moss hung from the cypress trees. The bright yellow hue from the swamp sunflowers reflected off the clear blue water. The day was quite warm. We swam in the tepid water.

Jacob and my body touched in the water. I felt his manhood awaken, hardening under my touch. He told me that we must wait until we were married. I know in my heart that this is true, but my body betrayed me. I wrapped my legs around his waist, not wanting to let go of him. His lips met mine and our kiss erupted in me a passion that I did not know could exist. His manhood pressed against my loins. I was breathless when he released me. He told me that we had to stop before it was too late.

We got out of the water to let our bodies dry in the sunshine. A balmy breeze blew over us while we lay in each other's arms. My head rested on his shoulder. We held hands, talking about our future.

Emily and Robert joined us on the lakeshore. We talked about our futures together. Emily shared her dreams that we would all be married and have families. Robert and Emily plan to marry when we reach our new home.

We will be sailing to a secluded place, called Ocracoke Island, on the North Carolina shore. Jacob told me he planned to marry me once his family is settled. I can hardly wait for the day that he is mine. His lips grazed over mine as he kissed me gently. We finished drying off and walked back to the sloop.

When we got back, all of the children were playing on the shoreline, under the watchful eyes of parents. Papa waved to us as we strode up. We had gathered oranges from a nearby grove. The little ones came running up to greet us. Their pink bodies and rosy cheeks glistened from their swim in the briny sea water. Each of them asked for an orange flavored treat. It made me sigh with sadness when I looked toward the sloop and saw my mama sitting topside, staring out into the unknown. She remains so lost within herself.

September 7, 1755—*The year and time are flying by. The cook made another scrumptious feast for us for Roger's going away party and for my eighteenth birthday. He used fresh fruit to make a heavenly, orange flavored icing to go on his special cake.*

We had fresh, flaky grilled fish and spicy shrimp for dinner. We also had a vegetable they called maize that the locals had grown. My papa said the native Indians introduced maize to the settlers. Cook called it corn. He grilled it over the fire. The kernels tasted like sugar. It was so sweet, just like honey. We sang and danced the night away.

Our friend, Roger was leaving to become a deckhand on his cousin Daniel's ship. Daniel watched our party from the shore. He caused my arms to have chill bumps. I felt his eyes on me when I danced with Jacob. I feared that Roger may be in peril.

Roger had made me another gift, a sketch that he placed in an ornate, carved wooden frame. He blushed furiously when he gave me my birthday gift. I thanked him and kissed him on his tanned cheek. I told him that I will miss him. He shrugged and walked away.

At the end of our party, he walked back to join his cousin's crew. Daniel winked and tipped his hat at me. I hid behind Jacob. There was just something about his cousin that made me fear for my life. There are rumors of his pirating, raping, and pillaging. I thought Roger was making a huge mistake to want to be a pirate. Jacob said Roger wanted to try to go out on his own and sailing with his cousin was a way he could do that.

November 13, 1755—*It has been more than a year since we lost my little sister. Mama is still a shadow of herself. She rarely talks and most days she is lost in her own thoughts. My other siblings are growing up quickly.*

My sister Lizzie is fifteen, almost sixteen. She has curly brown hair and hazel eyes and a natural beauty about her. She has become quite fond of Emily's brother, David. He is a few years older and quite protective of her. She had her time. How I wish my mama could have helped me. I tried my best to ease Lizzie's fears and explained to her that she is now a woman. Tender tears streamed down Lizzie's face. She trembled in my arms.

My brothers have grown, almost doubled in size, since we left our country. I gave mama our clothes to patch. I wish she would come back to us.

Papa took me to the market with him to gather supplies for our family. We were able to buy fabric to make clothes. Emily's mother helped Lizzie and me make clothes for everyone. The boys have outgrown everything. The knees of their britches were worn threadbare and were much too short for them.

We plan to set sail for Ocracoke Island at year's end. The captain is waiting for another arrival of supplies from a place that is called Belize. I am anxious to get to our new home and become Jacob's wife.

We have been working on special Christmas outfits for our families. Emily is such a grand friend and big help to me. We talk excitedly about our plans to be married one day.

Jacob wants to see his family set up before he and I wed. I am so impatient for the day he becomes my husband. Emily and I dream and speak about our children growing up together. We bought silky fabric, lace, and beads to make our wedding gowns. Emily's mama helped us design the patterns for our dresses. It is tedious work to sew the beads into the neckline. I cannot wait to see them on us. Emily is going to be such a beautiful bride. I dream of my wedding day, too.

December 25, 1755—*We had another Christmas on the ship. We are still on this beautiful land called Florida. Our families have become so close over the last year. It is hard for me to believe that more than a year has passed since we left our homeland. Emily, her mother, and I gave out the outfits we made for everyone. We all felt a loss at Roger not being here with us. His presence was truly missed.*

Jacob made me a beautiful dowry chest. The reddish golden wood that he used is called cedar. It has a spicy, heavenly scent. He carved delicate hearts and flowers with our initials in the center of the chest. He whispered in my ear that I could use this chest to hold all the treasures for our new life together. We stole a kiss in our secret hiding place. Robert made a dowry chest, also, for my dear friend Emily.

I made Jacob an apron to hold his tools when he does his woodworking. We gathered top side to sing Christmas carols with the lutes and mandolins. We held a special prayer service after dinner.

Papa told the story of Jesus's birth. My heart went out to Mary and Joseph looking for a place to stay. The stars shone brightly that Christmas night, like the night of Our Lord's birth. The weather has gotten much colder at night. Flesh bumps covered my arms from the chilly ocean breeze.

Papa held my mama's hand. We have all prayed that she will come back to us, but she is still lost. Emily's mother comes to help me care for her and our family. I do not know how I would handle it on my own. We all spoke of how blessed we felt that our bellies were full and that we were all healthy this year.

January 10, 1756—*We have finally set sail for Ocracoke Island. The supplies that the captain was waiting for were very late in coming. The land we are going to is said to be remote. We are all anxious to make our way to what will be our new home. It has been a long journey.*

I look forward to setting up our house and being off this sloop. It is hard to imagine what the new land will be like. We are told that there are pirates that roam the island. Jacob's father has decided it will be safer for their family to move further inland. When I marry and leave to live with Jacob, I will miss my family, but I look forward to sharing our life together. Jacob and I have planned to be married in the fall. Emily and Robert are planning to marry this summer.

February 1, 1756—*We reached our new homestead on Ocracoke Island. The sloop tugged into the wooden port. The glassy wake sloshed up over the bow of our ship. I'm told it is called Cockle Creek. It is quite beautiful. The sunbeams gleam off the water. It looks as if silver coins are shining in the sparkling water. Papa tells me that our family must stay close. He fears unknown dangers.*

We will be staying on the sloop tonight. Emily and her family are going to their new home. It is called the Shepard's Head Inn. There is a tavern, next to the inn, called the Oxford Pub. Her papa acquired the property before leaving England.

All of our families bought property on Ocracoke Island before leaving England. Our home is a little farther down the lane past Emily's new home. Papa said he would take Robert with him to determine what we need to move into our new home. He wants me to keep a close eye on my mama and the little ones.

Jacob's family will stay at the inn with Emily's family until they leave to go further inland. I fear that the distance between Jacob's home and ours will mean we cannot see each other frequently. Jacob came by to see me before he left the sloop. He held me gently and brushed away the tears that fell down my cheeks. I told him that I would miss him dearly and miss being with him every day. He told me not to worry, that we would be together soon.

March 7, 1756—*My heart breaks a little bit every day when I think about being apart from Jacob. I understand that he must help settle his family in this place called Virginia. My mama continues in her melancholy. I cannot leave her to go be with Jacob. He tells me that he will come back for me when he can.*

I met Jacob tonight in one of the little wooden barns, behind the ponies' pens. We came together to say goodbye. He gave me a silver necklace with a pretty trinket—half of a heart—dangling from it. He said his papa had given him two silver spoons and he used them to make two identical necklaces, one for each of us. He engraved the two half hearts with our initials. I am to wear his initials, JH. He will wear mine, EA. He told me that it will be a reminder of when we will be together forever.

He slipped the necklace around my neck and kissed me gently. I reached my arms around his broad shoulders. When our lips met, a passion erupted between us. Our clothes fell off as we lay in the hay. Uncontained emotion spiraled around us. I wrapped my legs around him. His manhood drove into my moist loins. We shuddered when we became one soul. We lay in each other's arms in the barn. Tears fell down our cheeks. He told me not to fear for he would be back for me soon.

My body betrayed me, but I do not regret our union. I am glad I gave myself to him. But my heart broke a little bit more when we dressed and walked back hand-in-hand to my home. He kissed me goodbye. I watched him stride away and tears cascaded down my face, my lips quivering.

My sister, Lizzie, saw me and came out to hold me while I cried in her arms. I thanked heaven that she was my sister and that she is here to help me through this time. I told her that I gave myself to Jacob. She stroked my hair and said she knew how much I loved him and that we planned to wed. She told me everything was going to be all right.

June 3, 1756—*I have been taking long walks on this beautiful island, along the dunes on the sandy shores. It is quite lovely and there are so many birds. I watch them dance on the sand, running in and out of the surf. It gives me peace.*

Papa has warned me to stay close, but the sea soothes my soul. I received a letter from Jacob telling me that it would be a while longer before he could bring me back to him to be his bride. He wrote that his father had died of malaria. That made me sad. I always loved Jacob's father, just like my own. He said they had just arrived in their new home when his father became sick. Now that Jacob is the man of his family, he must stay to help settle things before he comes for me.

I find myself spending more and more time on the beach. I love to sing into the wind. My tears fall and are dried by the warm balmy breeze. I keep busy setting up our new home. Mama is not much help. Papa said he doesn't think Mama will ever get over losing our baby Anna. Lizzie and Robert have been my greatest help.

I have been making my wedding dress with some of the fabric that, so many months ago, we found in the Canary Islands. Emily is making hers, too. We found pearl beading to embellish the necklines. Mine has sleeves that fall loosely from my shoulders and flutter when I move. It also has a tiny waistline and a short train. I like things that are simple, not too elaborate.

I spend a lot of time daydreaming about when Jacob and I marry. I picture myself walking down the stairs at the inn in Emily's home. The church is still being built, so I asked Emily's mother if we could wed at the inn. She said she would be delighted to have our wedding in their home. She told me that she loved me like a daughter.

"And the story ended there," I tell the group as I close the journal.

There isn't a dry eye in our group. We are all thinking about the young couple, so in love, who were never to see one another again.

Sarah speaks first. "Do you think there is another journal hidden somewhere on the island about the rest of Evangeline's life? Can you imagine how it was back then having to rely on letters to communicate with everyone?"

"Maybe there are other journals where her family lived or here in one of her chests in the attic," Emily suggests. "We will have to keep looking to see if we can find them." Then Emily holds up her phone. "Do you all realize how spoiled we are, being able to call, text, or email the ones that we love? Back then, family members didn't know for weeks—or even months or years—when one of their loved ones had died.

"Just think about the Lost Colonists," she continues. "They still don't know to this day what happened to them."

Chapter 7

A Celebration

"This story of these star-crossed lovers is just so sad. I need to shake this off," I say. "I don't know about the rest of you, but I'm up for a little beach time. It's still early afternoon. How about it? Anyone want to go to the beach?"

Mom nods. "Sure do. I've been dreaming all spring about going for a walk on the beach." She turns to my sister and adds, "Sally, you should come with us. It will probably be good for you to move around after that long car ride and all this sitting we've done listening to Evangeline's diary."

Sally laughs, holding her round belly in her hands. "I'll go up and put on my swimsuit. I'm sure the whales will think I am one of them."

We watch her waddle up the winding staircase to her room. Robert waits until she is out of earshot. He whispers, "Good. You keep her busy while we set up for her baby shower."

He turns to Emily, "Were you and Sarah able to get the food catered?" he asks. "I spoke to some of our friends earlier this week. They are supposed to be here later this afternoon. Boy, is Sally going to be excited!"

"Don't worry," I say, "we'll keep her busy while you guys decorate the pub. I don't think she suspects a thing. Robert, you should go upstairs while she is getting ready for our afternoon swim, so she doesn't get suspicious."

Robert agrees. "That's smart. I'll tell her I am going to hang out with Thomas, George, and Matt for a while."

We watch him leave, and I can hardly contain my excitement. We laugh about the surprise Sally has planned for Robert's thirtieth birthday.

"It is so cool. A surprise inside a surprise," I exclaim. "Sally said she was able to get ahold of several of Robert's closest school friends from high school and college. She was even able to invite some of their neighbors."

Mom points upstairs. "Angie, we better go up and get ready ourselves or she'll be back down here before us."

We walk up the steps together, linking arms. I smile. "It is so nice to be able to visit with you, Mom. I have really missed you."

When I reach my room, I tell my mother that I'll meet her downstairs in fifteen minutes. Her room is right down the hall from mine. It's nice having her so close to me. The creamy white door to my room creaks when I open it. I can feel Evangeline's presence. It never gets old, that feeling I get when I know she is around. I sense her but there's no sign of her. I wonder to myself when she will make her next appearance.

I finish getting dressed for the beach and meet up with my mom and Sally downstairs. We head down to the water for a quick afternoon dip in the dazzling sunshine and warm Pamlico Sound.

Earlier in the day, Emily and Sarah told me about all the decorations they had for the combination surprise baby shower and thirtieth birthday party. Since we were having the joint party on Ocracoke Island and Sally planned a beach theme in the baby's room, we decided to have a beach theme for the shower, too. They are going to transform the pub into a world of mermaids, seashells, and pirates.

Sally and Robert don't know if they are having a girl or boy—they want to wait until the birth and be surprised.

While the pub is being decorated, Sarah must check in all the out-of-town guests. The inn is bursting at the seams with happy people. You can feel the excitement in the air.

Robert hurries back downstairs after Sally has left for the beach. When people start arriving and checking in, Robert greets them—thinking they are here for Sally's baby shower. His college and high school friends have managed to stay hidden from his view, waiting for him in the pub.

Meanwhile, at the beach, my mom, Sally, and I catch up with each other while we float in the warm Carolina surf. We have been blessed with warm water from the Gulf Stream that arrived earlier this week.

Sally turns to me. "So, tell me about what's been happening between Thomas and you."

I shrug. "Evangeline sent me to see Thomas at the cottage, but it's really weird. I just met Thomas, but I feel like I have known him all my life.

"I can't believe that I never met him in all these years at the beach," I continue. "I mean, we stayed here every summer. And he even went to Georgetown University. It's only a mile from my old apartment. Evangeline said what Dad had told me about the time being right, whatever that means.

"When Thomas and I first saw that vision of Evangeline and Jacob, it felt like we were in a dream. It was so real and so sad. My heart was breaking for them," I say. "And to find the journal and letter, too! Do you think we'll find the treasure?"

I know I am rambling. Mom and Sally are staring at me in disbelief. Then Sally smiles.

"Where is Angie, that sad, depressed girl I saw at Mom's house just last weekend? You are like another person since you got here. This island is good for you," she says. "The girls and I knew that you would hit it off with Thomas. I just didn't think you'd end up kissing him the first day you met. Who would have figured?"

I blush a crimson red. "It just happened. I got so excited finding the necklace, the journal, and the love letter from Daniel to Evangeline. You had to be there."

Mom smiles as she watches us. She reaches out and takes our hands in hers. "I'm so glad we are all here. I have missed this place. It has always felt like home to me," she says.

I nod in agreement. "Mom, that's so funny you say that. It's the same thing I said to myself when I got off the ferry today. I know I'm only supposed to be staying for the summer, but it was just like coming home for me."

"Me too," Sally agrees. "I told Robert the same thing."

I feel my skin prickle, and I touch my necklace. Suddenly I hear a tinkling of laughter coming from the sandy dunes. Evangeline and Jacob appear before us. Sally and my mom both stare at the vision with open mouths, surprised at the apparition. Evangeline looks at me and says, "Angie, you must know that all things needed to fall into place before you could meet Thomas. The time is right. Trust him. He is a good man."

Then she turns to Sally and whispers, "Sally, don't be worried. I will take care of you. You and your little ones will be safe. I will protect all of you." Both Evangeline and Jacob smile at us, then they vanish into the mist on the seashore.

Holding her chest, Mom stammers, "I have always felt Evangeline's presence, but I have never seen her until earlier today in the inn when she appeared before us. This island is such a magical place."

Sally tenderly holds her very pregnant belly. "I feel relief knowing that she is here protecting us, but she said 'little ones?' What is that supposed to mean? As far as we know, there is only one baby. I wonder if we should be worried?"

Mom takes her hand, trying to comfort her.

"Sally, your doctor wouldn't have let you come if he thought there was anything to worry about or if he thought you were having twins," Mom says. "Sarah has even hired a midwife to be close by if anything were to happen. She's staying at the inn. Remember Georgia? I have memories of her from when you girls were just babies in my belly.

"Georgia is very good at what she does. She delivered Emily and Sarah," Mom continues. "Plus, there is a pediatrician who lives right down the street from the inn. You'll be fine."

It is a beautiful June day. The sky is a cobalt blue, dotted with puffy white clouds. The seagrass sways on the shoreline. The warm Carolina breeze caresses our bodies, and the sun shines down on us. The temperature is perfect.

Sally's baby must have felt Evangeline's presence. The baby gives a couple good kicks and stretches out its tiny feet into Sally's ribs. It makes her wince, and she rubs her belly.

It is starting to get late in the day. It's almost 3:30 p.m. when I glance at my phone. "I think, on that note, we should head back to the inn. Sally, do you need to get some rest before dinner and Robert's party tonight at 6?"

"Yeah, I think I might take a little nap before the festivities," she responds. "I am a teensy bit tired. The ride from Clements, Maryland, seemed to take longer today.

"But before I lie down, I want to see what Robert and the others are up to. I also want to check on how things are going with the set up for the surprise birthday party. I'll stop by the pub on my way in."

I grin and try to discourage her. "Oh Sally, I really don't think that's a good idea. What if Robert wants to join you? The surprise will be ruined."

Sally sighs. "Oh, I didn't think of that. Good point. I guess I'll just go back to my room and rest for a while. The doctor told me not to overdo it. He said I should try to take a nap every day if I can."

Sally starts to get up from the sand, but I remain on the beach, sitting and daydreaming about my encounter with Thomas. I smile to myself and I wonder how it was possible, over twenty-six years, not to have met him. It's too crazy.

I think about how it felt to kiss him. It is mind bending. I am going to be so embarrassed to see him again after our kiss. I know I spent time with him while I was reading Evangeline's journal but just the thought of seeing him again makes me so nervous and embarrassed.

Sally laughs at me. "You're thinking about Thomas, aren't you? You were a million miles away. You know the girls and I have always thought that you and Thomas would make a great couple. Even Robert thinks so.

"I guess we'll just have to see what happens?" she adds.

I grimace. "I was thinking about Thomas and how embarrassed I'm going to be when I see him after that kiss. I want to hide from him if that's even possible," I say. "Besides, I have no intention of getting into another relationship anytime soon. After Larry, I'm so through with men. I would rather get a dog, than a boyfriend."

Sally stands beside me, brushing sand off her arms. "That's so funny. That's what Thomas says, too," she says.

Mom is listening to our conversation smiling, thinking how lovely it is to have both of her daughters with her while she walks down to the shoreline to rinse the sand from her feet.

We finish gathering up the blue striped beach towels that Sarah loaned us and our beach bags. The three of us head across the dusty, sandy road to the B&B. As we walk up the front steps to the inn, the air holds the floral scent of the roses that line the veranda. I breathe in deeply. "Those flowers smell heavenly. I love this time of year when everything is blooming," I say.

I open the door and am almost knocked off balance by Max. I kneel to greet Thomas' excited puppy, who jumps up on me, barks, and smothers me in wet kisses. Thomas is standing in the parlor talking to George after Robert has left to go upstairs. He rushes over to grab Max's collar, flabbergasted. "I'm so sorry Angie. He doesn't usually act this way towards people he doesn't know," Thomas says. "It's a sign he really likes you."

Thomas helps me up off the veranda's hardwood floor. I feel his warm breath on my cheek as I rise, my hand in his. Our eyes meet. Heat rises into my chest, into my neck and face. I blush. His eyes—brilliant green and flickering with dazzling golden flecks—smolder into mine.

My heart skips a beat. I bend over to ruffle Max's ears. "Really, I don't mind. I just wasn't expecting him to be here," I say. "I love animals. When I lived in D.C., I had several foster dogs—I miss having them around."

"What happened to them?" Thomas asks.

"Oh, I wasn't able to keep them," I reply, remembering when Larry made me get rid of the animals. Just one more thing my old boyfriend made me do that I didn't want.

Thomas turns to see my mother and sister on the veranda, too. He wraps his arms around both, gathering them into a big bear hug. "I'm so glad you both were able to make it this summer," he says as he kisses each on the cheek. Still red from embarrassment, I watch the scene unfold, astonished as he teases my sister. He touches her belly. "Wow, Sally, some beachball you have there." Sally laughs and rubs her belly. "I know, right? I didn't need to bring a ball this year—this one is attached."

This is so weird. I can't believe that they all know each other so well.

Thomas winks at me. "Sorry again about Max, Angie. I'll see you guys later tonight at Robert's party. Boy, is he going to be surprised," He picks up his happy puppy and heads down the front steps of the inn.

Both Mom and Sally tease me. "Oooh, I think somebody likes you," Sally says with a laugh.

Flustered, I grab my things and stomp up the stairs toward my room. At the top of the stairs, I try to catch my breath. I can't seem to control my feelings toward Thomas. My heart races at just the thought of him.

I hear Sally and Mom coming up the stairs behind me. Then Mom says to us. "Don't forget, girls. The photographer will be meeting us before dinner at six for family pictures. I want to get some photos of all of us before the new baby arrives. It's a family tradition."

Mom has hired one of the local photographers. Her name is Jenni. Epic Shutter Photography is her company. She grew up with Sarah and Emily.

Sally nods to Mom. "I invited Robert's dad, David, to come for pictures, too. I hope that is okay, Mom. He's here for the surprise party for Robert," Sally says. "Robert's brother, Joseph, and his family are here, too. Is it too much to include them since they're here?"

"No, I think that's perfect. It will be so special to get all of us together for pictures. After all, we are family," Mom responds. "David has been so nice this past year. We've been spending a lot of time together. He's been helping me with the loss of your father. I don't know what I would have done without him. He told me our time together has helped him, too, since losing his wife, Samantha, two years ago to cancer."

Sally squeezes my mom's hand. "Mom, we are all here for you. I'm so glad that you came this year. You will be able to spend time with everyone."

As Sally leaves Mom at our mother's room, my sister grins at the thought of the surprise she has in store for Robert. She opens the creamy white door to their room and finds Robert resting on their bed with his arms folded behind his head. He grins from ear to ear when she comes over to him. Sally plants a playful kiss on his lips.

Robert grins. "So how was the beach and your visit with Angie and your mom? Did you have a nice time?" Sally sits down on the bed, and he nuzzles his wife's neck and nibbles on her earlobes. It makes goosebumps appear on her arms. She remembers the first time Robert nibbled on her earlobes. They were sitting on the beach by a crackling bonfire. Above them, the most brilliant stars were glistening and the fireworks were exploding in an incandescent Carolina sky—while mystical Silver Lake mirrored the scene.

Sally wraps her arms around Robert. "I can't believe it's been four years since our first kiss and two years since we had our wedding here on the island. You have made me so happy."

She looks around the room. "This place—this island—will always be special for me because it holds so many of our memories." She rubs her belly. "It seems like only yesterday that we were married. And to think, in another month, we'll be welcoming this little treasure into the world. I can't wait to hold this little angel in my arms." Robert encircles her body with his arms and strokes her belly.

He then turns and takes Sally's face in his hands. "It's going to feel just like Christmas when our little one is born," Robert says. "I'm so glad we decided to wait to see whether we are having a boy or girl. I know we like the name William Jacob for a boy, but we still need to choose a girl's name."

Sally responds, "It does make it a little hard to plan, not knowing if it's a boy or girl."

Sally thinks to herself that Robert has always made her feel loved even on these days when she feels like a beached whale. Her body is changing every day. Her breasts are swollen. And she's started to have what her doctor has told her are Braxton Hicks Contractions, even as he assured her that they were totally normal. He told her to stay active, take naps when she felt tired, and enjoy visiting with everyone on the island. She is thirty-four weeks into her pregnancy.

Sally wraps her arms around Robert's neck. She breathes in his familiar scent. She smiles as she thinks again about the surprise she has in store for him. She closes her eyes and naps for a short while.

Waking up, she touches Robert's shoulder and she says, "Honey, we need to get up and get ready. Mom wants to take family pictures before dinner. We need to be in the Oxford Pub by six."

They roll off the bed and head to the bathroom. Under the spray of the shower, Robert helps wash her oversized belly.

"Sally, you look so beautiful. You just don't know how much I love you," he says. "You're having my baby," he teases her as he starts to sing the song. He takes her hand and brings it to his lips. "The love I feel for you makes my heart swell. I feel so lucky."

As they dress for the photos, Sally glances in the old-fashioned mirror at the coral sundress that flows over her pregnant body. "I look like a big round pumpkin," she declares.

"No, you don't," Robert says, laughing. "You look adorable."

Robert wears a tropical shirt, peach with tan-colored seashells. They make a handsome couple as they hold hands and make their way down the winding staircase to the first floor of the inn. Each is ecstatic thinking about the surprise they have in store for the other.

Chapter 8
Surprises

Our family and friends are waiting anxiously behind the huge wooden doors of the pub. The decorations for the surprise baby shower and birthday party look festive. Little seashells, turtles, and tropical fish hang from the bar to carry through on the beach theme. As my sister and her husband push open the rust-colored doors of the pub, bellows of "surprise" ring out, and the startled couple bursts into laughter. They wrap their arms around each other, and then begin hugging and bantering with the well-wishers around them.

Eyes wide and with huge smiles, they face the people who love them. Tears start to stream down Sally's face. "Oh Robert. How did you manage to pull this off?" she asks. "Look at everyone here!"

Robert laughs. "Me? What about you? I can't believe you got my college friends to come. I just don't know what to say."

"Well, we especially need to thank Sarah, Emily, and the others for helping me to pull this off," Sally says. "Without them, it would have never happened."

Sally turns to the girls, the Whites, and her family and envelopes them all in hugs. "I can't thank everyone enough."

Robert is especially touched to see his father in the pub. David Brown has managed to make the long trek here from his home in Indian Head, Maryland. Robert knows how hard it is for his father to come back to the island since his mom died two years earlier. His mother and father first met on the island when they were teenagers.

Robert's father seems happy today. He is standing next to my mother, Isabella. Robert knows his father and Isabella have been keeping each other company since my father passed away last October, and he's glad they have each other to lean on. I am, too. My mother and David have been friends for as long as I can remember. Our families shared many summer vacations together.

Sally glows with all the attention she is receiving, and she is smiling from ear to ear. The photographer was able to get some lovely pictures of my sister and Robert being surprised. We take family pictures after the party has started. Isabella is on one side of the ecstatic couple and David is on the other side.

Thomas stands and watches my family's tender interactions, and he feels his heart melt. He shakes his head and wonders what is wrong with him. "I just met Angie. I don't want or need a relationship. I'm entirely too busy to get involved with anyone," he thinks to himself. "I need to shake myself out of this."

Thomas is gazing at me, although I am oblivious. Emily, standing next to Sarah, nudges her and points in Thomas's direction. Emily laughs. "Look at him. I think he's smitten." They both watch him and giggle. When he spots them, his cheeks flame red in embarrassment. Even his brother George, who is standing next to Thomas, is shocked to see his big brother so intensely observing me with love-struck eyes.

Matt, too, notices Thomas's gaze. Matt loves to tease me and Sally and, as I find out later, he's not going to let me hear the end of this.

Sarah stands back watching Matt, and her heart tugs a little. Matt looks over and Sarah catches his eyes, the color of the sea. Like mine, they change color—from sea foam green to brilliant cobalt blue to aqua blue, depending on Matt's moods. Matt grins at Sarah and winks, making her blush profusely.

Sarah confided to me many years ago that she has feelings for Matt. Sarah and Matt grew up together on the shores of Ocracoke Island. Matt gave Sarah her first kiss when they were teenagers, right here on the island's dunes. Sarah wonders how she is going to make it through the summer with Matt nearby? "I'll have to keep myself busy at the inn to keep my mind off him," she thinks.

It is time for Sally and Robert to open the gifts that guests have brought for the baby. I lean over to Emily. "I like this new trend, to invite the guys to baby showers. I think that the dads should be involved."

Emily agrees with me. "Yeah, it is a good trend. Years ago, they were left out of all of it," she says, before adding, "Hey, do you know if Sally and Robert have done their nursery at home?"

"Not yet," I reply. "They just painted the room a pale green since they didn't know whether it's a boy or girl."

The happy couple unwraps lots of cute onesies in yellow, green, white, and cream hues. They also receive plenty of diapers, baby bottles, and formula. Sarah and Emily have sewn a tropical-yellow and foam-green quilt that has tiny seashells, turtles, and palm trees on it. It is so quaint. And just perfect for the baby.

Sally holds up the quilt. "Oh girls, I just love this! It's so cute."

That's when Thomas brings out his present, with the help of his brother George. "I wanted to make you something special, to treasure and pass down to your little one," Thomas says to Robert and my sister. "Sally, I remember how much you loved the story of Evangeline and Jacob, so I made you guys this cradle. I carved a heart and added Evangeline and Jacob's initials. I thought it would be something you might like."

Sally is so excited that she jumps up and down and wraps her arms around Thomas and Robert. "Oh, Thomas, I love it! I'm so touched. We will treasure it always."

The beautiful golden oak cradle amazes me, and I say to Emily, "I didn't know that Thomas, Sally, and Robert were such close friends. How have I missed that?"

Emily smiles. "Didn't you know he used to come to their home for visits when he lived in D.C.? He used to tell me about it whenever he came home from college."

I shake my head. "Wow. That is crazy."

I reach up to touch my heart-shaped necklace. I feel the tears stream down my face. I wonder why am I so emotional?

After I'm able to compose myself, it's time for my gift.

"I hope you don't mind but I wrote a song for your new baby about your love story. I plan to record it on my next album. I hope you like it."

I grab my guitar. My heart flutters. I am so nervous. My voice and guitar echo through the tiny pub as I sing the heartfelt story of the romance between Robert and Sally—and how their child was a sign of their great love for one another. The two of them made one.

I feel Evangeline's presence as I sing, although I cannot see her. The whole room is quiet as my voice vibrates through the little bar. Some of the eyes in the room are moist with emotion. Cheers erupt when I finish my song. Robert and Sally race up to embrace me.

Sally has happy tears in her eyes. "Oh Angie, what special gift. We can't wait to get a copy of your new album and our song. We are so touched."

Robert hugs me. "That was great. We really love it."

I wipe the tears from Sally's cheeks. "The song will be released on your anniversary. I told my manager to have the royalty checks from my song go into a trust fund for your baby. Let's hope this song goes all the way to No. 1!"

Sally embraces me again. "Angie, I don't know what to say. Thank you so much."

Thomas watches. He doesn't say anything. I could feel his eyes on me while I was playing.

Thomas shakes his head and again wonders how he could feel the way he does about someone he just met. "This is crazy. What is happening to me?" he asks himself.

The gift-giving isn't over yet. Robert's father, David, has something for Sally and his son. Something extraordinary. He pulls Joseph, his other son, and Joseph's wife Rebecca close in. He hands the two brothers and their wives the keys to the beach home where the widower experienced so many wonderful moments with his wife.

"I want your families to share all the special memories that our family has shared over the years," he says to Robert and Joseph. "I want you boys and your families to share the beach home. Your mother would have wanted this."

Sally squeals and hugs her father-in-law. "We will cherish it always."

Robert takes the keys and hugs David. "Thanks Dad. We'll make you proud. We'll take care of it the way that our families have done over the years."

The house, a six-bedroom bungalow built back in the 1700s, has been passed down through the generations. Originally, it belonged to Roger Brown. David points to Thomas. "Thomas is going to help us renovate the house once he finishes with the cottage that Angie's staying in this summer," he says. "He wants to restore it to its original splendor. George will be updating the plumbing, heating, and air conditioning systems."

David turns to Thomas. "I can't believe my luck that you came back to the island, Thomas, and with a plan renovate all the old homes."

So many amazing things are happening on this wonderful evening, but the surprises within surprises aren't over yet. Robert's brother, Joseph, confesses a secret.

"Thanks so much, Dad. That is so nice of you, but Rebecca and I have a surprise, too. We just bought a beach house on the island. I planned to tell everyone tomorrow. I didn't want to steal any of Robert and Sally's thunder by mentioning it tonight."

David embraces Joseph and Rebecca. "I'm so happy for the two of you and your family. Your children will love spending their summers on the island."

Joseph steps over to Thomas and says, "You might have a new customer. We just bought that antiquated, five-bedroom home from the 1700s down on Howard Street. It needs a lot of work, so we are going to need a good contractor to help us."

George pats Thomas on the back. "We have all kinds of jobs lining up, left and right. Looks like we are going to have a busy summer."

Robert and his friends laugh as they reminisce about their previous times spent together. They then do a celebratory toast to Robert's 30th birthday.

The festivities continue and the cakes are cut. The drinks flow as I pick up my guitar again to sing my songs. A lot are about times I've spent on the Outer Banks and on Ocracoke Island. Some of my old friends from the island are here to help us celebrate. They listen to my melodies and music, which relax the heart and soothe the soul.

The night goes on until Sally and Robert announce that they are exhausted and excuse themselves, thanking everyone profusely for the gifts and well wishes. Robert has his arm delicately around Sally's shoulder. "Thank you all, but I must get my little princess up to bed," he says. "It's been a very long day."

Sally yawns, rubbing her belly. "Yes, everyone, thank you all for making this such a special celebration. I will treasure this day, always. When this baby is old enough, I will tell him or her all about all of our dear friends and family and the night you all shared with us. Good night all. Thanks, again."

George comes around the bar to help Emily. He pats her on the back. "Emily, you have really outdone yourself tonight. Boy, were they surprised."

I look at George and Emily together, and I just can't understand why these two have not become a romantic couple in all these years. It just doesn't make any sense to me.

Sarah and Matt help us take down all the decorations. We wrap up the remaining food to take back to the B&B with us. As we work, Sarah whispers to me, "Angie, I had forgotten how much I liked being around your brother. What am I going to do?"

I laugh. "Just stop fretting about it. Enjoy each other's company. You worry too much."

David, Mom, the Whites, and my grandparents join in to help us to clear up the clutter from the celebration. When I glance over at my mother, her eyes look sad, but only for a moment, as she watches us. She turns to me. "Your dad would have loved this and your beautiful song."

I wrap my arms around her. "I know Mom. Sometimes, I forget he's not with us. It's almost as if I can feel him here, even though I know that isn't possible."

David is standing beside my mother and he reaches over to squeeze her shoulder. "I know it's hard, but I'll help you get through this. You've got this, Isabella," he tells her. "I remember that when Samantha died, everything was a struggle. I know how you are feeling.

"Samantha would have loved this, too," he adds as he gives my mother a hug.

David is spending the night at Shepard's Head B&B with the rest of our family. He told us earlier, now that he retired a few months ago, that he plans to stay the whole summer on the island to help with the renovations of the beach house.

"I don't need to rush home to an empty home in Maryland. I love and miss being here on the island," he says. "What I need is here."

Chapter 9

The Dream

The party is all cleared away, but Emily isn't ready to end the reunion. "Anyone up for a little post-party bonfire on the beach, for old time's sake?" she asks with a laugh. "We can raid the bar. I know the owners."

George chuckles. "For sure. I think that sounds like a great idea. It's been a long time." Then she adds: "I'll give you a hand raiding the bar."

With drinks in hand, Emily, George, Matt, Sarah, Thomas, and I walk down to the beach. My mind wanders back to earlier times together by the bonfire, enjoying each other's company. Tonight, is a gorgeous evening. We watch the waves gently roll up onto the serene shore, then recede, while a crescent moon beams off the briny sea. The crimson and orange embers of the fire crackle, and the smell of the burning cinders teases my nose. It brings back so many fond memories of my blessed childhood.

Sarah lies back on a well-worn blue patchwork quilt that covers the silky sand. "Look at how brightly the stars are shining tonight. I have really missed the times we would sit here in this same spot. It seems like only yesterday," she says.

Matt plops down beside Sarah and takes her soft hand in his. He lifts it to his lips. "To think it has been over five years since I've come down on the beach for a bonfire with all of you. I have really missed doing this." Sarah looks like she is going to swoon as she gazes into Matt's cobalt blue eyes sparkling in the light from the fire.

We're quiet for a minute, before Matt speaks again.

"So, Thomas and Angie, tell me what happened at the cottage," he says. "I caught the tail end of it when I got here today."

I rub my hands over my face. "Matt, you would not believe it, even if we told you. It was like a dream. Right Thomas?"

I pause, then continue. "It was like being drawn into a time warp. Like we were thrown back into the past as we watched Evangeline and Jacob saying goodbye to each other. It was so surreal and so incredibly sad.

"They didn't know it was going to be the last time that they would see each other," I explain. "Thomas, do you think it would work if we showed him?"

For reasons that he can't explain, Thomas placed the heart pendant necklace around his neck after he found it and he has been wearing it ever since. I take my heart necklace in my hand, and I reach out for Thomas's hand. Once again, the vision materializes in front of us. Emily, Sarah, and I have tears in our eyes as we watch the scene unfold.

Matt is in shock. "Wow, that's so wild!" he finally says. "Who would have thought?

Then he turns to Thomas and me. "Angie, why do you think this is happening?" he asks. "Everybody always said you looked like Evangeline. Thomas, you look like some of the pictures I've seen of Jacob. Do you think that you two are linked because of the necklaces, or for some other reason, like soulmates or something?"

Thomas shrugs. "I don't know. I'm not sure what it all means. It's like she's trying to guide us somewhere or to something," he responds. "The letter we found gave us a clue to the whereabouts of Blackbeard's treasure map. Maybe that's it. Maybe she wants us to find the treasure."

George swats Thomas on the back. "Wouldn't that be so cool? Can you imagine?" Then George looks over toward all of us. "Don't you guys remember when we were kids how we used to search for pirate's treasures? We would go down to Springer's Point and dig holes in the sand, always searching for that gold coin or buried treasure chest."

I yawn. It has been a long, emotional roller-coaster day. "Well, according to the letter and Evangeline's note, we need to find the next clue," I say. "The handwritten note said we would need to search 'where the Tiger meets the inlet on the land where the Bankers roam free, and the Yaupon meets the pines.'

"So, if we think it is probably somewhere on Springer's Point or by the ponies' pen, I guess that is where we will need to search next," I add.

Emily looks at me and my brother. "You and Matt must be tired. It's been a long day for you two. Angie, you said you left your house at 5 a.m. What time did you start out Matt?"

Matt runs his hands through his curly black hair. "Same here. I left my house at 5 a.m., too. Yeah, I'm about ready to hit the hay."

Thomas ruffles Max's ears. The puppy wakes up and whines. Thomas reaches down to attach Max's lease to his pretty blue collar.

"I think we wore poor old Max out. Angie, he has been sleeping on your feet since we sat down. I think I need to get my poor little pup home," Thomas says. "George, are you about ready to head home?"

Thomas has been living with George until he can find an old island home of his own to remodel. George's house is right down the lane from the Oxford Pub—and Emily. Thomas has explained to Emily that he has his eye on a home off the beaten path, a house he can update while preserving its original charm.

When he came back from Georgetown University, Thomas had told Emily: "There are so many old houses on the island that are just waiting to be refurbished. A lot of them are standing empty. They are literally falling down and in disrepair, We want to restore as many of them as possible to their natural beauty."

Thomas and George live beside their parents in an antiquated colonial plantation home built back in the 1700s. It is right next to Teach's Hole, reportedly a gathering spot for pirates some three hundred years ago. Famous buccaneers like Blackbeard and Calico Jack hung out at Teach's Hole, carousing, drinking ale and rum. Some people believe treasure was once hidden in that area on the island.

We all get up to leave the beach. George tosses sand over what's left of the bonfire embers. "So long my little fire. We'll come back later," he says. We all laugh at him.

Thomas and George stand at the bottom of the steps of the inn. "See you all tomorrow," they say in unison before heading off in the direction of their home.

Sarah, Emily, and I walk up the stairs to the inn, arm in arm. We go over and sit on the white porch glider. Matt rolls his eyes as he listens to us giggle and daydream out loud about buried treasures and lost loves. Standing at the bottom of the stairs, he calls out, "See you later. It's been fun. You girls never change," he adds. "Still giggly teenagers."

We wave goodbye as he heads to where he's staying, one of the renovated cottages next to the B&B. Sarah sighs and points at Matt as he walks away. "Oh Angie, your brother still makes my heart skip beats. This is going to be a long summer. He told me earlier today that he plans to stay and help Thomas renovate your cottage."

Emily laughs. "Well, this should be an interesting summer between you and Matt, and Thomas and Angie."

Then she turns to tease me. "Wow, Angie, there sure are some sparks between you and Thomas. What's the deal? 'Fess up."

I raise my hand. "There's really nothing to 'fess up about. Come on, Emily. I just met him. And you talk about me, but what about you and George? He's obviously so head over heels in love with you—still. When are you two going to open your eyes? You need to give him a big ole lip lock, to seal the deal."

Emily, exasperated, blushes. "We're just friends. George doesn't feel that way about me."

I shake my head. "Are you kidding me? Are you blind? He can't keep his eyes off you. He's always around you. He helps you in the pub every day."

Sarah chimes in. "I agree with Angie. Give it time. It will happen."

Putting my hands on my hips, I say to Sarah, "Well, what about you, young lady? Are you ever going to tell Matt how you feel about him?"

Sarah shakes her blonde head. "No way. He still thinks of me as a little kid."

I take Sarah by the arm and lock into her jade green eyes. "I think you are wrong. Matt seems different this year," I say. "What about him taking your hand on the beach? That looked to me like he was hitting on you."

Sarah huffs. "Whatever. We aren't going to solve this tonight. Tomorrow is another day. I don't know about you girls, but I'm beat."

We get up off the glider and walk Emily over to her wood-shingled cottage beside the B&B, then Sarah and I climb the gray-and-tan stone steps of the mansion and then up the winding white stairs inside the inn. I hug my friend in front of my bedroom. "Good night. I'll see you in the morning."

I open the door to my room, fully expecting to see Evangeline, but the room is quiet. I smile and deeply inhale the fragrant scent of the yellow roses Sarah left in my room.

I call out to Evangeline, Evie, when I am alone. I shrug, then say aloud to the empty room, "Evie, I guess you aren't going to come see me tonight. Did you visit us enough today? Thanks for all the neat things we found in your cottage. I am just not sure what you are trying to tell us. Or what you mean by 'the time is right?'

"Well, if you're not going to talk to me, I think I'm going to bed. I'm exhausted," I add.

After getting ready for bed, I climb into the golden oak four-poster bed. The feather mattress is so soft. I sink down under the handsewn yellow-and-turquoise patchwork quilt that Sarah and Emily made for the room. I think to myself, these girls are so crafty. I hope, maybe, while I'm here this summer that it will rub off on me.

I smell the heavenly scent of Downy on the sheets. I can barely keep my eyes open. Weary after my long day of travel and partying, I close my eyes and I dream of Evangeline, of pirates, of a beautiful tropical island with silky pink sand.

In my dream, Evangeline is holding a little boy. His feathery white hair curls around his cherubic face. He snuggles up to her. I hear her whisper in his tiny ear, "Oh Jacob, if only you could see our child. William reminds me so much of you. Would you come to rescue us if you knew where we were?"

Tears stream down her face. "I must keep you safe, my little one. No one will ever know that you belong to Jacob. If Daniel ever figured out that you didn't belong to him, our lives would surely be in peril."

It's as if I can read her mind in my dream. I know what she is thinking. Everyone on the island assumes the child is Daniel Teach's son. Daniel believes that William is his. He keeps Evangeline and the boy well protected and loved. I feel that Daniel truly loves Evangeline. I see her read one of the love letters he wrote her. In my dream, Daniel tells her, "Evangeline, my love, I will give you clues to find Blackbeard's treasures. If anything were to ever happen to me, you and William will not be poor."

I see him lavish Evangeline with jewels and baubles from his pirating excursions. I see her beg him, "Daniel, I miss my family. Please let me go home, if only just to visit them." He sneers, grabbing her roughly by her shift. He swears, "I will never share you with anyone. You belong to me and only me."

She cries in his arms, knowing in her heart that the only way she will go back home to Ocracoke Island is if she and William escape.

Later in my dream, Evangeline rocks young William in a pretty, wooden rocking chair. I hear what she is thinking. She loves her time with her son. Then a tall, dark-haired man walks onto the porch where she sits. She looks up at him. "Hello, Roger," she says.

Roger Brown. I remember him from stories we heard about Evangeline. She traveled across the ocean on the same ship as him. He is a good comrade of her love, Jacob.

Roger blushes. "I'm so glad you are able to use the rocking chair that Daniel and I made for you."

Evangeline smiles up at him, "Roger, I just love my chair and so does William. If he is fretting, I soothe him in it. I am glad you come to visit me. You feel like home to me.

"Oh, Roger, how I miss my family," she continues, "but fear I will never get back home." She tells Roger about her conversation with Daniel and how he said he would never share her with anyone.

I see the exotic island in my dreams. It is a beautiful tropical paradise with billowing palm trees and lush blossoms scattered along the pink sand beach. I can almost smell their heavenly floral scent. It is so real, just like I am there.

Roger makes a promise. "Evangeline, fear not. I will see William and you safely home one day. I just have to wait for an opportune time. Daniel is a dangerous man. He would kill both of us if he ever found out that I plan to help you escape."

Then, in my dream, Evangeline is walking down a narrow path lined with green vines, her son hitched on her slender hip. The path is lined with bushy seagrass and small brambles. The bushes prickle her legs as she passed them. She must push them aside as she continues walking.

I feel her excitement when she reaches a clearing that reveals an aqua-colored lagoon. The water is so clear that beautiful tropical fish are visible swimming around a brightly colored reef. A spectacular waterfall cascades over the lagoon. It seems so real in my dream.

Angeline speaks to William. "We are here, my son. We can play here without fear of eyes watching us. This will be our special place. I will teach you to swim, just like my papa taught me.

"But we will only come here when your papa is away at sea."

Evangeline takes William behind the waterfall, into a space hidden from the outside world. She lays the tired child on a quilt on the cavernous floor. She kisses her son's chubby little cheek.

"One day, I will take you home to my family. They will love you," she whispers. "You have a papa, a grandpapa, and lots of uncles and aunts. And probably cousins by now. They will be so surprised. One day, my dear child, one day."

She daydreams of her escape and return to her family. She imagines reuniting with Jacob. She wonders if he still thinks of her. It has been three long years since she was captured. Daniel has been good to her. She no longer fears him, but she knows not to cross him. She has given up on trying to escape from his grasp.

Next in my dream, I see Daniel coming home from his latest exploits. He drapes sparkling trinkets and jewels around Evangeline's neck and over her hands. He tells her he has hidden more diamonds, rubies, emeralds, and sapphires in his treasure chest on the island.

In a flash forward, I see Roger dash into Evangeline's home, agitated. "Evangeline, we must hurry! The time has come for our escape. Daniel has perished. He fell overboard from the sloop and drowned in a drunken stupor.

"The other pirates here do not yet know of his demise. We are in danger if we do not leave now. Gather young William and your chest of belongings," Roger says with urgency. "Have you sewn your jewels into your gowns as I told you?"

Evangeline rushes out of the cabin down the path to the port, to Daniel's ship. William is in her arms, trembling and crying on her shoulder. "Where is my poppa? Momma, I am scared," the child says.

Fear and despair are written all over his tiny face. "Baby, we are taking you home," Evangeline coos. "All is well. You will see."

I can feel William's little heart beating wildly against me as he wonders where Daniel is. He doesn't understand all the commotion or why they are leaving the only place he has ever called home. Aboard Teach's ship, Evangeline holds her son close as they watch the lush island become smaller.

Roger has his arm around Evangeline. "I promised I would see you home," he declares. I can feel the love he has for Evangeline and William. It shines in his eyes. Then I, too, see the island disappear as the ship sails farther away.

I wake up, roll over in the comfortable feather bed, and rub my eyes. I wonder if the dream is real. Did Evangeline just show me part of her life on the island where she was held captive? I really wonder if Evangeline is trying to show me something.

Chapter 10

More Dreams

I hear a tinkling of Evangeline's laughter when I rush downstairs to tell the others about my vivid dream. The bright sun already beams through the ancient glass windowpanes and sends rainbow-colored reflections onto the pale, yellow walls.

I run down the winding, white stairs, down into the welcoming parlor. The aroma of smoky, hickory bacon and freshly brewed coffee fills my nose as I find my way into the cozy, warm kitchen. My mother, Sarah White, and the girls are busy cooking a feast for breakfast. "Man, that smells so good?" I ask. "I have missed our family breakfasts here on the island. What can I do to help?"

Sarah hands me a paring knife and points to the fruit. "If you want, you can cut up the fresh fruit. I was able to get melons and peaches at the farmers market yesterday before you guys got here. Isabella is making her famous biscuits. Emily is making her ever popular veggie scrambled eggs. Mom is also making her yummy sausage and gravy to go over the buttery biscuits."

Emily looks at me, "How did you sleep? Any more visits from Evangeline last night?"

I start to slice the juicy peaches and melons. "Funny, you should ask. I had the strangest dreams last night. I think I dreamed about Evangeline's life on the island. It was so real. The dream was about her son, William, and about Daniel and her friend, Roger. She was on this tropical island. She was swimming in a secluded, aqua-colored lagoon with her son. I could even feel the warmth of the water while she and William floated in the prettiest turquoise water I've ever seen. I even felt tiny fish nibble on my ankles. It was so weird. There was this cascading waterfall, behind it. There was a cavern. Evangeline said it was their secret hiding place.

"Then, it's like it flashed forward to another time and she's back in the cottage that she shared with Daniel," I continue. "I saw Roger come run into her home to help her escape the island. I've never experienced anything like it before. Do you think she is trying to show me her life?"

Sarah scratches her head. "That's really neat. Maybe you should write it all down just in case it helps us with our treasure hunting. You never know. Maybe she was trying to give us more clues."

My sister Sally shrugs her shoulder. "I think she's really trying to tell us how to find the treasure. Maybe you can use it in the novel that you plan to write while you're here this summer. What a perfect place to write about their love story. You said all along you wanted to tell their story. Maybe now is the time."

I nibble on one of my mother's biscuits. It melts in my mouth. "I wonder if I will dream anymore about her life."

After a pause, I'm pulled back to reality. "What time are we leaving for the beach today? It looks like it's going to be a beautiful day," I say. "Look at those puffy white clouds and how blue the sky is."

Emily pulls her hair up into a ponytail. "Matt and Robert already made sandwiches to take for our picnic lunch on the beach. And Thomas and George should be here any time. They're bringing Max. You should see that puppy running in and out of the surf. Your Mom has Skippy and Ace ready to go, too. They are going to love the beach."

At that, we hear Max barking, excited at seeing the other dogs and people. The storm door opens, and I feel my face flush when I look up at Thomas. Max barks and whines trying to come over to greet me but Thomas hasn't let him off his leash yet. He jumps up on me, trying to get my attention.

We take the short bumpy ride down to milepost 42. I hitch a ride in George's red 4x4 Jeep with Emily and Thomas. We drive onto the sandy beach. I gaze out at the crystal, aquamarine-colored water. It feels so serene and I am the happiest I have been in ages.

It's going to be another glorious day. Clouds that look like cotton balls float across a dazzling sky the splendid cobalt blue you see after a storm has cleared out. A gentle breeze ruffles the seagrass on the reedy dunes while iridescent waves slowly roll onto the velvety tan shoreline. The warm temperatures and calm water are perfect for floating in the lovely Atlantic swells. Sally can even loll in the surf today, with her ever-growing belly.

All my cousins' children splash and play in the surf under the watchful eyes of their parents. I overhear Sally ask Robert, "What do you think our little one is going to look like? Dark hair? Blonde hair? I am getting so excited. It could be any time now."

"Just think, this time next year our baby will be splashing in the water," Robert adds. "Sally, you just lay back on me and relax. Let the water ease your aching back. The water is so warm today. The Gulf Stream must have come up this way early."

The crystalline water is so clear today that I can see my feet even while standing waist deep. Silver minnows nibble at my ankles. We swim and float for hours. It tickles me when I think that Thomas looks just like a pirate, with his long blonde hair braided down his back. All he needs is an eye patch.

Thomas swims in my direction. When he pops up from the water, he gazes into my face. "Angie, did you know your eyes are the color of the water? They are so pretty. It amazes me that we never met before this year."

I smile. "I said the exact same thing to the girls just last night about never meeting you." No one talks that day of buried treasures or pirates. We just enjoy each other's company.

As the day wears on, some of our family and friends head back to their beach homes early. I tell the others I want to stay and watch the sun melt into the sea. "I don't want this day to end. It's so peaceful. I have missed the days we spent over the years on this beach," I think.

Nightfall comes down upon us. We sit on the shore and watch as the sun dips into the Atlantic, its water reflecting colors of lavender, coral, magenta, pearl, gold, and tangerine. I watch in awe. "I don't think there is anywhere on this earth that there is a more spectacular sunset than here on Ocracoke Island," I say. "I hate to leave."

Sarah consoles me. "Don't worry, Angie. We'll have many more sunrises and sunsets. You're going to be here all summer this year."

I grin in response. "I should have done this years ago."

The time comes when we have to head back to the inn. We gather all our belongings and pack up the vehicles. Emily, George, Thomas, Max, and I all climb into George's truck and set out on our way back to the B&B. Max is worn out after frolicking in the surf with the children and my mother's dogs, Skippy and Ace. He falls asleep, his head of golden hair in my lap.

Thomas turns to glance toward the back seat and he sees Max. "Angie, sorry about Max. I can bring him up here with me if he's bothering you."

I rub Max's furry head. "No, don't do that. I'm really enjoying him. I miss being around dogs—but that's another story, for another day."

The rest of the gang—Sally, Robert, Matt, and Sarah—follow us home in Matt's blue Chevy 4x4 truck. No one wants the beautiful day to end. Sarah and Emily's parents have taken on inn duties to give Sarah the day off.

Sarah tells our group, "It's so nice having our parents back home. They have been such a big help. I didn't realize how stressful it is to be as busy as we've been so far this summer. It'll be nice having us all together tonight without having to work. Even Emily is off with the pub being closed today."

We return to the Shepard's Head Inn in time to join the rest of the family and friends for a delicious dinner of local seafood. My mouth waters as we enter the inn. I catch rich aromas wafting from the kitchen: shrimp, oysters, fish, and clams. "Sarah, everything smells heavenly," I say. "Thank you so much for having tonight's dinner catered. You think of everything."

Sarah shrugs off the compliment. "I can't take all the credit. It was a joint effort," she answers. "Mom, Dad, and Emily helped plan the evening. It's just nice that fresh seafood and vegetables are easy to get this time of year at the farmer's market."

The day ends so quickly, leaving me exhausted again. I collapse into my soft bed, curl up, and fall asleep almost instantly. It's another dream-filled night. Again, I'm transported back in time to watch Evangeline's life unfold. She is back on Ocracoke Island after returning from her captivity. William looks to be about five or six years old. Her family—nieces, nephews, brothers, sister, and her father—are around her. I can feel the love that encircles them.

I watch her younger brother, Stephen, get married to Mary Albright. Evangeline has stepped back into her matriarch role in the family. Her friend, Roger, stands beside her at the wedding. He beams at her. After the wedding, I see Roger take William and Evangeline home to her tiny beach cottage. "I am so glad Emily and Robert let us move into this cabin," Evangeline says. "It is so different being home with William."

Next, I see Evangeline speaking to her very pregnant friend, Emily. "I can't believe you and Robert are having another baby," she says. "I missed the first baby. I'm so glad I get to be here for this one. Thank you again for letting William and me stay in the cottage. I just love it."

Emily hugs her old friend. "I, too, am glad you are here," she says. "Our first baby did not want to come into the world. I had such a hard time. It is a comfort that you are here for me. I am glad you'll be here with me when our babe is born."

Then I see Evangeline running up the steps of the inn to help Emily deliver her baby. Emily is a tiny woman, and it has been a difficult pregnancy. The room where the birth will occur bursts with tension. I feel Evangeline's relief when the baby enters the world, turning pink. He wails and his loud cries fill the room.

When I wake up in the morning, I again wonder if I am watching Evangeline's real life unfold in my dreams. After breakfast, I decide to check on the progress of my cottage. As I open the door, I'm greeted by Max, his tail wagging. I bend down to pet him and I'm rewarded with lapping kisses. My face is wet with puppy love.

Thomas is already busy. I watch him pull the old wooden mantel off the time-worn hearth. There's something underneath. A new discovery! Apparently, Evangeline likes to hide her treasures behind the mantel. Thomas find another tiny cedar box. Inside the coffer is a tiny silver locket that holds a small sepia picture of Evangeline's little William, as well as a lock of what must have been the child's curly blond hair.

The box also contains a tiny golden ring and a beautiful ruby necklace with a note saying "Daniel gave this to me when William was born." It is signed by

Evangeline. A letter is also enclosed. It is another of Daniel's letters in which he vows his love for Evangeline and provides another clue to the treasure map.

As I reach to examine the items in the little box, my hand grazes Thomas's. We are transported back in time again. In this vision, we watch Daniel bend down on one knee. He vows his love to Evangeline and asks her to marry him. "Evangeline, you have given me a son and given me the greatest happiness I have ever known. Be mine forever with this golden ring I offer thee."

He slips the ring onto her tiny pale finger. Evangeline looks at the gold band. "You are the father of my son. I accept your proposal," she replies. The scene vanishes, and Thomas and I are back in the present time.

"I feel in my heart that she felt she had no other choice," I say aloud to Thomas. "She told me in my dream that she knew that Jacob had moved on. She accepted her fate even though she would always long to be with her family and with her true love. It's weird that I can feel these things about her, almost as if I am part of her. Do you think that you and I linked because of the necklaces?"

Thomas exhales. "You might be right. Since finding the necklace, I have felt drawn to you as if I have known you forever."

"Thomas, ever since you found the other half of the necklace I've been having dreams of Evangeline's past life. It's as if she wants me to see what happened to her," I say.

We sit in silence for a minute and then I tell him the reason I came to the cottage this morning. "I would really love to help you guys with the renovation. Would it be okay with you and Matt?"

Thomas runs his hand across the old wooden mantel. "It's fine with me and I'm sure it will fine with Matt. Today I was just going to take down the rest of these fireplace stones. I'd like to reuse as many of them as I can," he says.

Thomas glances around the cottage. "It's as if time hasn't touched the place," he says. "The ancient fireplace stands as it did when Evangeline was cooking meals here so many years ago."

We both start taking down the stones, lost in our own thoughts. We think about Evangeline's past life. At one point, Thomas chuckles. "I wonder how many other treasures we'll find in here," he says.

Before I can answer, there's a knock on the door and there are giggles and laughter as Sally, Emily, and Sarah come in to see what magic Thomas and Matt have worked with my tiny summer home. I tell the girls what we found. I hand the locket to my sister.

"Sally, look at what's inside the locket. There is a letter saying the picture is of Evangeline's son, William. The gold ring and the ruby necklace were given to her by Daniel when he proposed after William was born."

Then I add: "Thomas and I saw another vision of Evangeline's life." Excitedly, I start to tell them about our latest vision and how Evangeline's life has been coming to me in my dreams, but I stop when I hear Sally gasp.

The locket is open and she is staring at the picture of William's face. Her heart tugs and she instinctively reaches down and rubs her hands over her belly.

"It's so weird. I feel drawn to Evangeline's son. I can't explain it," she marvels. "I believe you must be linked because of the necklaces. But why do I feel connected to William?

"I know I already told you, Angie, but you need to write down all these dreams and visions so you can use them in your novel," she adds.

I hold the letter in my hand. "I know. I have been writing it all down. I'm taking your advice—I'm going to write a novel based on the story of Evangeline and Jacob."

Sally and the girls are subdued as they peek around the cottage, looking at Thomas's progress. I know they're thinking about Evangeline and Jacob and Blackbeard's treasure. Sally breaks the silence. "We stopped on our way for a walk on the beach. Angie, do you want to join us?"

Max hears the word "walk" and barks. He wags his whole body, wanting to join us.

I look at Thomas. "Sorry. I hope you don't mind me bailing already. Do you think Max can come with us?"

Thomas's green-and-gold eyes sparkle as he ruffles Max's ears. "How can I say no to that? Have fun. We'll show the others the latest box and its new treasures later today. Do you want to put them somewhere for safekeeping?"

I race back to the inn with the new treasures. I can't wait to show my grandfather. He should be able to give us some insight into the history of the trinkets in the box. I put the box in the drawer, quickly slip into my bathing suit, and bounce back down the stairs and run out the door. I catch up to the girls.

Emily, Sarah, and Sally tease me. "What's the scoop on Thomas and you?"

I point to the cottage where Thomas is working. "Guys, I already told you. I'm not ready to get involved with anyone else right now. Thomas and I are just friends. End of story," I say. "I just left Larry a month ago. It's going to be a while before I'm ready for anyone new. I will say, though, that I continue to have that strange feeling that I've known Thomas forever."

Emily cracks up. "Oh Angie, I think it's obvious to everyone that there are sparks flying between the two of you."

I throw my arms up in the air. "Okay. I won't deny that there's some chemistry between the two of us, but I think it's because of all the stories about Evangeline and Jacob."

After a pause, I ask: "Do you guys believe in fate or that there is such a thing as a soulmate for everybody?"

The girls start to giggle. Sarah nods. "You're just an old romantic soul. I do believe in soulmates. In my heart, I have always wished that Matt and I would end up together. Who knows? Maybe it will happen one day. The bigger question is whether two soulmates can travel from one lifetime to another? Do you think that Evangeline is guiding you to Thomas?"

Lost in thought, we walk down the same path that we did when we were little girls talking of buried treasure and forgotten loves. Times haven't changed. We are still dreaming of buried treasures and lost loves.

Max races ahead of us. He runs down the overgrown sandy pathway that leads to the land where the Banker horses roamed free, the place called Springer's Point. As we hike down the well-worn path, I point to the cedars. "I see the yaupons meeting the old pines. I wonder if this could be the place mentioned in the treasure note?"

Farther down the path, Max is furiously digging. The girls and I run to see what he's found. Sally waddles up behind us. In the bottom of the hole the dog has created, the corner of an old wooden box pokes out of the sand. I reach down to pick it up.

"It looks just like the ones we found in Evangeline's home, near her fireplace," I exclaim, excitedly.

We gather around as I open the box. Suddenly Evangeline stands before us in a mystical haze. She points to the little coffer in my hand. "Inside you will find a letter. It will lead you to another clue that will help you find the treasure map."

Then she disappears.

My hands are shaking with excitement as I gently lift the letter out and hand the box to Emily to hold. I begin to read aloud what is written on the weather-worn page. 'Go to the Place where the Sun melts into the Sound and Sailors look for a Guiding Light to bring them Home." We stand there, awestruck.

Max barks at us as he runs down the path toward the beach. He snaps us back to reality. Emily hands me the little box and I tuck the letter inside. We hurry to follow Thomas's pup over the dunes. As Max chases seagulls in and out of the rolling surf, we are all talking at once.

Sally tries to catch her breath. "Can you believe we just found another clue! Do you really think it's possible to find Blackbeard's treasure map?" she asks.

I am holding the little coffer in my hands. "Who knows? Evangeline keeps saying, the time is right," I reply. "Maybe anything is possible."

We watch as the waves roll gently onto the shore. The water is a translucent blue. White clouds above reflect off the water.

I dip my toes in the rollers. The ocean is surprisingly warm for this time of year. "We are lucky. The Gulf Stream has made an early visit this year," I say. "We can soak here in the surf for hours."

It is about noon when Emily looks at her Fitbit. "I gotta' get back to the house. The pub is opening today at 2 p.m.," she says.

Sarah sighs. "I guess I should get back to check on things at the inn. I need to relieve Mom and Dad. We are fully booked."

"And tonight is my first official night singing in the pub," I chime in. "I'm so nervous."

Sally touches my shoulder. "You'll be fine once you get up there and start singing. You'll know most of the crowd listening," she says. "I need to get back to the inn now, too. I'm supposed to meet Robert and the others at SmacNally's Bar and Grill today for lunch. I've been dreaming all morning about those mouthwatering fish tacos. I might even have time to rest for a bit before we meet."

Sally's doctors want her to stay active but they have also urged her to get some rest on the island. Her belly has grown noticeably larger in the two weeks since we arrived on the island. She had a sonagram early in her pregnancy but she and Robert bypassed a later one that would reveal the baby's gender—and her doctors were fine with that because she was healthy. Her healthy pregnancy is also why they said it was okay to travel to the island on vacation. Sally estimates that she still has about four more weeks to go, give or take a week.

She and Robert are leaving the island in a week. They want to be home in time for the delivery but they don't want to miss the Fourth of July celebration on the island. The Fourth is their special day—the anniversary of when they met again and fell in love and, later, when they married, all on the island.

Emily pulls out her cell phone and calls her dad. "Can you have everyone meet us in the B&B? We found another clue at Springer's Point. Make sure you let Thomas know. He needs to hear this, too."

The girls and I meet with the whole crew in the parlor when we get back from our beach trip. We tell them about our latest discovery. Max is in the middle of the mix, eager to play again with his new friends, my mother's dogs Skippy and Ace. Mom's dogs are still a little timid around Max, who is in the puppy phase and animated. After he hears Max barking, Thomas opens the patio door to let the puppies out into the fenced in back yard.

We all gather around the little wooden box Max found. I feel the excitement in the air when we show the others the latest letter. Thomas asks me to get the box that he and I found earlier in the day at the cottage, so I run upstairs and retrieve it. When we hold the two boxes side by side, everyone is in awe at the similarities.

Thomas examines one of the small boxes. He finds a false bottom. "Is anything in here?" he wonders as he slips his fingers into the space. We are astonished when he pulls out gold coins and a beautiful emerald ring.

My grandfather, Paul, is amazed. He takes a gold doubloon and holds it up to examines it. "When I was a young boy, a fisherman I knew told me a tale about Evangeline. The sailor claimed that Evangeline found Blackbeard's treasure and had hidden it in various locations around the island."

I think to myself that it must be true. So far, we have found a gold ring, ruby necklace, emerald ring, and several Spanish gold coins.

Sally examines the emerald ring. "I wonder what we will find next time?" she asks.

That's my cue to pull out the clue from the latest letter. "Listen, this is where we need to look next," I announce as I begin to read out loud. "'You must go to the place where sailors look for a guiding light to bring them home.' Maybe somewhere near the lighthouse? What do you guys think?" I ask.

Paul says he has some old maps. We wait while he gets them and spreads them out on the big parlor table.

"There has been so much erosion on the island and many renovations over the years in the area you're talking about. Let's look at my old maps of the island," he says. "I gathered a lot of historical data while I was researching Ocracoke history and Blackbeard. Maybe we can get some sense of the likeliest places to look."

Emily points to a map. "We'll need to find an area that has remained untouched. Remember that a lot has changed on this island over the last three hundred years." Paul nods in agreement. He puts his finger on the map, near the shoreline. "I think we should look in this area."

"Yeah and we should bring Max with us since he found the last box," I say.

Sally yawns. "Let's plan to take a walk tomorrow. We can explore around the point."

Paul gathers up his maps. "I'll pull out some of my history books and study them this afternoon. Maybe, I can find some old landmarks that will be helpful to look around.

"Of course," he adds, "if the treasure's was hidden three centuries ago, someone might already have found it without realizing what they have. This is going to be really challenging."

Chapter 11

My New Life

I run upstairs to get ready for my first night playing in the pub. I can't believe how nervous I am. I have performed in so many clubs and bars over the last five years but, for some reason, this gig feels different than all the others. I think, with amusement, that maybe it's because all my other jobs were performed for people I didn't know. Here at the Oxford Pub, I will be playing for people I grew up with. At least Emily will be in the pub to help shoo away my nervous butterflies.

I have my usual playlist with me. I love to play songs like "Sitting on the Dock of the Bay" or "Brandy." These are always big hits. I also plan to play several of the songs I've written over the last three months.

I hope I'm able to write some new pieces while I'm on the island. Many of my best songs were written on Ocracoke. The music just seems to flow right out of me when I'm at the beach.

I love to go down to the water with my guitar and my wire-bound notebook. I think of the magical nights and sunshine-filled days sitting on the secluded shoreline, writing music and lyrics. I have some ideas for a new song. A catchy little tune has playing in my head since I arrived at the B&B.

I pick up my guitar, take a breath, and get ready to kick off my new life. I haven't told anyone yet but, more and more, I'm thinking I may stay on the island permanently. It depends on how this summer works out.

Emily is already hard at work when I walk outside to the tiki bar. When it's nice outside, we open the tiki bar and close the pub inside. She usually starts work around 2 p.m. stays at it until the pub closes at midnight. My hours will vary, depending on how many people are in the bar. We have worked out an arrangement in which I work from 3 to 10 p.m. For the first hour, I help Emily set up the pub, then throughout the night I plan to play four hour-long sets. I'll play to the crowd since it's not a set schedule, I can adjust the times if I want to. If the pub is busy, I'll also help wait on tables and bartend. I worked many a night as a bartender over the years at my old job in D.C.

Everything is so different here. For starters, we are on island time. I love the slower pace after my hectic D.C. lifestyle. I was so accustomed to always being in a hurry in my old life. I feel at home here at the B&B and pub—and I can't wait to get moved into my little cottage.

Emily has opened the tiki bar, and I will be playing outside. All the regulars are here at the bar to enjoy the beautiful weather and heavenly music, and I receive a lot of hugs and kisses from the locals as they arrive. There is a balmy breeze blowing through the palm trees and seagrass. I keep wondering to myself if it would be possible to move here permanently. It has always been a dream of mine to live on the island.

As I start my shift, I see that Sally and Robert have joined Matt and my mother and David for an early dinner in the pub. They hug me and cheer me on. Having my family in the audience helps me feel a little bit more relaxed when I go outside to play on the tiki bar's open-air stage. It's a beautiful afternoon and the sun is shining down on us as I play my music.

I sit down on an old wooden tavern stool. I begin to strum my trusty acoustical guitar, my fingers picking out an inspiring old melody. I love harmonies and I gravitate to easy-listening folk ballads. In addition to my regular playlist, I like to play requests. Tonight, as most nights, I will start my set with "Under the Boardwalk." I love to perform rock classics. A lot of times I gear what I play to the type of audience that's in for the night. I'm good at gauging what my listeners might like.

I delight in performing songs by Fleetwood Mac, Heart, Carole King, and James Taylor, even though they were way before my time. My Mom used to listen to them in our old gold-and-brown striped Chevy station wagon when I was just a kid, and we would drive down to Ocracoke Island. I can even play a few songs from the '50s for the older crowds.

When I'm on break, Emily says, "Look at the massive crowd. It's almost like a concert. The tiki bar is packed."

Emily looks pleased. "I told everyone I knew that you would be playing tonight. I put it on Facebook, our Instagram page, and our website. Your old friends from the island couldn't wait to hear you play. You are really great for our business."

I sing the song I wrote about my father. I explain to the crowd how my father was such an inspiration to me and was always supportive of my music career. I tell them how special this island and my friends here are to me. The crowd erupts into applause and shouts out, "Go Angie. We love you, too."

I have been playing for about an hour when I see George and Thomas arrive. My heart does a little pitter patter when I spot Thomas walk in. I feel the heat rise in my chest. George and Thomas sit with my mom and the others. Emily laughs when she sees how Thomas's presence is affecting me.

I grin right back at her when I see her reaction when George steps up to the bar to order drinks for everyone. I can tell her heart is melting. During my break, George comes to where I'm standing with Emily. He smiles, his dimples showing. "Hi girls. Can I get two menus for us from my favorite dinner spot?" he asks, before adding, "Boy, you really have a huge crowd this evening!"

I look out to see who's here. I spot Thomas and George's parents. I have known Elizabeth and Joseph Alexander forever. In fact, my family has known their family for over forty years—which again makes me puzzle how I never managed to cross paths with Thomas before now. Sarah and Emily's parents, Sally and Jim White, are here, too. They told me the other day that they have really missed being on the island and seeing their old friends. I spot my cousins. They've turned out to offer their support. Sarah, who thinks of everything, even hired a nanny to help take care of all the little kids in the family.

It is going to be fun having us all together.

Even Max is here. The pub and tiki bar have a relaxed atmosphere when it comes to pets. Once Max sees me, he trots up, wags his whole body, and greets me by plopping his paws in my lap. I tousle his furry head. He lays down at my feet.

Thomas walks over, apologizes, and tries to retrieve his puppy. I wave him off. "It's okay. I love having him nearby," I say. "He can be my mascot."

The night speeds by and finally comes to an end. I help Emily close the tiki bar. George stays to help us close the pub, too. This is his routine: He always helps Emily whenever he is at the bar.

Thomas stops by the bar on his way out with Max. "I'll see you guys later. I had a busy day today and I'm tired" he says. Then he turns to me. "Great job, Angie. Everyone loved your music."

Emily laughs and teases me once Thomas is gone. "He's definitely smitten with you."

George is ready to leave right after Thomas. Before he goes, he hugs me. "I loved your sets," he says. "And I think Emily is right. I've never seen my brother act this way."

George's comment gets me thinking about another brother who is acting differently this summer. Matt. My brother has grown up a lot since my father died last October and, more than in past summers, he has been hanging around with us. Sarah has told me more than once that she hadn't realized how much she missed his company. She wonders if this summer they might rekindle some of the old feelings they had for each other years ago.

I think back to earlier in the night, when I was between sets in the pub, and I saw Sarah leave with Matt. Earlier, I'd overheard him ask her if she wants to go for a walk. "Sarah, it's such a pretty night. Let's grab some wine and head down to the beach."

Sarah had come up to the bar, grabbed a couple of glasses and bottle of crisp white wine before winking at me. "Wish me luck. Fingers crossed, she said, before walking off toward the beach.

Chapter 12

Wishing on a Star

Sarah and Matt sit on the rocks overlooking the bay. Matt pops the cork on the wine and pours each of them a glass. The crescent moon is beaming off the water. They sit back, and the two old friends gaze up at the ebony-colored sky peppered with a million brightly shining stars.

"Do you remember when we used to lay on the beach and watch the meteor showers?" Matt asks, contentedly. "It seems like a lifetime ago."

They spot a falling star as it shoots across the sky. They laugh then say, at the same time, "Make a wish. I bet you don't know what I wished for?"

Sarah blushes. "I bet it wasn't the same thing I wished for."

"Was it this?" Matt asks. The next thing Sarah knows, Matt is encircling her in his arms. Their lips meet. He kisses her ever so delicately. Old flames of desire are reignited and spread through each one of them.

Matt smells Sarah's light, citrusy perfume and feels the warmth of her skin under his hands. Suddenly, he pulls back and apologizes. "I'm sorry, Sarah. I got swept up away by the moment," he says. Then he adds, "I've wanted to kiss you for such a long time."

Sarah shakes her silky blonde head in warning. "It isn't fair for you to play with my heart, Matt," she says. "You have to know how much I care for you."

He pulls her back into his arms. He holds her gently as he whispers in her ear. "Sarah, I have no intention of hurting you. I have dreamed of this moment. I've just been too afraid before now to let myself care for you," he says.

"Last October when Dad died, I finally realized that I had to tell you how I feel. But I had to wait until the time was right," he continues. "Tonight, is that time."

In the distance, up on the dunes, Sarah and Matt see two figures watching them. Suddenly they realize it is Evangeline and Jacob looking down at them, smiling. Neither can believe their eyes. They are astounded that the two long-ago lovers are with them on the beach.

Then they hear Evangeline murmur to them, as if she is right there on the rocks. "Just let it happen. Do not be afraid. It is meant to be. It is written in the stars."

With that, Evangeline and Jacob vanish into thin air.

Matt strokes Sarah's velvety hair. "Sarah, just rest your head on my shoulder. Everything shall be as it should."

Sarah takes Matt's hand in hers "We need to take things slow," she cautions. "I don't want to get hurt, again. You mean too much to me."

Later, as they walk down the beach and over the dunes back to the B&B, their fingers are entwined, and they are smiling. Matt feels like he is floating on air. Sarah is exhilarated, too, but she is also thinking to herself—and worrying—about Matt's history with women over the last few years.

Matt hugs Sarah tightly. It's as if he can read her thoughts. "I guess I'm just going to have to prove myself to you," he says. "I'm really serious about you. You're not one of my summer flings."

Sarah's heart melts.

Then Matt confides, "I haven't told anyone except Thomas and George, but I plan to move down here to the island permanently. I'm going to stay here and work with Thomas and George renovating the old homes here."

He pats himself on the back and smiles. "As you know, I'm an excellent woodworker and carver," Matt continues. "Have you forgotten that I got my degree in architecture at Georgetown University, just like Thomas? I can't wait to bring some of the wood in the homes back to its original splendor."

Sarah raises her eyebrows. "Why is this the first time I'm hearing about your plans?"

He shrugs. "I wanted to surprise you. I haven't been able to keep my mind off of you since last summer. I just hope that you feel the same way."

Emily and I are sitting on the front porch, rocking in the white wooden rocking chairs, when we see Sarah and Matt walk up to the B&B—still holding hands. Emily and I jump up and rush down to them, laughing.

We chuckle and Emily swats Matt on the shoulder, "What took you so long?" Emily laughs as she adds, "Evangeline must be casting love spells on everyone."

Sarah smiles. "That is so funny that you said that. Evangeline and Jacob were watching us from the dunes."

Matt kisses Sarah on the cheek, "Goodnight, Sarah, girls. I'll see you tomorrow. I have an early day."

We watch as Matt walks off, back to his little bungalow. After a few paces, he turns to wave goodbye. As soon as he continues on his journey, Emily and I dissolve into oohs and ahhs. We tease Sarah, and she turns bright red, but she is smiling from ear to ear.

Not far away, Matt walks into his cottage and closes the door behind him. He then leans back against it with a sigh, before speaking aloud. "I hope that I have done the right thing. I don't want to hurt Sarah. She is just too special to me," he says. "I know in my heart that I can be a one-woman man."

He moves across the room and puts his hand on the fireplace mantel. Evangeline appears before him. Matt jumps, but then calms himself.

Evangeline points to his heart. "Listen to your heart, Matt. Be not afraid. You know that you have been in love with Sarah all your life. She has always been your true love. Sarah is the part of you that you have been missing all these years. Reach out and tell her how you feel."

No sooner does Matt remove his hand from the mantel than Evangeline vanishes into thin air. He shakes himself. He thinks he must be dreaming. "Well, I am standing up, so I must be awake. Who would have figured?" he tells himself.

He sits down on his bed, suddenly tired, and falls asleep. He dreams that night of his future with Sarah. When he wakes up, he feels nervous and excited about the prospect of a new life that includes her.

Tomorrow morning everyone plans to meet and walk over to the lighthouse in search of more clues to Blackbeard's hidden treasure. Matt decides that tomorrow will be the day when he breaks the news of his plans to stay on the island.

His one reservation is his mother. He worries what she might think about his plan. And he is concerned that if he moves to the island, he won't be living close to her. He has been so apprehensive about her since he lost his father, and she lost her husband.

Matt hears a knock on his door. "Come on in."

In saunters George and Thomas, along with a happy Max. Matt puts on his bright blue baseball cap. "Hey were your ears burning? I was just thinking about you guys," he says.

"What's up, man?" Thomas responds.

Thomas and George have known Sarah her whole life. Matt is not sure how his friends will react to what he says next.

"Well, guess what, guys? After all these years I told Sarah how I feel about her," he says. "I haven't been able to stop thinking about her since last summer. I finally got up the nerve to kiss her last night on the beach.

"I just hope I did the right thing. You know me, man. I've never been one for settling down," he adds. "But this just feels right."

Thomas pats Matt on the back. "Well, it's about time! You have been head over heels for her as long as I can remember."

Matt nods in agreement. "I told Sarah last night about my plans to join your company and work with you and George. She was so cute."

As Matt looks at Thomas, he again wonders how Angie managed to avoid meeting him over all these years. Thomas and Matt have been friends for as long as he can remember. When they were teenagers, they played on the beach and rode the waves in the Atlantic. Any time Thomas was in the pub, Angie must have been off, Matt thinks.

"I know I'm changing the subject here, Thomas, but I was just thinking how weird it is that you never met Angie before now?"

Thomas shakes his head. "I don't know. Who knows? Maybe it was meant to happen this way," he says. "Anyway, let's get going. We were supposed to meet the others at the inn this morning at nine. We're going to the lighthouse to look for more clues."

As the three men walk across the grass and up the oyster shell driveway toward the B&B, the tan and white shells crunch under their feet. Matt and Thomas are laughing about how things have been turning out when they look over and see me and Sarah on the front porch. We both blush. Emily is with us, watching it all, and she cracks up. "You two are too funny," she tells me and Sarah as the three of us start laughing, "but it's so cool."

George seems oblivious. "What did I miss? Emily, what are y'all laughing about?"

"Apparently, Evangeline has been casting love spells all over Ocracoke Island," Emily says.

George watches as Matt steps up to Sarah, takes her hand, and then brings it up to his lips. "Well, who didn't know that was going to happen?" George declares. "And just in time for tomorrow's Fourth of July celebration and fireworks!"

Matt then turns to Emily and me. "I might as well tell you guys now—I'll tell the rest of the family when they join us. I'm relocating to the island permanently. I'm joining Thomas and George as part of the Back in Time Renovation Company."

I squeal with delight. "That's so funny. I've been thinking about making the island my home, too," I say. "Before long, we will have the whole family moving here!"

With that, Thomas, George, and Matt start talking shop, including how impatient they are to get working on Robert's father's home. David's house is one of the oldest on the island. As they jabber on about their projects, George turns to me. "Oh, by the way, your mom's A/C should be up and running soon. I'm just waiting for a part to come in."

Sarah interrupts us. "Come on. Let's go into the parlor. I had the bakery bring over some pastries for a quick breakfast. I hope everyone's hungry," she says. "I even managed to get some fresh fruit from the local produce stand.

"Sally texted earlier to say that she and the others will be down shortly," Sarah continues. "So, we are just waiting for Robert and Sally, Isabella, and David. Angie and Matt, your grandparents are already in the sunroom with my parents."

Emily's stomach growls. "Breakfast sounds good. I'm getting hungry. All I've had so far this morning is a cup of coffee," she says. "Once everyone's done eating, we can walk over to the point by the lighthouse. This is so exciting. I wonder if we'll find anything?"

Just as we sit down, the others join us. While we eat, my grandfather, Paul, pulls out the old maps he has collected since he started researching the history of Ocracoke Island. He finds Ocracoke Village on one and points.

"This was where the lighthouse was built in 1798. Originally the town was called Pilot Town. It was later changed to Ocracoke Village. The current lighthouse tower wasn't lit until 1823. Before that time, it is believed that families took turns waiting with lanterns on the point if they knew a loved one would be returning to port. There were many a vessel that capsized while trying to navigate off the coast of the Outer Banks of North Carolina, and most ship captains knew it was dangerous to try to maneuver their sloops into the channel if it was dark or stormy."

Emily is amazed. "Paul, I can't believe you gathered together all these documents. What do you think? When we begin today's search, where do you think we should look first?"

Paul moves his finger on and off several spots on the ancient maps. "We will need to look at these areas around the lighthouse and on the point. I think we should split up into two groups," he says. "We also need to remember that these maps are very old, and there has been a lot of erosion over the last three hundred years. It's very possible that our next clue might be underwater or even lost at sea."

We split up into two groups of six. Thomas, Emily, George, Matt, and Sarah are in my group with Max as our guide dog. Sally, Robert, his father David, my mother Isabella, and my grandparents Paul and Mary are in the other group with my mom's dogs, Ace and Skippy. Mom must keep her two boys on a leash. They are famous for trying to escape, plus it's an island rule.

There are two acres of land that we need to explore. My grandfather, because he's a local historian, has special permission to walk inside the fence surrounding the lighthouse. We search around the grounds of the lighthouse and on the beach. We are looking for any areas that a coffer could be hidden. Thomas spies an area on the grassy shoreline and digs around in the sand looking for any special hiding places that Evangeline might have used. "This is really going to be difficult. Think about it and how much this area has changed over the last two hundred and fifty years," he says.

Further down the beach with Sarah by his side, Matt is using his metal detector, "Well, if anything is here, hopefully this detector will pick up gold or silver."

After an hour or so, Sally rubs her back, "I need to take a little rest. I'm going to sit in the shade for a while," she says. "I'll take the puppies with me. They look tired—and they could probably do with some water."

She told me just after breakfast that the baby is active today and then proved it by showing me how its arms and legs are poking at her belly and ribs. She also told me her belly has been tightening all morning, but she thinks it is just Braxton Hicks. She still has more than two weeks before she is due. Sally could have stayed at the inn while we traipsed off in search of treasure, but she didn't want to miss out on any fun. She had to come along.

Sally finds a wooden bench to sit on. Skip and Ace search for shade at the base of an old, crooked oak tree nearby. The dogs start to dig a little hole, where it will be cooler in the leaves. When Sally walks over to put water in their bowl, she notices a little stone buried in the dirt close to where the dogs are sitting. She takes a stick and starts to dig around the stone. The dogs, thinking it is a game, bark in excitement and start to help by pawing at the ground.

Underneath the stone, her stick hits somethings. Later, Sally tells me that there was a moment when, all a sudden, she felt goosebumps on her arms. She prods into the dirt a bit longer and realizes she has discovered a little box—just like the other boxes we've found.

Sally calls out. "Guys, I think I have something over here!"

Sally brushes the dirt off the little box and then starts to open it. Immediately, she sees Evangeline, who exclaims, "The babes time is near." Then Evangeline vanishes.

Sally stands there—amazed—her mouth hanging open. She yells again. "Guys, I've found something!"

When we dash over and gather around her. Paul takes the box and slowly looks inside—at a beautiful blue sapphire necklace. Paul hands the necklace to me. "Angie, this sapphire is as blue as your eyes. He glances back into the little box and spots a piece of paper. "Look here's another letter—and I think it has a clue!"

Paul carefully lifts up the paper and reads: "Look to Where Blackbeard Had Rested his Head."

We are beside ourselves. Another hint in this ongoing riddle. "Way to go, honey! You found another clue," Robert says to my sister. Then I hear him gasp. I look up and see Sally grab her belly, bend over, and wince in pain.

Chapter 13

The Arrival

Robert sees Sally is in distress, and he quickly takes her arm. "Honey, are you okay? Do you need to sit back down?"

Sally wipes the sweat from her forehead. Robert helps her slide back down to sit. "I think I just got a little overheated. That's why I came over to sit in the shade," she says. "Evangeline was here. She said the babes time is near."

Sally starts to stand up again. "I'm fine. Really," she says. Suddenly she feels a little trickle run down her leg. "Oh my God, Robert, she was right. The baby is coming!"

Robert lifts her in his arms. He thinks to himself how thankful he is that he goes to the gym frequently. "I've got you, honey. Don't worry," he says. Then he turns to the rest of us. "Sarah! Call Georgia."

As Robert carries Sally toward the inn, we follow closely behind. As we go, Sarah reaches into her faded blue jeans shorts and pulls out her cell phone. "Georgia's staying in one of the rooms at the inn. She wanted to be nearby just in case Sally needed her." As she punches in the phone number, she adds: "Georgia and I prepared a childbirth room just in case Sally went into early labor. Boy, I never thought that we would need it!"

Sally is thirty-eight weeks pregnant. She and Robert planned to leave the island the day after the 4th of July to get home in time for the birth of their first child with help from their local midwife.

We get Sally settled into the makeshift birthing room, and Georgia examines her.

"Sally is in early labor. Her contractions are only eight minutes apart. It could still be hours before this baby is born," she says. Then she turns to my sister. "Sally, are you sure you are not farther along? Your belly is measuring bigger than thirty-eight weeks."

Sally rubs Robert's arm. "My dates have been pretty accurate. I think I even remember the day we conceived. Maybe it's just a big baby."

Emily and I step out of the room, leaving Robert with Sally, my mother—soon to be a grandmother—and David and Sarah. After a minute, Georgia comes out of the room, too, and says to us, "It's probably going to be awhile. She's only in early labor." She then steps back into the birthing room.

Emily turns to me. "I'm going to get ready to open the pub. You can stay here and be with your sister if you want."

I shake my head. "No, that's okay. Tomorrow's the Fourth of July, which means you're probably going get slammed today. I'll go let Sally know that I'm going to go to work with you. It sounds like it is going to be awhile before anything happens.

"Did I tell you that I read one of Sally's books the other day, and it said some labors can last for twelve hours or even longer?" I add.

When I go back into the birthing room to see Sally before I leave for the pub, she and Robert are pacing the floor. Sally rubs her back as a contraction wracks her body. Once the contraction is over, I hug my sister. "I'm going to work for a while. Georgia says it could be a while before the baby comes."

Sally rubs her hands over her belly. "That makes sense. Who knows when I will have this baby? It could be tomorrow, for all we know."

Robert looks nervous and is kneading his hands together. "I can't believe the time is here already. I thought we had another couple of weeks. Georgia said her belly is measuring over forty weeks—and to tell you the truth, I thought it looked bigger lately. Maybe our dates are off?"

Georgia answers him in a reassuring tone, shaking her head. "Don't worry, Robert. I've delivered many a babe. Everything will be fine," she says. "Sarah and I are just going to finish getting things ready for your wee one, for when the time comes."

David and Isabella say in unison, "We can stay and help out if you need us, too."

My mom looks excited, and her cheeks are flushed. "I can't wait to see my new grandbaby!" she declares.

Sally smiles. "Of course. I want you both to be here. Don't worry. Sarah even called the local pediatrician to check on our baby when the time comes. All we have to do now is wait."

There's a knock on the door before it swings open and Matt comes into the room to see our older sister. "The rest of our friends and extended family are downstairs watching football on the TV in the den," he says. Matt's worried expression touches Sally's heart. She grins and looks at Sarah. "Hey, what did you do with my brother? He's being so nice…"

She doesn't finish the sentence. Another contraction rips through her body. Robert rubs her back and helps with her breathing exercises.

Sally turns to Robert. "You know, I think I do better if I stand up again," she says. "I'm so glad we took those childbirth classes early—and before we left for this trip. The breathing exercises do really seem to help to ease the pain."

Georgia waits until the contraction is over, then says, "Let me check the baby's heart rate." As Georgia listens, she has a puzzled look on her face. But she doesn't say anything. "The beat is strong," she simply says.

Over the next hours, the labor progresses. Emily and I are working. The rest of the family remains congregated downstairs in the den. There is a lot of last-minute speculation on whether it will be a boy or a girl. It is around midnight when Georgia checks Sally and says with a smile, "We're getting close now. You are ten centimeters. I can feel the baby's head."

Emily and I are able to join Robert, Mom, David, and Sarah to watch this miracle. It is now about twelve hours since Sally's first contraction. One more contraction and Sally exclaims, "I think the baby's coming!" With that, her son makes his entry into the world. He has curly blond hair and rosy, red cheeks. His loud wail echoes and his cries pierce the warm delivery room. The room erupts in laughter and tears of joy. Oohs and awes can be heard as we all gaze down at his little cherubic face. Sally and Robert have tears streaming down their cheeks. They take in the moment and look at their precious little bundle.

Georgia is feeling Sally's belly. Suddenly she speaks up. "Sally, we're not done yet. I think Robert and you are in for a big surprise. Give me one more push."

With one final push, a red-haired princess makes her appearance into the world, a little fireball child squealing to announce her own arrival. Robert reaches down to bring up their daughter and gently sets her down beside their precious prince, who is resting on Sally's chest. Robert and Sally laugh, but they still look a little stunned by the unexpected appearance of twins. Robert gazes down at the babies. "Honey," he says to Sally, "I guess we need to find a little girl's name, too."

Emily and I had popped back upstairs to see how things were going, so happy to arrive just in time to witness the birth of their little miracles. Georgia wipes Sally's forehead then says, "I could feel Evangeline's soul here with us as she guided me through your delivery. It's as if you had two midwives present."

I laugh then think about Evangeline. I sense her spirit, entangling with all our joy and filling us with a golden peace.

I stroke the little cheeks of my new niece and nephew. "I guess it's a good thing we gave you guys a baby shower. Those gifts you two received will definitely come in handy, especially since there are two of them."

Emily chuckles and looks at her sister. "Come on, Sarah. Let's run downstairs and tell the guys we have babies. Plural!"

Sarah and Emily bound down the stairs with the big announcement. "Guys, you won't believe this, but Sally and Robert just had twins! Sally had not one, but two babies," Emily says. Then Sarah adds, "One girl and one boy. The boy has curly, blond hair and the little girl has strawberry blonde hair. They are so cute."

Emily nods. "Georgia examined both babies and called the pediatrician. He's on his way to check them over. He should be here at any time.

"They both had healthy cries," she adds. "I bet you could hear them all the way down here."

Matt smiles, holding Sarah's hand. "Wow, that makes me an uncle times two. Who would have thought it could happen?"

Up in Sally and Robert's room, I sense Evangeline. Then I see her and Jacob arrive to witness Sally and Robert's little miracles—before vanishing without a trace. I wasn't the only one who saw them. Sally turns to Robert, "Did you see? They are watching over us. Let's name our little girl after Evangeline since we are naming our son after Evangeline's son."

They agree on the babies' names. Their son will be William Jacob but they have decided to call him Jacob. Sally looks at Georgia and places her hand over hers. "For our little girl, we want to name her Georgia Evangeline for my dad George and for you, if that's okay, Georgia?"

Tears sparkle in Georgia's bright blue eyes, and she puts her hand over her heart. "Of course, it's okay. I'm so touched."

Robert picks up their little angel and kisses her rosy cheeks. "I think we'll have to call you Evie." Then he looks at his son. "You two babies have already stolen our hearts."

Evie stretches her tiny legs and wiggles in her father's arms. She is going to be a feisty little girl.

I watch my mom as she holds her new grandbabies, one in each arm. Tears of joy come into her pretty, pale-blue eyes. "Oh, how I wish my George could have seen these two. Your father would have spoiled them rotten."

David reaches down to squeeze Isabella's arm. "Somehow, I think he's here in spirit, just as Robert's mother, Samantha, is here too, looking down on all of us."

I smile, thinking again how happy I am that my mom has such a good friend in David. They have given each other support when they needed it over the last couple of years. It makes me sad to think that Robert's mother and my father can't be here to witness this happy miracle.

Robert and Georgia take the babies and place them in their new cradle that Thomas made. Sarah has come back upstairs with Matt, who is anxious to meet his niece and nephew. I watch my brother pick up our precious little Evie. He holds her in one arm as he wraps the other around Sarah and pulls her close. I hear him whisper to her, "One day, I would love for us to have a tiny girl of our own." I see Sarah melt up against him as they gaze down at the infant. Clearly things have rapidly blossomed between those two.

I laugh and ask Sarah, "Hey, where did you put my brother?" Matt blushes. "That's so funny. Sally said the same thing to me earlier today," my brother says. "I guess I have always been in love with Sarah. I just wouldn't let myself feel it until now."

Isabella watches us. I can tell from my mother's expression that she is bursting with love. David feels the same way as he watches his family and its new additions—the beginning of the next generation. It is such a happy gathering.

The pediatrician arrives and we all leave the room except for Sally, Robert, and Georgia. Both babies are given a seal of approval from this experienced country doctor. He looks over the twins and tells their parents, "I have examined a lot of newborn babies, but this is a first. Most couples know when they are going to have twins, especially with all the sonograms these days."

The doctor weighs the babies. Jacob is the bigger of the two. He weighs 6 pounds while his sister weighs 5 pounds and 12 ounces. The doctor chuckles. "These two are perfect in every sense. I am amazed that they are so healthy and at such a good weight."

We rejoin the new parents, who beam as they gaze down at their two little angels. Sally lies down on the soft feather bed and Robert places the two babies at her side. My mom pulls out her red Cannon Elph camera and starts taking photos. Mom can't hide her smile, even as tears of joy glisten on her cheeks.

"These two are our little miracle babies. Who would have thought you would have had them here on the island?" she says, before adding: "Sally, it's almost two in the morning and it's been less than two hours since you gave birth. I think it's time we left you so you can get some rest. Besides, the rest of us have to get some sleep, too, so we're in gear for today's Fourth of July celebrations."

Sally grins and looks at Robert. "Can you believe we had them on the same day that we were married? Our two-year anniversary and our babies' birthday all on the same day!" she exclaims. "And the fourth anniversary from when we were reunited."

Robert rubs Sally's shoulders and kisses her on the cheek. "Your mom's right. This is going to be a long day. The Fourth of July is one of the busiest days on Ocracoke Island. We should all try to get some sleep."

Sarah yawns. "Yeah, it's going to be a very early morning start for all of us. Why don't I take the clothes you received from the baby shower? I will ask my night shift girls to wash them—and the bottles—so that we can dress and feed these little ones. Luckily, Georgia thought to have a set of onesies and blankets ready, just in case."

Sally turns to Georgia. "I plan to breastfeed the twins but from what I've read, it could take several days to get my milk going. I'm so glad someone thought to give us some baby formula. Everything has worked out perfectly, almost as if we had some type of divine intervention."

With that, Georgia says she has something to share. She tells us that Evangeline has just whispered a message in her ear. "She told me, 'It was not luck. Everything happens for a reason, even if we do not know what the reason is at the time,'" Georgia says. Everyone stares at her in disbelief.

Georgia then picks up Jacob and cuddles the infant. "Evangeline has given me lots of support over the years and often has intervened in times when I have needed her," Georgia says. "I've gotten used to having her here to offer me support and comfort when I deliver babies."

I think about Evangeline as I go downstairs to give Thomas and George an update on the birth of the twins. I enter the den. Max spots me; the drowsy puppy lifts his head up from Thomas's foot and starts wagging his tail.

"You should see the babies! They are perfect in every way. They are tiny but alert," I say, excited. "They named their little boy Jacob. He has curly blond hair. His little sister has reddish-blonde hair. They named her Georgia Evangeline after our father George, Georgia, and Evangeline. They are going to call her Evie."

"Wow, I can't believe they had twins!" George says. "They didn't know it would be twins, did they? This must have really been a shock to them for them!"

I laugh then try to stifle a yawn. "Thomas, the best part is that the cradle you made for them already has their initials carved into it! We didn't realize it until after Sally and Robert named the babies and Georgia and Robert placed them in the cradle. It was crazy when we discovered it."

I yawned again. "I'm exhausted. So, on that note, I'm heading to bed. I'll see you guys in the morning."

I climb back upstairs to my cozy room. My head barely touches my cool white pillow when suddenly I am back with Evangeline.

Chapter 14

The Fourth of July Celebration

In my dream, I am transported back to the Caribbean Island where Evangeline spent her captivity. I watch her son, William, as he sits on a hard dirt floor beside his mother's tanned bare feet. He appears to be about two years old, and he is playing with carved wooden toys. His curly blond hair cascades around his tiny, cherub face. His bright green eyes look up at Evangeline as a small, black kitten wanders over to join the child.

I see Daniel walk into the room and take Evangeline in an embrace. I feel her relax in his arms. She whispers to me in my dream, almost as if I can hear her thoughts. "I no longer resist his love. Our survival depends on me accepting my fate of being his woman and keeping Daniel happy," she tells me. "He is not a bad man. He has proven his love to me and my son over the last three years."

Her feelings wash over me. She is amazed at how lucky she is to be on this lush Island. Daniel's home is a tropical paradise with gorgeous pink sandy beaches, heavenly orchids, and fragrant fruits. I watch as Evangeline feeds William a chunk of ripe pineapple, its juice dripping down the child's chin. William licks his lips. "Yummy, Mummy!" he calls out.

It is sweet to watch this little boy delight in the delectable fruit. As Evangeline looks down on her son, I watch as Daniel places a stunning, pearl necklace around her neck. He nibbles on her ear, then murmurs into it. "There are more jewels like this hidden in my treasure chest. I have a fortune in jewels and gold coins. One day, I will show you where my fortune is buried in Bain Town."

Bain Town. The Bahamas. I recall reading about a lake there where it is said that mermaids live in its depths. I wonder in my dream if this is where the treasure is hidden, the place where I saw Evangeline take young William to swim.

I awaken from my slumber relishing the fact that my dreams are letting me watch Evangeline's life unfold. I keep a little notepad on my nightstand to document my vivid dreams, and I hastily write down everything I can remember. I hope these encounters when I am unconscious will provide more clues as to the whereabouts of Blackbeard's treasure. Sarah really feels that these dreams are important. For me, it's as if Evangeline is trying to tell me where the treasure can be found. I reach up to touch my precious half-heart necklace and I feel Evangeline's presence.

The warm shower cascades over me as I try to wake up after last night's excitement and too little sleep. My thoughts jump between my latest dream and the birth of the twins. I feel so much joy and love toward my new niece and nephew. I can't wait to see those two darling angels.

I am still stunned to think that my sister has twins. I didn't see that coming. Last night, after the birth, Robert mentioned that there were several sets of twins in his family. His great aunt has twins. I guess twins run in his family.

I finish my shower and dress for the Fourth of July celebration. I decide to wear my favorite faded blue jean shorts and my lacy red, white, and blue tank top. The Fourth of July is one of my favorite holidays and it has always been a busy day on the island. As I start to run down the winding white stairs, the rich aroma of coffee hits me and awakens my senses. I am late, as always. The rest of the family is already gathered around the huge parlor table. Everyone is talking about the events from the previous day: The twins' birth and the discovery of more treasure clues.

The two babies are already awake and making their first public appearance. They look like little cherubs. Their grandparents, Isabella and David, have proudly taken up their roles as Nana and Pop Pop. Each one holds a baby. Isabella is rocking Jacob in her arms and little Evie is squirming in David's arms, her bright blue eyes staring up at her grandfather.

Sally looks tired but happy in her new role as a mother. Robert looks like the cat that got the cream. His smile shines as he watches his twins resting in their grandparents' arms. Sarah, Emily, and I wait impatiently for our turns to hold the babies. Out of the corner of my eye, I glimpse Jacob and Evangeline watching our happy group.

Georgia is at the table, too, standing by to offer her help if it is needed. I am so relieved that Sarah had asked Georgia to join us. She certainly is a lifesaver. As a midwife, Georgia gives her all. She has helped Sarah's staff arrange and organize all the baby shower gifts so they are ready for the twins.

I say to Sarah, "I'm so glad that you asked Georgia to come stay with us. Was that ever a good idea! Never in a million years did I ever think that Sally would have the babies here on the island."

"You know, it's funny," Sarah answers. "I had forgotten, but it came to me in a dream. Evangeline told me to have Georgia come here to stay."

Everyone in the room turns around, staring at Sarah in disbelief. "It's true!" she exclaims. "I had totally forgotten."

Sarah looks at her watch. "Sorry, I hate to leave you, but I really need to go prepare for today festivities. Remember, later in the day, I'm the first in line for holding the babies. And let me know later what you all think about our latest clue to the treasure."

The clue from yesterday's discoveries tells us to "Look where Blackbeard had rested his head." My grandfather, Paul, rubs his chin as he sits back, deep in thought. "We need to think about all the places Blackbeard might have stayed when he was alive. I pulled out these dusty, old maps of historic homes on the island from my collection. We need to look for homes that would have been around in the 1700s, starting with the ones that are still in existence today. There aren't many of those still standing."

He jots down notes as he pores over the documents, then scratches his head. He looks up and smiles. "Believe it or not, the first building we should check out is the Shepard's Head B&B. David and George, your family homes also date back to the time we're talking about. Our home, Mary, was Evangeline's family home," my grandfather says. "All of these homes were built in the 1700s."

We listen as he explains how we should go about searching.

"I figure we will need to explore the rooms and look for secret passageways where pirates might have hidden something all those years ago. The Shepard's Head was renovated, but we have to remember that some of the original features are still present. Besides, when it was being renovated, no one was thinking about looking for hidden panels or rooms."

David grins. "My house is a perfect candidate because Thomas and George are planning to start renovating it once they finish Evangeline's cottage. My home once belonged to Roger Brown. Who knows what we might find there? I'm sure you all remember that Brown was Blackbeard's grandson and the man who helped Evangeline escape from Daniel Teach, one of Blackbeard's other grandsons."

It's George's turn to chime in. "After we finish your home, David, we were planning to renovate our childhood home—unless we get another job lined up first. It will be interesting to see what we might find at our place," he says.

"All of this brings back so many memories of when we were kids and we would search for hidden treasure," George continues. "Matt and Thomas, remember how we used to search the beaches and marshes for pirate booty? We'd come back covered in mosquito bites, sunburned, and empty-handed!"

Emily's dad, Jim White, suggests that we meet up tomorrow to begin the search. For now, though, he suggests that we concentrate on today's celebration plan.

"Does anyone need any help with setting up for the party? I have the pig roasting, and I could some extra hands with the grill," he says. "Thomas, George, and Matt, I hope you guys are still going to be able to help me grill some burgers, brats and hot dogs."

Robert jumps in to say that he, his dad, and his brother Joseph are heading down to the beach to set up tarps, tents, and chairs after breakfast. "Joseph is going to be surprised when he hears that we had twins last night! He didn't expect to be an uncle so soon—and certainly not twice over. Sally and I decided to wait and surprise him and Rebecca with the news this morning."

Emily turns to me. "Angie, can you help me set up the tiki bar and the stage for your performance today? Once that is all done, we can relax and enjoy the day."

"I wouldn't have it any other way," I answer as I put my arm around Emily and smile.

The town of Ocracoke Island hires a pyrotechnic specialist to set off the fireworks display, and it is always a grand affair. The tiki bar is usually overflowing. I am starting to get antsy and nervous about my performance before the whole town.

George is to help Emily and me set up today. "Emily, I'll be over shortly to help you," he says. "I'm going to help Jim and the other guys set up the grills first. Do you need me to get extra ice for the drinks?"

Emily nods. "That would be great. We have a lot, but it's pretty warm outside already. Looks like it's going to be hot today."

David and Isabella help Sally and Robert with the twins. Georgia gently takes little Jacob from Sally. "Sally don't forget to take it easy today. I will watch the twins this afternoon."

Sarah, the planner that she is, with the help of Georgia, has sent some of her staff inland to pick up extra supplies for the babies. What a special day for Sally and Robert—their anniversary and the birth of their beautiful babies, all on the Fourth of July.

It is a balmy summer day, with a refreshing breeze blowing across the bay. The seagrass is willowing on the sunny dunes. Hungry little sandpipers are busy in their search for sand fleas, as they race in and out of the surf. The children are at the water, making sandcastles and swimming in the bay. They jump in and out of the waves under the watchful eyes of their parents, who are floating in the tranquil Gulf Stream water.

As the morning progresses, Sally is resting on the porch on one of the white glider swings. Georgia is upstairs keeping a watchful eye over the twins, who are asleep in their new cradle. Sally loves the Fourth of July festivities. Normally, my sister is in the heart of everything, but this year she will only be allowed to watch.

I sit down beside Sally in the other white glider. There is a huge glass pitcher of ice-cold lemonade sitting on the pretty yellow table. It looks so inviting that I can't resist having a cool drink. I take a long sip of the tangy drink. "I don't think there is anything quite as refreshing as lemonade on a hot summer day," I say.

Sally stretches, suddenly feeling very tired, when she spots Thomas and Max headed our way. She swats me on my shoulder. "Enjoy. It looks like you have company coming to join you. I think I'm going to go upstairs and take a nap before the evening fun begins."

She waves at Thomas and turns to me. "I'm off to bed. Tell Thomas I'll see him later," she says as she heads toward the door of the inn.

Max beats Thomas up the stone stairs to the wide porch and rushes over to see me. He's wagging his whole body and jumping up and down, excited to see me. I pet his head. "Come and join me, Thomas," I say. "This lemonade is the bomb."

"Sure. Thanks. I never could turn down a cold drink on a hot day," Thomas says as he accepts an icy glass of lemonade and sits down in the other glider.

"When we were growing up, we used to rock these gliders so hard we'd almost rock them off their casters," I say, laughing. "It's so funny how you remember the things you did when you were a kid."

Thomas nods at me. "George, Sarah, Emily, and I used to do the exact same thing. It's so strange that you and I never crossed paths during all that time. I can even remember rocking on these with Sarah and Matt."

He looks down the driveway. He points to Sarah and Matt. "Speak of the devils themselves, look who's arriving now."

Matt is holding Sarah's hand as they climb up the old stone steps "That lemonade looks good. I think we'll join you," Matt says. "Emily and George should be coming along soon, too. We just saw them leave the tiki bar."

Before long, everyone is sitting on the timeworn veranda, keeping cool in the shade of the porch, and sipping on glasses of lemonade. We are done with our setting-up duties for the day, and now we can relax for a bit. Sarah is smiling, facing into a cool breeze that sends tendrils of her wispy blond hair blowing around her face. "Emily, I'm so glad we hired extra help this year," she says. "Now, all we have to do is supervise."

Emily and Sarah's dad, Jim, arrives a short time later. He chats with us for a bit then looks at his daughters. "I'm so proud of you two," he says. "You've done so well taking care of the inn and the pub since we retired."

The girls' mother, Sally White, is beside him. "We had forgotten how much we missed this place and the people," she says. "Your father and I have been talking. We've decided to move back to the island permanently. We aren't coming out of retirement, mind you, we just want to be close to everything that makes us happy. We asked Thomas and George to renovate one of the other old cottages. We plan to move when it is done."

Emily and Sarah squeal with delight then hug their parents. "That is fantastic news! This place hasn't been the same without you around," Emily says. "We have missed y'all."

Sarah is ecstatic. "Emily is right. It's like a piece of a puzzle was missing with the two of you not being here. I was so used to being able to walk down the hall to ask you a question or just enjoy your company."

I think to myself. It is going to be a busy—and exciting—summer with so many new plans. For my part, I am looking forward to lots of fun with my family and friends. Sally and Robert have decided to stay the whole summer, too, with their twins. The plan is for all of them to move into Mom's old family beach home at the end of this weekend.

George fixed my mom's air conditioner, and it's now up and running. Since Robert and Sally are both teachers, they have the summer off. Their decision means I will get to spend more precious time with my adorable niece and nephew. Sally and Robert's coworker is housesitting their home in Clements, Maryland, while they are away. He needed a place to stay, anyway. Now he can just stay there for the summer.

My mom and Robert's father, David, have also decided to stay for the summer. "I want to hang around to help renovate my old house, plus I want to spend time with my new grandchildren," David says. "I'm going to stay at Isabella's home with her, Robert, Sally, and the twins during my house's renovation."

I suspect my mom is loving the idea of having her whole family here for the summer and spending time with the babies. It is reassuring to see her happy again. The arrival of the twins has been good for her.

Everything seems to be falling into place as my grandparents, also, have decided to stay for the summer. My grandfather perks up and hugs Grandma. "I can't think of a reason to go back to our home in Ripley, Maryland, while our whole family is here on the island. Mary is in heaven, and I can't wait to be able to investigate our latest pirate clues."

Paul—my grandfather—has been spending his days and evenings enjoying, examining, and researching each of clues in the old letters as we've stumbled onto them. He has been researching Blackbeard's treasure, the history of Ocracoke, Hatteras, and Roanoke Island for most of his life.

"I have dreamed of one day being able to find the treasure maps that were rumored to be here on this island," Paul says. "I love to listen to the locals tell stories about the island's history and folklore."

My mind wanders back to a time years ago when I watched him, and my father ponder over all their historic documents.

My grandmother, Mary, is thrilled about the summer plan, which will let her spend time with her children, grandchildren, and now, great grandchildren. Earlier today she told me, "I feel so old knowing that I have great grandchildren. I love this island and our family. You know, I met your grandfather here on this island when we were teenagers. That's over sixty years ago. Ocracoke will always hold a special place in our hearts."

I sit back, watching my friends and my family and thinking of how lucky I am to have them. Yet I miss my father and I can't stop my heart from aching. It is like a toothache that throbs. My grief sneaks up on me at times, washing me in pain and carrying my soul into the depths of sorrow and gloom. The twins have helped to ease some of my despair, but the grief is always there.

Today I plan to sing my song about my love for my father as a tribute to his life and memory. But I fret about that decision.

"Emily, I am afraid if I sing my song, it might spoil everyone's mood," I tell her when we have a minute to ourselves. Emily hugs me. "Angie, I think you need to sing your song. You need to sing, not just for yourself, but for all the others who loved him," she says. "By remembering him, you will help the rest of us accept his death. We will never forget him—he touched so many lives, especially those of us who will be here today."

Shortly I will climb up on the small wooden stage and sing for the whole town of Ocracoke. Emily is busy overseeing the tiki bar schedule and plans. She wants me to sing my first set between 4 and 6 p.m. I feel so honored to be chosen to perform for their annual Fourth of July celebration. As usual, I also have pre-performance butterflies. I feel my heart beating in my throat. I hate these pre-stage jitters and wonder if I will ever get over them. For now, I remind myself to take slow deep breaths.

"Tonight, is my official public debut since coming to Ocracoke Island evening," I think. "Sure, I played for everyone at Sally and Robert's combination baby-shower-and-surprise-birthday-party, but somehow this is different. In so many ways, it feels like this a new beginning, the start of my new life."

I am daydreaming, thinking about my decision I've made to stay on the island permanently. I know that my hours at the pub will be cut drastically after the summer rush is over, but that creates a perfect opportunity to start writing my novel. I've had a rough draft in progress since I began having dreams about Evangeline's life.

I am on the porch, lost in thought, when Thomas touches my arm. It startles me for a minute and, instinctively, I reach up and touch the heart-shaped pendant on my necklace. We both gasp as we feel an electric current spark between us. Evangeline and Jacob appear before us, smiling. Surprised by their appearance, I drop the little heart. The two immediately vanish. We are speechless. Everyone in our little group has witnessed the encounter, they all start to speak at once. "Do you think anyone else saw that?" I ask.

We all look around to make sure, but no one else roaming around near the B&B acts like they've witnessed the extraordinary appearance of the two bygone lovers.

Paul speaks thoughtfully. "Maybe the reason we can see their spirits is because we are all somehow connected to them," my grandfather says. "You all know this, but I love to tell the story of the connection between Emily and Evangeline. Emily White was married to Evangeline's brother, Robert Alexander. Evangeline and Emily were grand friends, like sisters. They traveled across the Atlantic Ocean together with their families. When Evangeline disappeared, Emily told everyone that she could still feel her presence. She was the only one who thought Evangeline was still alive, and she was correct."

George looks at Emily's mom, Sally. "I remember you told us that you named our Emily after Emily White. And that we are all descendants of the original settlers to Ocracoke Island, "he says.

Sally White smiles. "Yes. I so loved to hear all those stories that I named her after the old Emily White. It's funny, now, how Angie and my Emily seem as close as Evangeline and the old Emily White. I wonder if one day the two of you will be linked?"

Matt squeezes his grandfather's shoulder. "Your folklore and tales about the island are part of what makes the summers here so special. I know the Ocracoke Historical Society is happy to have you back for the summer. I heard you're even planning a lecture on the Lost Colony of Roanoke at the museum next week."

Paul looks excited. "Yes, I can't wait. You know how much I love to talk about the history of the Outer Banks," he says. "On that note, I must warn everyone to please be careful not to leak any information regarding the clues to Blackbeard's treasure maps. There are way too many treasure-hunting fanatics out there. It could be dangerous for us.

"Jim, I'm thankful you decided to keep our clues, letters, and jewels hidden in your safe at the inn," he adds.

Jim White shrugs. "No problem, Paul. And I agree. There are a couple of hoodlums who still live on the island. If they had been around back in the day, they would be called pirates."

Emily looks at her watch. "Well Angie, it's almost time. You and I must get ready for your big debut. I don't know about the rest of you, but I need a nice hot shower."

Thomas wipes his forehead. "Yeah, I guess George and I should take Max home and get ourselves cleaned up. I'm going to let Max stay here with us until the fireworks start tonight," Thomas says. "Jim, what time do you want to start grilling? I was thinking around 2 p.m. Would that work?"

Jim agrees. "Two o'clock sounds just about right. I'll see you guys in a little while."

As Thomas and George walk toward their home, George notices that Thomas is deep in thought. "So, what's up with you, Thomas? You're awfully quiet."

Thomas wonders if he should say anything, but finally answers. "I don't know, man. Do you believe in love at first sight or in soulmates? I feel like I've known Angie forever. I just met her two weeks ago, but it feels like I've known her my whole life. It's just crazy. I can't stop thinking about her."

Laughing, George teases his older brother. "You know me. I've always believed in that kind of stuff. I think there is someone for everyone and everyone has a kindred spirit or a soulmate. The problem is most people don't open up their hearts to the possibility. Most of the time people are not lucky enough to meet their soulmates."

Max whines because no one is paying any attention to him, and he wants to be fed. The brothers' conversation ends and Thomas is left with a lot to think about. He feeds his anxious puppy and plays with Max to calm the pup's nerves. As he rubs Max's ears, he talks to the dog. "Max, I am going to take you home tonight before the fireworks start. The fireworks will probably scare you." He laughs at himself because he is talking to Max like he will understand him.

Thomas reaches up to touch the little half-heart he now wears around his neck all the time. A calmness washes over him and he hears Evangeline whisper. "All will be as it is supposed be. All will be well if you only trust your heart."

Thomas shakes his head and wonders if he is starting to hear things. Max just wags his tail and licks Thomas on his hand.

Back in the inn, I am looking in my mirror. I decide to take a little extra time to make sure that I look good for my big debut. A short time later, as I walk down the staircase, past the parlor, and into the Oxford Pub, a déjà-vu comes over me.

I open the doors into the pub. Emily has set up the tiki bar for the festivities tonight. George has just delivered some extra ice for the drinks and is now positioned at Emily's side. He is always around to help her, if only she could just see how that reflects the depth of his love for her. The weather is perfect. It feels great to be outside. This is shaping up to be a fantastic Fourth of July.

Tan-colored canopies have been put up to provide shade and block the sun. Emily's fair skin is already turning pink from the work to set up earlier today. Her cute brown freckles pop out and give her a wholesome look. A refreshing wind lightly fans us while we get final touches in place for tonight.

"I'll help you mix up your special planter's punch," I tell Emily. "That Oxford Brew really has a kick—and it's a great seller at the tiki bar. With all the local, fresh fruit we have, the drink should be a big hit today."

I mix up the fruity rum drink and take a sip. "This is excellent. Do you want to try it?" Emily takes a slow sip and grins. "Yummy. I'll have to have one of those later tonight."

It is time for me to get settled up on my small stage. I listen as Kate McNally finishes her set. Her soulful music makes everyone sway and tap their toes. As Kate steps off the stage, I take a deep breath and hug her. "Great job, Kate. I just loved your set."

She welcomes me with her easy smile and swings her guitar over her shoulder as she exits the stage. "Thanks, Angie. I can't wait to hear you play. I've been following you on the radio."

My palms are sweaty. My heart is racing. I sit down and hold my trusty guitar close to me, like a shield against my nerves. I breathe in deeply. My nervousness dissolves when I look into the crowd and spot my mother, brother, sister, and my friends in the audience. They are here to cheer me on.

I take the mic in my hands and my voice rings out. "Hello Ocracoke. So great to see all of you here on this lovely Fourth of July." The performer in me emerges.

I always feel like I am on a tropical island when I am on Ocracoke Island. I can smell the burgers and brats, making my mouth water, and hear the sizzling from the grill. The guys stop cooking to come over to watch me play. I see Thomas and think about the kiss I gave him the first time we met. My cheeks flame hot and red.

I begin my set. My first song is about my love for the island. "This is a song I wrote while sitting on the beach of Ocracoke," I say. "I plan to donate some of the royalties to the Ocracats."

The crowd cheers and sings along. Ocracats is a nonprofit organization formed to help feed, spay, and neuter feral cats on the island. All of my life, I have loved to watch the ocracats—as the island's felines are known—lounging on the porches of businesses and meandering around the island. They laze and bask in the glorious sunshine, without a care in the world. The cats are a part of the culture that makes Ocracoke Island such an old-fashioned place to live and visit.

I wrote the second song in my set when I struggled to deal with my relationship with my ex- boyfriend, Larry. I remember that when the song came out he didn't even realize that I was talking about him in it. He was totally oblivious—one of the reasons we're no longer together. *Ces't la vie.* So true—such is life.

I passionately sing my nostalgic songs. My voice radiates through the sound system and wafts across the town. A balmy breeze blows through my long wavy hair. My coral-colored peasant shirt flows over me as the air drifts off Silver Lake. A lot of locals have come to welcome me home and I see them in the audience as I go from song to song. My jitters are replaced with the same warm, fuzzy feeling you get when you arrive home after a long journey.

Oxford Pub and Shepard's Head B&B have always been the center of activity on the holiday. Their location overlooking Silver Lake—*the* place to be for the holiday—makes them a hub of the Fourth of July. The town has a spectacular firework's display every year after the sun sets. The fireworks reflect off the translucent water.

The friendly pub and the quaint inn also help make the day a momentous occasion for everyone. This year, I'm part of the entertainment. As I move into my set for the afternoon, I play two of my new songs and I am surprised by how many people are singing along with me. It is really surreal. I see my brother-in-law Robert and sister Sally reclining on blue lawn chairs under the shade of the majestic oak tree in front of the inn. Sally gives me a thumbs up. She yells, "Go, Angie!"

You would have never known that she just had twins the night before.

Georgia had warned her: "It will be good to go out and get some fresh air. Just don't overdo it." I am delighted to see all my family out in the audience.

I have been working on the song about my father ever since his death back in October. I sent it to my agent last week. The lyrics talk about the love that I had for my dad and how he inspired me over the years. After listening to it, my manager called me. "I think you might just have another No. 1 song on your hands. I can see this being a song that brides play when they dance with their fathers on their wedding day. It is so, heartfelt."

Soon—maybe by the end of the summer—I'll have enough songs to make my first album. I only have three more to write to finish my collection. I plan to write a song about Evangeline and Jacob to go along with my novel about them. I laugh to myself. Maybe one day, it will become a movie, like a Harlequin movie. I love the idea of a song to use as a marketing tool for launching a new book—once I write it.

I plan to spend time on the beach this week to work on some of my music. The lyrics of my music flow right out of me when I sit and gaze out at the waves that lap the shoreline. I feel my tense shoulders relax when I reflect about the moments that I spend on the seashore. And I remember the story about how Evangeline used to sit on the dunes when she pined away for her Jacob. It is rumored that she sang into the Carolina gale. Even to this day, both locals and visitors on the island say they can hear woeful tunes echoing in the breeze.

The tiki bar is packed. People are seated, lounging on chairs and blankets all over the sandy beach and on the fresh green lawn of the Shepard's Head Inn. Not far away, we hear the happy yells of excited children splashing in the cool water of Silver Lake. The golden sun beams down on everyone. I smell a fruity coconut bouquet from the suntan lotion people have slathered on. An easy way to tell locals apart from tourists is to look at their skin. Most of the locals have tans. Not the visitors—their white skin is already turning pink from the strong sun, me included.

Several of the restaurants on the island have catered the celebration. Along with the grilling meat at Emily's place, I catch the aroma of spicy shrimp and the smoky scent of tangy barbeque and roasted pork. I will definitely need to find some time for dinner when I finish my set.

Fourth of July on Ocracoke Island is shaped by many fun traditions. The island attracts patriotic people who are proud to be Americans. I love the flag-raising ceremony and the way children are involved in each year's celebration, often through a patriotic skit. The youngsters are taught at a tender age to love this country. It is a nice change from where I lived in Washington, D.C. There is so much negativity in the capital. It is such a shame.

Earlier today, I took a hike down to the beach to take a look at the contenders in the annual sand sculpture contest. I am amazed at the things that can be sculpted out of sand. Most of the sculptures and carvings are truly works of art. One of our locals designed and carved a turtle with a dolphin inside a sand dollar. It is absolutely beautiful. Another tradition in the village is the Annual Classic Old Time Parade. It contains floats, bikes, and golf carts decorated in red, white, and blue. Some are even decorated like pirate ships. It is always great fun.

The celestial sky is crystal blue with puffy white clouds reflecting off Silver Lake. I feel a need to pinch myself because I can't believe I am here, living the dream. A new beginning full of dreams and aspirations has opened before me.

Thomas, George, and their parents are sitting beside my mom and David. My Aunt Marie and my Uncle Allen are at the beach with their children, my cousins. They wave to me. The gorgeous sunlight is starting to melt into glorious glistening, orange-colored flames as this amazing afternoon shifts into the evening. Words can't adequately capture the beauty of the colors of the sunset. Those that come to mind are golden, amber, rose, and flaming crimson. The sunsets here are never the same. Tonight, is no exception.

I play the sincere song that I have written about my father. My emotions floods out in my music. "You held my heart from the day I was born. Your strong hands reached out to me. You were always there to pick me up and support me. Your life was short but full."

I feel tears escaping down my cheek as I strum my guitar and sing for the crowd. I hang my head and bow to my friends, family, and visitors when I finish the tribute to my father. The audience stands, claps, and cheers me with a standing ovation. I am touched by the outpouring.

My mom, sister, and brother come up onto the stage and wrap me in a big bear hug. My Mom wipes away a tear. "Oh honey, I loved it. Your music and the lyrics touched my heart and spoke to how much we loved your father. Your father would be so proud of you."

Sarah joins us after we leave the stage. She hugs me, too. "Angie, that was just wonderful."

I can feel my father's presence, warm and feathery, caressing my face. I sometimes wonder if my father is here with us, just like Evangeline.

The evening has just begun. Sarah has a special surprise for Sally and Robert. She has planned a small anniversary party. It is a thoughtful gesture on her part. Sally and Robert are so touched by all the attention.

Sally has tears in her eyes. She embraces Sarah. "Sarah, you have thought of everything. I don't know what we would have done if you hadn't arranged for Georgia to stay at the inn. I never in a million years dreamed that I would give birth here on the island, much less to twins. We can't thank you enough for all that you have done."

Sarah, too, has tears dropping onto her cheeks. "Sally, you have always been like a sister to me. I hope that you will always feel at home here."

Sally dabs at her sparkling blue eyes. "Must be hormones. I've never been such a cry baby."

"You must be tired, too, sweetheart," Robert says. He rubs her back and adds: "I know I am."

Sally yawns. "I'm going to bed right after the fireworks. You know how much I love fireworks. I can't miss them. It just wouldn't be right."

"Okay. Just don't overdo it. You heard what Georgia said before we left," Robert says. "Georgia's a lifesaver."

Emily and George join us, and Emily points to the pontoon boat on the sound. "I think the fireworks are getting ready to start. I just checked on our staff and everything is cool," she says. "And guess what? Sarah, we have the rest of the night off. Dad said he would take care of any problems that might come up. I'm so stoked. How often does that happen?"

Everyone stakes out a place on the worn tarps, blankets, or beach chairs that they have brought from home to watch the fireworks display. The mayor announces, "Folks, the fireworks are about to begin. The local preacher will say a prayer to bless this town and all the locals and all our visitors."

The voice of Kenneth, the Methodist clergyman, then rings out. "Bless this town and this country. Keep us all safe." The national anthem is performed by the high school marching band. These annual traditions are part of the reason why I love this town.

Thomas shows up after taking Max home as the last note of the anthem is performed. "Is it okay if I sit with you, Angie?" he asks, as he moves to plop down beside me. I smile and pat the green army tarp where I'm sitting. "Sure. There is plenty of room here. Did you take Max home?"

He nods. "Yeah, I'm pretty sure he would be terrified by the explosions and loud blasts from the fireworks."

The golden sun has set, and the calm sea slowly rolls up on the sandy shore. The woosh of the waves is tranquil. Fireflies twinkle in the woods behind the B&B. Music plays in the background. Don McLean's song, "American Pie." I sigh. It is so peaceful. "It's beautiful tonight," I say.

The first of the rockets blare overhead. The fireworks are spectacular. A flaming brocade of lavender, red, green, blue, and gold appear above us and reflect off the water of the lake. Intricate aerial spinners, fish, comets, and starbursts fill the ebony sky. It is a fabulous eruption of dazzling lights in the warm Carolina night. The fireworks team's music pulsates along with the pyrotechnic display. The grand finale sends explosions of brilliant vibrating lights. It is a spectacular end to a wonderful display. The crowd bursts into appreciative cheers when the fireworks come to an end.

Some of the locals and visitors will continue their celebration, but not our little crowd. I look around me and see most of us are yawning. I know for a fact that I am exhausted.

Chapter 15

More Dreams

Sally and Robert are the first to leave us. My sister looks so happy. I give her a hug before she heads off to bed. "I can't believe that I am an aunt to your two sweet angelic babies and that you are a new mother. Good night, Sally. It was a perfect day."

"I know what you mean," she replies. "I want to pinch myself—it feels like I am in a dream. And to think we have two beautiful babies not just one!" Sally then steps back and announces to everyone, "I don't know about the rest of you, but I'm whipped. 'Night everyone."

Robert yawns and wraps his arms around her. "Good night, everybody. Time to get this little momma to bed."

Everyone leaves to get home for a long-deserved sleep. Not long afterward, up in my room in the inn, I reminisce about the day's events. I'm sitting in the cozy window seat that overlooks Silver Lake. Most of the Fourth of July crowd has dispersed for the evening.

I have a tingling sensation and gooseflesh appears on my skin. I feel Evangeline's presence before I see her ghostly shape. "Angie, you will find true love before the summer's end," she says. "Open your heart. You will find what you have always been searching for, if you will only allow it to happen." Then—poof—she is gone. It startles me each time she appears, but I never feel threatened.

I am overtired and decide that I need to get some rest before the morning comes. I must get up early tomorrow to help the others clean up from the festivities. I fall into the soft down feather bed wrapping the covers around me. Before long, I am sound asleep. I magically dream again about Evangeline.

In this dream, Evangeline is with her friend, Roger Brown. I watch as she sews her jewels into the hems and pockets of her shift. Roger seems edgy, nervous. "Be ready, Evangeline. When we escape, we will need to disappear quickly. You must be ready to go at a moment's notice," he says.

Then time flashes forward and I see when Roger is taking Evangeline back to Ocracoke Island. He takes her directly to the home of her father, Robert Alexander. It has been four years since Evangeline's capture. She left the island as a seventeen-year-old captive and now returns as a twenty-one-year-old mother. Her precious son, William, clings to her neck. He rests his wee face in the crook of Evangeline's neck and has his tiny little arms wrapped tightly around her. He is frightened, and his forest green eyes are wide and round. The pirate island is all he has ever known. Everything here is so new to him.

I see Evangeline's father open the door to his home and gasp when he finds Evangeline, William, and Roger standing on his doorstop. He is shocked to see her. His big hands shake as he takes his daughter and grandson into his burly arms. He cries huge tears of joy. Tears roll down Evangeline's face, too.

He embraces her, not wanting to let her go. "My dear child, we thought you had perished in the sea. God is good. But how is it possible that you are here? Where have you been?" He looks from Evangeline to Roger in question.

Evangeline clings to her father. "Poppa, I was captured by Daniel, Roger's cousin. He held me captive on his island. Roger helped me to escape."

Elizabeth, Evangeline's sister, and her husband David, hear the commotion and come running to the doorway. A baby on her hip, Elizabeth rushes out to see what has happened. She reaches out to Evangeline to welcome her home, even as she cries with happiness. "Evangeline, where have you been? We searched the shores for you. We thought that you had drowned yourself in misery in the surf."

Evangeline rushes to tell them. "I was on the beach. I was reading a letter from Jacob when these scruffy, vicious pirates came upon me. They dragged me to their ship," she explains. "I was kidnapped by Daniel Teach's crew! He kept against my will on an island.

"You remember Daniel Teach, don't you? He leered at me when we were in Florida and then again here on this island. I always feared him. He was Blackbeard's grandson, a wicked pirate and Roger's cousin. Roger rescued me. Thank God, he was part of Daniel's crew, or I would still be there on the island. Daniel drowned at sea. Roger helped me to escape and brought me home."

I watch as Roger reaches down to scoop up little William. The scared child is caught up in the excitement and tightly wraps his tanned skinny arms around Roger's neck. His eyes are the size of saucers. He looks at these strangers that are his family, people he does not know. He has only heard his mother tell him about their existence.

"This is my son, William," Evangeline says as she introduces the little boy to her family. Evangeline's sister, Elizabeth, gently takes her nephew into her arms. She kisses him on his soft cheek. "Come to me, my little lad. Your momma is my sister. I am your Auntie Elizabeth." She points to her children. "These are your baby cousins."

Little William grins at her. "You look like my momma."

Evangeline looks at her sister's family—her husband David and their two children. "I have a lot of catching up to do," Evangeline says. "You will need to tell me all that I have missed while I was captive."

"Remember before you left, I told you of my feelings for David? I married Emily's brother now two years gone by. These are your nephews, Adam and Levi. We have been living here with Poppa, helping him with the home. David has been helping run the Oxford Pub since your capture.

"Our brother Stephen married Anna Albright a year ago. They are about to have their first babe," Elizabeth continues. She wraps her arms around her sister and gently walks her into the kitchen. "We will have some tea and I will tell you everything else you have missed."

Evangeline looks around for her other brother. "But where is Robert?"

Elizabeth and her father laugh. Her Poppa grins and nods. "Now, that is another story. Your friend Emily White married your brother, not long after you were missing. He is helping them run the Shepard's Head Inn. They will be so surprised to see you," he says. "It's so funny. Emily has said all along that she felt that you were still alive. She kept telling us that she felt your presence. We will need to go visit them. But first, we must get you and our precious William settled."

Evangeline's father tenderly reaches over to take little William into his arms. "Come here my grandson. I am your Grand Poppa. My, but aren't you a handsome little fella." He plants a kiss on his grandson's cheek, with a small tear sliding down his bearded face.

Evangeline exclaims as she hugs her Poppa. "I have missed so much. Poppa, it is so good to be home. I have longed for home. Daniel would not allow me to come home. It was only in his death that we were able to escape his grasp."

I awaken from my dream to find sunlight beaming through the old windowpanes and making prisms on the creamy yellow walls. I roll out of bed and rub the sleep from my eyes. I wonder again if Evangeline is trying to show me her life through my dreams. I reach down on the golden oak nightstand for my little notebook and begin writing. With this dream, as in the others, I have the feeling that I was witnessing something that has really happened in the past. My face is wet, and I realize that I had tears of joy to match the tears running down Evangeline's olive-colored profile when she is reunited with her family.

After I finish my journal entry, I jump into a hot shower. By the time I dress, I feel revitalized. I rush down to my family and friends, ready to start my day. My life has purpose since I have arrived on the island.

Downstairs, everyone is already seated eating their breakfast. The smell of hickory-smoked bacon and perked coffee fills the air and makes my mouth water. I sit down and take a bite of a homemade cinnamon bun that melts in my mouth. The pastry is so buttery. We have fresh strawberries, melon, and cantaloupe from the local produce market to go along with our pastries.

This year, Sarah and Emily have hired extra staff to help with the Fourth of July cleanup. The food leftover from yesterday was wrapped up by staff last night and refrigerated. We will share it today at our evening meal with friends and family—another of our traditions.

Excited about my latest dream, I burst out, "Last night, I had another dream about Evangeline. In it, she was rescued by Roger and brought back here to her home on Ocracoke Island. Her friend, Emily, is linked to Evangeline. Emily always felt that Evangeline was still alive."

I tell them more details about the dream.

"That's fascinating. Maybe she is trying to lead you to the treasure maps," my grandfather, Paul, says. "There were always rumors that Emily and Evangeline were somehow linked spiritually. My grandmother and your grandmother were also able to see visions of Evangeline."

"What?" I say. "I never knew that."

I sit for a minute, thinking about my dream. "I watched Evangeline sew her jewels and baubles into the hems and secret pockets of her gowns. Her friend, Roger Brown, was so in love with her. I could sense the passion he felt for her in my dream. She was fond of Roger, but her heart and soul belonged to Jacob. Evangeline told Roger that he would always hold a special place in her heart, but it was not fair for her to marry him since she could never give him her heart fully.

"She also told Roger that he did not belong on a pirate ship. His compassion for others would never allow him to hurt others," I say. "His nature was too honorable."

My grandfather had been sitting, quietly thinking. "Robert and David, as you know, Roger Brown was your ancestor. He was adopted by the Brown family," Paul says. "The stories describe him as a ruggedly handsome man with coal black hair and eyes of chocolate brown. He loved Evangeline with all his heart. Because she could not give him her heart, he had numerous lovers, just like his grandfather, Blackbeard.

"Roger Brown lived in your house, David," my grandfather continues. "It will be interesting to see if we will be able to find any of his belongings there. To this day, not much has been found about him. It makes me wonder if it there might be something hidden away somewhere in your home."

"I wonder if Roger might have left a journal somewhere in my house. It would be interesting to see everything from his point of view," David responds. "Paul, isn't it true that after he brought Evangeline and her son back to Ocracoke, he worked for her father, Robert Alexander? Robert Alexander operated a cargo company that shipped between Ocracoke and Hatteras Island using the pirate ship Roger brought with him.

"I guess we will need to keep doing more research. We need to find out everything we can about them," David adds.

Chapter 16

Where Pirates Gather

Paul opens up his maps and reads the latest clue. "It says, 'Look to a place where Blackbeard lay his head.' To me, that means we need to look at places that Blackbeard might have stayed or slept when he stayed on the island, meaning places that were around between 1712 and 1718.

"This is a is a census showing all the residences that were standing in those years," he continues, pointing to a document he has pulled out. "Surprisingly, David, your home; also, the Shepard's Head B&B; and your parent's place, Thomas and George, are among the homes that were around at that time. My home and, Isabella, your home, are also listed on the census."

Jim White, Emily and Sarah's father, speaks up. "It is fascinating to think that we might be able to find more clues in our homes. I can't wait to see what we come across in your place, David, when Thomas and Matt renovate it, since it once belonged to Roger Brown."

Thomas nods. "I know, and I can't wait to get started." Thomas turns to me and continues speaking. "We expect to finish the renovation on your cottage today, Angie. Look at what we have found there already. Who knows what else we might come across this afternoon."

Thomas's look suddenly became serious. "I am getting worried, though, about anyone finding out what we have discovered so far. There are some really shady characters here on the island—I heard that Rusty Gamble and Ricky Pervell were recently released from prison. Remember them? They were arrested a couple of years ago for B&E and robbing the Ocracoke Health Center. They were looking for drugs. Scared poor old Lucy to death when they broke in. Luckily, she heard them and hid under one of the desks.

"When we were in high school, they terrorized some of the teenage girls on the island," he continues. "Word was that they even raped one, but they couldn't prosecute him because she left the island. I heard that they threatened to kill her."

"Hey, and don't forget that it was those two who blew up a rabbit and left its bloody body on the church steps," George says. "They were heavy into drugs and always getting into trouble "Yes, we need to keep this quiet about what we're doing. We can't talk about this with anyone except our group."

Matt shakes his head. "I agree. I haven't seen those two this summer, but they have a reputation. You girls need to stay as far away from them as possible—and let's stay in groups to be safe."

"What do they look like?" I ask.

Paul frowns. "Unsavory characters. Both have ponytails—ratty, oily, dirty blond hair. Most of the time they wear grimy T-shirts and tattered blue jeans or dirty frayed jean shorts. They cuss like sailors—or pirates," Paul says.

I surprise everyone when I say, "Evangeline keeps warning me in my dreams that there could be danger."

Paul points on his list to the B&B and David's home. "We need to figure out what direction to look in for the next clue—and other places Blackbeard may have rested his head. Let's sit down later today to brainstorm.

"Robert, do you want to go with me to the library and the Ocracoke Preservation Society Museum?" he continues. "I need to do some more research on Blackbeard. I know you like doing that sort of thing."

We spend the rest of the morning cleaning up the island. The local residents turn out to help us pick up all the trash and clutter that was left after yesterday's Fourth of July celebration. As Emily and I work, I groan in exasperation. "Some people just don't clean up after themselves," I say. "I don't get it. I was always taught to leave everything a little bit better than how I found it."

Emily throws discarded paper streamers and candy wrappers into the heavy green dumpster. "I know, Angie. Some people just aren't like us. It's the way they were raised."

I think on how much I love this little community. "I have missed small town life. I didn't feel any comradery with anyone when I lived in Washington, D.C.," I say. "I didn't even know the majority of my neighbors. People there didn't speak to you or even care to get to know you.

"It is so foreign to me after growing up in Ripley, Maryland, where we knew everyone. We played softball, rode our bikes or motorcycles. We were outside every day, especially in the summer, with our neighbors."

I continue talking as I'm swept into nostalgic memories. "I had an awesome childhood when I lived on my small dirt road, Hannon Drive. Emily, do you remember coming to visit our family that one summer? To this day, I am still friends with most of the people I grew up with there. I wouldn't have changed my youth for anything in the world. Ocracoke Island is so much like the little town that I grew up in so many years ago."

Matt wraps me in a hug. "Speaking of good things on the island, I can't wait to show you the special touches we added to your cottage, Angie. You're going to be surprised!"

"I know you guys are doing a fantastic job with it," I say.

We go back to cleaning up the little town. I'm working close to Emily, sweeping debris into piles. "It's crazy how much of a mess you create when you set off fireworks!" I say to her. "But it's great that the whole town helps with the cleanup. Look—we're almost done and it's not even 11 o'clock."

I gaze up at the dazzling indigo sky. "Look at this spectacular day. Perfect weather. It's going to be another great day for a picnic on the beach."

I point to my cottage. "I haven't told the others yet, but I think I'm going to stay on the island permanently. I have been mulling it over since I got here two weeks ago. What do you think—can I rent your cottage on a full-time basis?"

Emily whoops and embraces me. "Really Angie, that would be awesome! I'm sure it wouldn't be an issue having you rent full time. When are you going to tell everyone? I'll be busting at the seams to keep this a secret."

I smile. "I think I am going to tell everyone at our picnic today. The thing that worries me is my mom. With Matt staying, that only leaves Sally and Robert living close to her in Maryland. Sure, she has all her friends, but I still worry about her since Dad died."

Emily puts her arm around me. "I think she'll be alright. David and your Mom seem to be pretty tight. He seems really supportive of her," she says. "Besides, you never know, maybe she'll spend more time down here on the island with both you and Matt here—and those two precious grandbabies! For sure, she'll want to spend as much time with them as possible."

I nod. "Thanks, Emily. You're right. She'll be fine. And I can always visit her. As it is now, I have only been able to see her once a month. Also, Sally has asked Mom to babysit the twins when Sally goes back to her teaching job."

"Is she still teaching fourth grade at Father Andrew White Elementary School? Emily asks.

"Yep. The same place and the same grade since she graduated from Salisbury State University," I answer. "She told me the other day that she doesn't want to give up her class. She really enjoys teaching at the neighborhood school."

I point across the way to the tiny school on the island. "Sally told me the other day that Ocracoke School reminds her of her school at home. She and Robert stopped by Ocracoke School the other day. Did you know Robert is still teaching phys ed and coaching basketball at Chapticon High School? He started after he graduated from college and he's still at it. He told me his principal has been very accommodating—and let him take off whenever he needed to take Sally to her OB appointments."

Emily laughs. "God, wouldn't it be cool if Sally and Robert would move to the island, too? I'd love to have all of you living here all the time," she says "I told Robert the other day that they needed help coaching this summer. Mr. Able, the local PE teacher, hurt his back this past spring and is still out on a medical leave. I hear he's been thinking about retiring.

"There would be work here for Sally, too. We've got kindergarten through 12th grade, just like the school where she teaches now. I heard the other day that one of the teachers, Mary, is pregnant and wants to cut back her hours this fall," Emily says. "I know Sally loves our little island school."

I smile. "It would be fantastic if they moved here. I'd be able to spend more time with my new niece and nephew. Those twins are just too cute!"

Looking up at the bright blue sky, I exclaim, "We need to round up the others and head down to the beach. I need some sun and surf before we go to work at the pub."

Emily yawns. "I know, right? We open today at 2. And Sarah says she needs to be back at the inn at 2, also, to let her staff off. Hey—and speaking of Sarah," Emily points to the right, where Sarah is bagging trash with Matt. "I'll go ask if they're ready to go to the beach."

I stretch. "Good. While you do that, I'll find my Mom, David, and my grandparents to see if they're ready to go."

Emily says she spoke with her parents earlier and they are planning to head to the beach at noon. The others are going to meet us at the inn at 11:45 to go to the water together.

"I'm going to run up and get changed into my spiffy new royal blue bathing suit," I say. "It's a beauty. I can't wait to wear it."

Emily grins, walking towards her cottage. "Did I tell you that Thomas and Max plan to ride down to the beach with us? I'm sure you won't mind that. You two looked pretty chummy last night sitting on the tarps watching the fireworks."

I shake my head. "Emily, I told you, we're just friends. I'm not ready for a relationship with anyone anytime soon," I say. "But to be honest, I enjoy having him around. I feel comfortable with him, like I've known him all my life."

I find my mom, David, and my grandparents and tell them about our beach plans. My grandfather models his new turquoise blue bathing suit with tan seashells on it. "I'm ready to go whenever you are," he says. "I have my bathing suit on already."

Grandmom laughs. "Bathing suits are the only thing he wears when we are here on the island. He puts it on first thing in the morning, every morning. It's a good thing, he has seven bathing trunks, or he would get pretty funky," he says.

"Hey. You put your suit on first thing, too!" Paul replies.

"I knew we were going down to the point at noon," she replies. "I can't wait to have some of that leftover pork with that vinegar-based North Carolina barbeque sauce. I woke up dreaming about it. The thought of it makes my mouth water."

We pile into the vehicles and head to the parking area near the beach. Armed with beach towels, chairs, and a cooler, we all walk down to the point of Ocracoke Island. The seagrass on the sand dunes is swaying in the pleasant breeze. Waves roll gently onto the shoreline. The tan-and-white sandpipers search for their lunch, popping their tiny beaks in and out of the sand, looking for sandfleas.

I watch the pipers from my pink beach chair. "I sure have missed watching the birds play in the surf."

I pick up my blue iPhone, with its flowery case and get up from my chair. "I'm going to take some more pictures of them. It's almost impossible to capture their beauty, the way that they play cat-and-mouse in the surf. No matter how many shots I take, I never feel I'm capturing the charming way that they play in the water."

Before I walk toward the birds, I spray my arms and chest with my suntan lotion, catching its coconut and pineapple aroma. Unexpectedly, a breeze rolls by midspray, catches the lotion, and hits Thomas with it smack in the center of his muscular chest. I am so embarrassed.

"Sorry, Thomas," I apologize. "It's a little windy today. I didn't realize you were standing right behind me."

Thomas is screwing Emily's teal-and-white umbrella into the sand. "It's okay, Angie. I kinda' like smelling like a piña colada."

He looks over at me. "You might want to put some of that on your back and shoulders. You're already a little pink," he says. "Do you want some help?"

I blush, hand him the suntan spray, and turn my back to him. "Sure. That would be great. You can use some if you want."

Thomas takes the spray container. I squeal and jump away when the cold lotion hits my warm back. "Oh, that's cold!"

His hot hands rub in the spray. His callused hands are amazingly soft and I'm feeling weak in the knees. I try not to react, but my stomach clenches and I feel a passion growing up in me. I turn around and look up into his stormy green eyes. They swallow me whole, and I stutter, "Thanks, Thomas. Can I put some on your back too?"

He looks at me, his eyes smoldering, and hands back the sunscreen. "No, I'm good. Maybe later today."

He takes my hand in his, massaging some of the lotion onto my hand. I try not to melt. I dare not say anything, for I know that my voice will tremble and give me away. The photographs I was planning to take are quickly forgotten as our passion starts to smolder.

Emily is watching us. She laughs and pushes us toward the waves. "Come on guys. Let's cool you two off. Time for a swim," she says. "What a pretty blue the water is today. It's like being in the tropics. Maybe we can come back later tonight after work."

She looks over at her mother and points up to the crystal-blue sky. "Mom, it reminds me of the color of your flow blue china."

Sarah is wading in the inviting water. Her olive-green bikini hugs her sensuous hips and small bosom. She epitomizes the perfect beach baby when she dives into the gentle waves. Her silky hair is woven into a French braid, and its highlights glimmer in the sunshine. Matt plunges into the warm waves beside her. She wraps her legs around his waist. They frolic in the ocean. I hear her laughter when he nibbles on her earlobes.

Emily throws a beach ball at Matt as she wades into the water. "Oh my God, you two, get a room! There are children here," she teases. "Let's play some beach volleyball. The ocean is calm enough."

Matt volleys the ball toward Thomas. "Heads up, Thomas. You, Emily, and Sarah against Angie, me and George."

Thomas slams the ball back at Matt and laughs. "You're on. We're going to slaughter you guys."

The white beach ball flies, its orange, red, blue, and green stripes a blur. Max is in the water and paddles around us and chases the ball. Our shouting fills the air. I am laughing so hard that I find it hard to hit the ball.

A rogue wave comes up and wipes all of us out. Sally is up on the shore with her cell phone, videotaping us. "That was great. I caught the wave on video," she yells to us. "It's going to look wild on TikTok and Facebook."

Another huge wave rises up and knocks me under the water. My raven hair tumbles out of its clasp and falls into my eyes. I dive under the water to straighten my hair and run smack into Thomas. I accidentally grab his butt when I try to get up out of the water.

He yelps and laughs. "Oh, Angie. I'm not that kind of guy. We haven't even been on our first date yet."

Matt howls with laughter. "Oh my God. So funny! Angie, you should see your face. You're the color of a strawberry."

I blush and stutter. "Stop, Matt. It was an accident. I didn't see Thomas. My hair was in my face."

Emily laughs. "That was classic. I don't know who was blushing more, you or Thomas."

I put my hands over my eyes and peek through my fingers at my friends. It is so embarrassing.

Sarah looks at her Fitbit and calls to Emily and me. "Oh no. You aren't going to believe this but it's already 1:30. We gotta' get back to the inn. I told the staff that I'd let them off at 2 pm. I gotta' fly. Can somebody give us a ride back?"

Sally yawns. "Robert will take us. I need to get back to the twins. They need to be fed and I'm starting to get a little tired."

Robert stands up, wrapping a towel around his waist, "I'll pack up the truck and get you back in plenty of time."

Matt gathers up his gear. "Sarah, I can give you a ride."

Mom looks at David. "I think I'm ready to go back, too. What about you, David?" She starts tucking her things into her new white-and-teal canvas beach bag from L.L.Bean. David stands up and puts on his bright yellow T-shirt with the red OBX symbol on the front. "I'm ready whenever you are. It is beautiful though. I could stay here all day."

We gather up all our beach supplies. George takes down our beach umbrella and knocks the sand off its anchor. He packs it back into its bright blue bag, to be used the next time we come to the beach. "Looks like we are all going to head back. Even Max looks like he is ready to go," George says. "I think we wore him out in the water. Look at him, Thomas. He's passed out under your chair."

Chapter 17
A Special Gift

Emily and I are down in the pub before 2 p.m. My guitar is swung over my back. I slip it off and set it on my guitar stand up on the small wooden stage. I smile, do a little jig, and say to Emily, "This is my new life. How awesome and magical is this island? It's like always being on vacation."

I help Emily pull the chairs off the tables and make Oxford Brew. The tropical punch is filled with pineapples, strawberries, and oranges. Its sweet nectar is as refreshing as wild honey. Orange and berry-flavored rum adds a tang—and a kick. It'll sneak up on you if you aren't careful. I remember one night we took a whole gallon of the fruity brew out onto the beach. We poured it into red Solo cups and sat around a blazing bonfire.

Oh, how those memories of moments shared with my friends are still so fresh. I feel so lucky to be living here on the island. I know we'll have many more treasured days and nights.

The vibe outside the pub is always fun. Guests sit at picnic tables or hang their toes into the refreshingly warm water of Silver Lake. People arrive by both water and land. The guests that come by water are picked up by the water taxi after they have spent time sailing or cruising on sparkling Pamlico Sound.

The Oxford Pub's water taxi driver, Sam Brown, is a distant cousin of my brother-in-law, Robert. He wears his long bleached-blonde hair long pulled back in a ponytail, and he sometimes braids his beard. He was hired by Emily many years ago. They've known each other since kindergarten. He is loved by all the guests for his happy-go-lucky personality, and he's always ready with a witty comment or joke. Sam Brown loves to surf, just like Emily, and he spends most of his mornings on the beach, surfing in the ocean before work.

The outside tiki bar is popular, but Emily always keeps the pub open inside, too, for those seeking air conditioning. The pub menu can vary, but it usually includes pizza, hamburgers, barbeque, steamed shrimp, fresh mahi-mahi, fish tacos, conch fritters, and fried oysters. The seafood is supplied by the local fishermen. The succulent steamer baskets are a favorite among the pub patrons, me included. The pizza comes from Ocracoke Pizza Company. Emily has carved out a pretty good deal with the business, one that benefits both the pizzeria and the pub.

The pub's kitchen stays open from 2 p.m. until 9 p.m. Most of Emily's customers know her summer schedule and frequent her establishment on a regular basis. Some people eat at the pub every night. George is one of them, but I think he just loves being around Emily.

Now that Emily knows I'm staying on the island, we talk about the details. "In the off season, your hours will vary depending on the size of the crowds," she tells me. "I'll still be able to give you a credit on your rent when you play for us in the pub.

Then she adds: "I quickly spoke to Sarah about your plan—I hope you don't mind—and she would love to have you rent the cabin on a permanent basis."

"I should have no problem paying for my rent," I respond. "I have been getting a pretty good-sized royalty check from my songs. My manager listened to my latest songs, and she thinks they could possibly go to No. 1 on the charts, too."

Emily nods. "I wondered about that. I love hearing your songs on the radio. The other day I heard a disc jockey say one of the songs was at No. 4 and seemed to be steadily going up," she says, before adding, "Are you nervous about playing tonight?"

I laugh, running my fingers through my long hair. "I'm always nervous before I play," I answer. "I know it seems silly, but I just can't help it. I'm always afraid I'll bomb out and... Hey, look, here comes your friend, Cindy! I haven't seen her in years."

Emily waves at Cindy. "She went to college in Delaware at Salisbury State. She just moved back a couple weeks ago. She finished her bachelor's degree in nursing," Emily says. "Cindy's fun to be around. Do you remember her from our bonfires on the beach?"

I nod my head. "I do. She had a big crush on Matt," I say. "We better tip her off that Matt is with Sarah now. You know what a woman magnet Matt is. I know in my heart that he's always been in love with Sarah, but he is such a flirt. He better not break Sarah's heart."

Emily waves to Cindy, who steps over to join us. "Long time, no see, lady. How have you been?" Emily says as she gives her friend a hug. "Did you start working at the hospital yet?" Emily points to me. "Do you remember Angie?"

Cindy hugs Emily back. "Hi, ladies. How are you two doing? And to answer your questions, 'yes' to both.

"Angie, it's been a long time," Cindy continues. "I just love your song about Ocracoke Island. I heard it on the radio the other day. Are you playing tonight?"

I shake my head in the affirmative. "Yeah, I'm playing in a little bit. Right now, I'm helping Emily set up the tiki bar. I just finished making some of her famous Oxford Brew," I say as I hand Cindy a cup. "Would you like some? It's a really good batch if I do say so myself."

Cindy smiles. "How can I say 'no'? I love this stuff. It's the best on a hot day," she responds. "So, Angie, is Matt here? Someone told me he was here on the island this year working with Thomas."

Emily smiles broadly. "Cindy, you'll never guess. Remember how Matt always had a thing for Sarah? He and my sister finally got together after all these years. It's so romantic."

Cindy sighs. "Darn. But good for them. I can't believe it didn't happen long before now."

She spots the water taxi driver and points to him. "Oh look, there's Sam. Gotta' go. I wanted to ask him if he can run me out to Henry and Samantha's boat. I was out with them earlier today and left my sunscreen on the boat. I need to go get it before I get fried."

She looks around the tiki bar. "Boy, this place is getting packed already! It's just past two o'clock. See you two in a little bit—I won't be gone long."

We continue to set up. Soon the place is overflowing. There are people in the tiki bar area, out in the water, and overflowing onto the pub's dirt driveway. I feel like I am getting ready to perform a huge concert. My nerves bubble over as I look out at the masses. Emily sees me looking pensive, comes over, and squeezes my shoulder. "You've got this Angie. You know most of these people. Just pretend we are sitting on the beach and you are playing for us."

My palms are sweating. "I know it's stupid. I just can't help it. Maybe one day I'll get over this nervousness I feel when I play for crowds. Now you know why I don't want to go on tour. I would just die."

Emily's cell phone rings and she answers it. "Okay, Matt, I'll tell her. She's having her usual nerves. It should help her get her mind off performing. This place is packed already."

Emily gets off her phone. "That was Matt. He wanted you to know that they're nearly finished the cottage in case you want to see it before your first set."

"Really? I can't wait to see it! You don't mind if I dash over before I play? I won't be long," I promise her.

I run down the dirt road and over the patchy grass and sandy yard. I open the porch's screen door. I am ecstatic, beside myself, overjoyed to see the finished work of the small cabin that will be my home from now on. It is only a two-bedroom with a combined kitchen, living room, and dining room. But it will be mine. Emily had told me earlier that Thomas and Matt were finishing up work today on the old wooden floors.

I take a deep breath and knock on the stained oak door behind the screened door. I hear Max barking in a frenzy. Matt opens the door with a big smile. "Voila, my dear sister. Come into your new parlor."

I am smiling from ear to ear as I take in all the unexpected details Matt and Thomas have added to my quaint cabin. My brother and Thomas are in the middle of sanding the old oak floors. Thomas is shirtless and sweat is glistening over his tight tanned abdomen. His worn jean shorts hold his muscular bottom. I take a deep breath and flush, turning my head.

Matt bursts out laughing at my reaction to Thomas. There are tears coming out of his eyes because he is laughing so hard. He teases me, "What's the matter, Angie? Never seen a bare chest before?"

I swat Matt on the back. "C'mon, stop teasing me. Just show me my new place."

Thomas is trying his best to contain Max, who is jumping up and down. Max scampers over to greet me. His whole body wags with excitement. As he jumps up and down, the puppy loosens a board in the floor. Thomas reaches down and pulls up the old wooden plank.

"Hey, you are not going to believe this. I think there's an opening here below this floorboard," he says.

"Could it be another one Evangeline's hiding places?" I wonder aloud.

Thomas shines a flashlight into a crevice below the floor. He gets on his knees, reaches into the space, and pulls out a small, ornately carved, wooden box. The small chest look like the others we found.

Thomas opens one box. Inside is a small burlap bag. It jingles when he shakes it. He loosens its tie and dumps out about twenty gold coins. Thomas holds up a couple to the light.

"These look like the Spanish gold doubloons we found the other day," he says. "They're dated 1757—that's around the same time Evangeline and her family moved to Ocracoke Island. Could these be part of Daniel's treasure?"

Thomas reaches into the hole again, stretching his arm further this time. He pulls out another box, "I wonder what's in this one?" he says. "Angie, you open it. I opened the first one." He grins and hands the box to me.

I gasp as I open the second box. "It's a beautiful pearl necklace. I wonder if this is the one Daniel gave Evangeline?"

I look back in the box and bring out a sparkly golden ring and a piece of parchment paper. "Look. Another diamond ring and another love letter from Daniel to Evangeline. Oh my gosh—it's a clue!"

I step closer to a window to read what's written.

"Look to Where Pirates Gathered and Near Teach's Hole," I announce.

Matt scratches his bearded chin. "This must be talking about Teach's Hole off Springer's Point. I love hiking through that park. There is so much wildlife. But it's said to be haunted by the spirit of Blackbeard."

Matt turns to Thomas. "Do you remember when you, George, and I camped there, under that gnarly old oak tree? We got spooked when we heard some weird noises, and then we thought we saw a gauzy, headless figure walking down the path through the woods towards us.

"It was crazy. I was scared shitless. We ran home and ended up camping out in your back yard," Matt says. "If I remember right, we were about twelve years old. I never told anyone about that. Did you? "

Thomas chuckles. "Oh yeah. I almost forgot about that. I remember my Mom asked us what we were doing back home so early. I told her we were getting eaten up by mosquitos, and that was why we came home to camp in the backyard.

I never told her what we saw that night. I was afraid she wouldn't believe us," he says, then turns to me. "Angie, you should have been there. It was the craziest, scariest thing I have ever seen. To this day, I thought it was Blackbeard. How ironic would that be if we found Blackbeard's treasure?"

My eyes are wide open in astonishment by this time. I look straight at my brother. "Matt, how come you never told me? You know how much I love all that scary stuff. Don't you remember how you would tell us girls ghost stories when we were young?"

We all become pensive. Suddenly I break the silence. "Enough of that. Show me my new cottage. I need to get back and play soon."

I walk over to the refurbished stone fireplace topped by a golden oak mantel. I run my hand over the smooth wood. "Did you make this, Thomas?" He nods.

"It's gorgeous. I can't wait to light my first fire in it." I turn toward the kitchen and smile. "And look at these kitchen cabinets. Their honey-colored oak matches the mantel and the floors. They're beautiful."

Matt steps into the living room. "You think those are pretty? Come and see what Thomas made for you. It's an oak stand for your guitar. Look he even carved two half hearts into it. They match the two hearts from your necklaces." The golden oak guitar stand is magnificent. It helps to make the room mine.

I wipe a tear that escaped my eye. "It's gorgeous. I'm speechless. This is so special. I will treasure it always."

I rub my hands over the guitar stand. No one has ever done anything so sentimental for me before. It is almost as if Thomas was reading my soul and understanding how important music is to me when he built it.

I blush when he looks at me. "I'm so glad you like it. I hoped you would. I know how much you love the story of Evangeline and Jacob," Thomas says. "It's got a little secret of its own. I created a hiding place behind the carved heart."

He points to a spot on the guitar stand. "Just push on this latch here and a crevice will open up for you," he explains. "Kind of like the wooden boxes that Jacob made for Evangeline or the wooden frames that Roger made for her."

"That's so neat. I can't wait to hide something in there. This is so special. Thomas, I don't know what to say." I hug him and kiss him on the cheek. I feel the heat rise in me and my cheek flame bright red.

"It's great. Isn't it?" Matt says. "But that's not all. Come look at the bathroom."

My brother watches my reaction as I follow him. "How do you like the pearly white tile in the shower? And what about this antique wooden bathroom vanity? We found it at an estate sale in Manteo. Do you like the seashell theme?"

I'm touched that my brother would remember how much I love the beach. My apartment back in D.C. was full of nautical things.

Thomas goes back to work on the floors. "I'm going to finish up the floors. I'm almost done with them. Matt, you go ahead and show Angie the rest of the house."

Matt takes me into one of the bedrooms "Angie this is the master bedroom. I think this was Evangeline's bedroom. How do you like the pale yellow we painted the walls? And look at the stained glass windowpanes. We found them stashed in the closet."

He guides me toward one of the windows. "Now take a peek out the window. You can see Silver Lake from here," he says as he opens the blind.

I am in awe of everything, "Oh, Matt. It's lovely. I'm going to be in heaven staying here. I can't wait to move in. I just adore the crown molding and the hardwood floors. It feels just like home already."

Matt hugs me. "I'm glad you like it. It has been fun working on it with Thomas," he says. Then he adds, in a whisper, "You know what, Angie? I think Thomas likes you a lot."

I look into my brother's bright blue eyes. "Matt, come on. You know we just met," I whisper back. "He's great, but I'm so *not* ready to be involved with anyone."

I change the subject. "We need to call the others. Or maybe we can just tell them tonight, when we see them, about the new clue," I say. "We can get everyone together tomorrow morning to show them what we've found. I'll tell Sarah and have her gather the troops in the parlor at the inn."

I have been carrying the two wooden boxes, and now I hand them to Matt. "Why don't you hide these in your toolbox and carry it across the driveway to the B&B. Jim can put the boxes in the safe.

"I know you're worried about these discoveries getting out," I continue. "I am worried, too, especially after hearing about Rusty and Ricky. We will need to be more careful and make sure all our clues are in safe places. In my dreams, Evangeline keeps warning me to be wary the dangers that finding the treasure might hold.

"Oh, look at the time! I need to leave," I say, rushing toward the door. "I'll see you guys over at the pub. You're coming to hear me play, aren't you?"

Matt and Thomas answer in unison. "We wouldn't miss it. See you over there later."

I walk across the gravel dirt driveway, down the steps behind the inn and out into the tiki bar. Emily is with George behind the cedar-planked watering hole. They both wave at me. I give them a thumbs up and run over to them.

"Emily, you have got to see my cottage. It is gorgeous and so me. It felt just like home when I walked in today," I say. "And we found another clue!"

I stop and look around, then lower my voice. "Max knocked a floor plank loose, and Thomas found two boxes hidden under it. One contained a clue.

There was also a diamond ring, a pearl necklace—and some more gold doubloons."

I look up and suddenly see a creepy guy nearby. It's gotta' be Rusty. He looks at me and raises his eyebrows. He walks past us and joins another grimy friend—Ricky—in the crowd. He didn't say anything when he walked by, but I grimace. "Oh God. Do you think he heard me? Oh no. I need to be more careful. We don't need anyone, especially him finding out about our clues."

George puts his finger to his lips. "I hope not. He's the last person we want to know about any of this," George says. "Did Matt say when he and Thomas might be coming over here? We all need to meet to go over the new clue.

"Do you think that diamond ring was from Daniel?" he asks.

I twirl my hair around my fingers. "I don't think it was from him. In my dream, Daniel gave her a small golden ring," I say. "Maybe I will have another dream that shows me where it came from."

Emily points to the stage, rubs my back. "You feel up to playing now? The customers are asking me what time the music starts. I told them you would be right back."

Picking up my guitar, I smile. "I'm ready. I was distracted from my jitters," I answer. "Has anyone given you any requests? I left a box on the stage for requests."

I sit down on my wooden stool and strap on my guitar. "How's everyone today? I'm so glad to be here with you all. I'm going to start out with a song about the summers I've stayed on the island. I hope you like it."

My music fills the air as I sing about the island and how much I love this place. I notice that some of the patrons are singing along with the lyrics. When I finish, the crowd erupts in cheers. I am amazed and touched that a lot of people know all the words to my songs.

I run through my first set and announce that I'm taking a short break. I step down off the stage and walk back to join Emily and George. I spot Joe, my favorite bartender from SmacNally's Raw Bar, and his wife June. We greet one another with warm hugs and smiles. June is one of my friends from our bonfires.

"Angie, it's so good to have you back on the island," June says. "I just love that song you sang about Ocracoke Island. I felt like I was back on the beach by one of the bonfires we used to have. How have you been?"

"Thanks June. I'm so glad you liked it," I answer. "And hey, congratulations on your wedding. I'm so happy for you and Joe. I'm sorry I couldn't make it down here last spring for the ceremony. I couldn't get off work."

June shakes her head. "It's okay. Emily told me that she spoke to you and that you couldn't get away. And it's not like D.C. is right down the street. It's quite a hike from here. Let's make plans and go to the beach one day soon."

I give her a thumbs up. "That sounds great. You know how much I love hanging out at the beach. Give me a call and we can set it up." As we trade cell phone numbers, Joe orders two Oxford Brews.

"Angie, we're going to go grab a table," he says. "Really love your music. It feels like old times." June waves goodbye and they make their way to a table by the shoreline.

Sarah comes over to where I'm standing at the bar. "Angie, that was great. The crowd really seemed to enjoy it and you know that I did."

She adds: "Matt called to tell me about what Thomas found. I talked to the others and we're going to meet in the parlor tomorrow. The two new boxes are in the safe."

At that moment, Thomas arrives with Max in tow. He walks straight up to us. "Sorry I missed your first set," he says. "I finished the floors. You are all set to move in whenever you're ready. The furniture Sarah ordered should be here tomorrow."

Sarah looks at me. "I think you're really going to like the country-style furniture I ordered for the cottage. The couch is a sage color. I tried to match it to the wall color. The bedroom set is a four-poster oak bed. Emily and I made a seafoam and pale yellow quilt for your bed last winter. I hope you like it."

"Really. That all sounds just right up my alley. You girls really know my style," I say and then grin.

When the evening ends, Emily congratulates me. "That was a great night. How are you feeling—think you're going to like playing in the pub?" she says. "The islanders and the visitors seem to love your music."

I pick up my guitar and slip the brown leather strap over my shoulder. "It was so much fun. It feels like I'm on vacation but I'm getting paid for it. I know one thing though. I'm beat," I say. "I'm going to head to bed early tonight. What about you guys?"

George yawns. "Me too. I feel like I've been up for two days. What about you, Thomas? Are you ready to go? Max slept under our table for an hour."

Thomas ruffles his dog's fluffy brown ears. "Max, what do you think? You ready to go, boy?" he says. "I'm ready. I'm not used to staying up late when I'm working. So, girls, I will bid you farewell. Sarah, what time are we meeting in the parlor tomorrow?"

Sarah checks the text that she sent the others. I told everyone to meet us at around 9 a.m. Is that okay with you guys?"

George looks at his watch. "I think that will be fine. I have an appointment at Conners tomorrow to do some routine maintenance on their air conditioner. That will give me time to catch the ferry over to Hatteras. So, on that note, I'll see you guys tomorrow."

Matt looks at Thomas and George. "One thing—Sarah said Angie's furniture should be here tomorrow. Can you guys give me a hand with it?"

Thomas shrugs his shoulders. "I'm sure we can make time for that. What do you think, George?"

"No problem," George says. "Just text me when the delivery gets here, and I'll come on over to help. Angie, do you have much you have to move from the inn?"

"Not much. Matt can help me with that," I say.

I take a final sip of my lemonade. "Just think. Tomorrow night I'll be sleeping in my new home. I can't wait," I say. "Thank you all. I just love everything you have done." I kneel and pet Max on the head. "Max you be a good boy and I'll see you tomorrow," I say, then look up at everyone else. "See you guys at 9."

Emily, Sarah, and I head toward the B&B and split off once we get to the inn. It's been another rewarding and fun-filled day. I yawn and open the door to my room. All is quiet—no signs of Evangeline tonight.

As I slip into sleep, I wonder what I will dream about.

Chapter 18

The Scare

I wake in the morning feeling refreshed. I realize I didn't have any dreams.

I am full of energy, ready to start my day, and get moved into my new home. I race down the winding staircase to join the others. As I enter the parlor, I see that Sarah is on her cell phone. "I understand," she murmurs. "Thanks for calling. I'll let everybody know."

She ends the call and turns to us. "Angie, glad you're here. That was the delivery company. They won't be able to bring the furniture until tomorrow."

"Ahh, man. I was really psyched to get moved into my new place. Guess I'll just have to wait another day," I say, trying not to show how disappointed I am.

Sarah tucks her cell phone back into the pocket of her cute peach-colored peasant top. "I heard from George, too. He and Thomas will be here shortly. The others are in the kitchen eating breakfast. I got more of those yummy croissants that you like and some fresh melon."

"Umm, sounds good to me. I am kind of hungry. Did you already eat?" I start to walk towards the kitchen.

"Yeah. I got an early start today. One of the girls called and said she was running late." Sarah holds up a stack of bathroom towels she has just folded.

We walk together into the cozy kitchen, where a cool summer breeze is blowing the lacy curtains at the window overlooking Silver Lake. The coffee smells heavenly and tastes even better. The twins are already up and being coddled by Mom and David. Their blue eyes follow me when I walk across the room and serve myself a buttery croissant with homemade fig jam.

"What a treat, Sarah," I say as I take my first bite. "You are spoiling us. None of us are going to want to leave."

Sarah laughs. "I try to pamper all my guests. It makes them come back."

Emily comes through the kitchen door. "Umm, it smells heavenly in here. If those are croissants from Ocracoke Bakery, I'm definitely having one," she says. "I saw Thomas and George down the lane. They should be here any minute. Oh, I think I hear Max now. Have we started yet?"

Paul holds up some documents. "Not really. I was just getting ready to go over what Robert and I found at the library. I figured it'd be better to do it all at once after everyone gets here."

The screen door opens. Thomas, George, and Max come into the kitchen. George makes a beeline for the coffeepot. "Ahh, just what I need, a nice hot cup of coffee and croissants, too," he says. "Thanks Sarah. You think of everything."

Thomas reaches for his favorite mug, a rust-colored ceramic one. He pours a steamy cup of coffee and adds vanilla creamer. "Sarah, you're a lifesaver. We were out of coffee at our house. I've been craving a cup all morning," Thomas says. "Definitely need to go to the grocery store after work today. So, what are the plans for today?"

Paul points to the parlor. "I think it would be easier if I spread everything out in the other room. Robert and I found a couple of really good articles on Blackbeard."

Sally picks up her little Evie. "Come on baby, let's have a look at what your daddy and great grandpa found."

Robert picks up even-tempered Jacob and kisses his pink cheeks. "We had fun. I had forgotten how much I liked doing research. Paul and I went to the library and the courthouse. We researched the census records for the time that Blackbeard was said to have roamed the island."

Sarah and Emily's father brings out the four cedar boxes from my cottage. Jim places them on the gleaming oval table. "I got the boxes out of the safe. I think we should spread out what we've found but make sure we keep the items grouped by where they were found. It might have some meaning that certain objects were hidden close together."

Paul opens up the first box, the one we found behind the stones of my cottage fireplace. "I think you're right. If Evangeline hid pieces of the map, we might need to find them in a certain order."

"Thomas and Angie found these things—Evangeline's necklace and a love letter from Daniel Teach in the stone fireplace in what was once Evangeline's home. The love letter contains this clue: 'If you have found this letter, you will need to find the next. You will need to go where the Tiger meets the inlet and the Bankers roam free and where the Yaupon meets the pines.'"

Paul points to Thomas. "Why don't you open the second box and go over the next clue."

Thomas opens the little wooden container and pulls out the items as he talks. "This is the second box we found in Angie's cottage. There's a silver locket with a picture of Evangeline's son, a lock of her son William's hair, a gold ring, and this ruby necklace. These were given to Evangeline by Daniel, according to Angie's dream. The gold ring was given to her when Daniel proposed to her. Daniel gave Evangeline the necklace when William was born. Later he gave her the locket."

He hands the locket to Sally and Robert. "The picture of William looks just like your son, Jacob."

Sally opens the clasp so she can view the picture, again. "The resemblance is amazing, isn't it? Robert, look at this—it's crazy." She holds the locket up beside her son's cherub face.

Robert takes the locket and shakes his head in amazement. "It feels like more than an unbelievable coincidence. I wonder if this means there will be some connection between Jacob and William—or Jacob and Evangeline? Maybe Evangeline will be our twins' guardian angel, protecting them."

Thomas opens the second letter and reads its clue. "Go to the Place where the Sun melts into the Sound and Sailors look for a Guiding Light to bring them Home."

Paul points to Matt. "Why don't you open the next box."

Matt opens the coffer and holds up the sapphire necklace. "This necklace is gorgeous. Look at how it shines. The color reminds me of your eyes, Angie," Matt says. "I wonder if Daniel brought this home to Evangeline after one of his pirating excursions. The box contains another letter from Daniel and the third clue.

"It says, 'Look to Where Blackbeard Had Rested his Head.'

I turn to my grandfather and Robert. "What did you find in the library?"

Paul lays out the documents he and Robert gathered when they reviewed the census. "According to the records, there are several existing places that were around when Blackbeard was alive," Paul says. "Our research shows that he was on the island from around 1712 to 1718. He docked his ship—Queen Anne's Revenge—in Ocracoke Inlet. It's believed that he was in cahoots with Charles Eden, the governor of North Carolina at the time. Blackbeard was killed by a Lieutenant Robert Maynard on November 22, in 1718."

He continues, "The first place associated with him is right here at the Shepard's Head B&B before the Whites bought the property. The next place was David's home. We're lucky that Thomas and Matt plan to renovate the house next week—it will give us an opportunity to search it carefully. The third place is Isabella's home.

"Our home is next. And fifth is what was formerly called Wahab Village Hotel. It was renamed back in 1936. Then Chip and Helena Stevens bought the inn in 2007 from his great uncle, Robert Stanley Wahab and changed the name to Blackbeard's Lodge. According to the records, it was built in 1742," Paul says. "Now, I know Blackbeard was not alive by that time, but Daniel or Evangeline might have stayed there and hidden more clues on the property. It's a thought.

"The next place would be your parents' home, Thomas and George," Paul continues. "So, there we are. Plenty of places to search."

Jim looks over the articles on the table and turns to Paul. "Did you see Betty Gamble when you were in the library? You know she is Rusty Gamble's aunt—

and from everything I know about her, the biggest gossip in the town. I hear that Rusty and Ricky have been staying on her farm since they were released from prison."

Paul looks shocked. "You're kidding me. I had no idea," he says. "I told her we were researching Blackbeard for a new book that I am writing in connection with the 300th anniversary of his death. She was pretty helpful. Do you think she's going to cause problems?"

Grimacing, Robert rubs his face. He looks worried. "I just keep remembering that Evangeline said to being careful as there may be danger," he says. "You girls make sure you stay together and don't go out alone."

I wonder to myself if Rusty might have overheard me talking to Emily and George yesterday, but I shrug it off and don't mention it to the others.

Paul hands me the fourth box to open. "Well, there's nothing we can do about it now, but Robert is right. Be careful going forward. You open up the next one, Angie."

My hand grasps the box and I take out a dazzling golden filagree diamond ring. I get that familiar sensation that pops up whenever Evangeline materializes, but she doesn't appear today.

"I wonder if Daniel gave this ring to Evangeline. He gave her a gold ring in my dream when he proposed to her," I say. I pick up the little burlap sack of gold Spanish coins and dump them onto the parlor table. I draw out the ancient parchment and read the latest clue.

"Look Near Teach's Hole and Where Pirates Liked to Gather."

Paul picks up the fragile paper and examines it. "This could mean a bar, or maybe down on Springer's Point," he says. He looks thoughtful for a minute. "I want to think that it is possibly the Oxford Pub. The records Robert and I looked at show the pub was around during the right timeframe."

Emily laughs. "I don't know how that would be possible. I'm in that pub every day and have never found anything."

Jim smiles as he speaks to his daughter. "Maybe it was because the time wasn't right or that we just haven't been looking in the right places," he says. "Maybe we need to search in the wine cellar where we keep our kegs—that's one place you don't stay in for too long. It was the original cellar. You've told me before that it gives you the heebie jeebies."

Paul scratches the stubble on his chin. He doesn't shave every day when he is on the island. "It would be a good idea to have a look in the cellar with a new set of eyes. We have a good start here toward finding the next clue."

George checks the time on his phone. "I've got to cut out now. I must go inland to Conner's store to work on the A/C. Thomas and Matt, what are your plans for today? And Isabella, by the way, your air conditioner is fixed. The part finally came in yesterday. I'm sure you guys are anxious to move back into your home. It's all ready to go."

Matt looks my way. "I had planned to help my sister move into her new place, but the furniture isn't coming until tomorrow." He then turns to his work partner. "Thomas, do you want to get a head start on David's home? We can look around and maybe do a little demolition work today."

Thomas looks happy. He turns to David, "Would that be alright with you, David, if we head to your place and get started? Do you have time to go over with us? I don't know what your plans are for today."

David looks excited. "Sure! That sounds good to me. I've been looking forward to renovating that house for so many years, so the sooner the better," he says. "But remember that it's Robert and Sally's home now.

"I can go now if you want. Isabella, do you mind if I go with the guys today? I can catch up with you later at the beach," David tells my mom.

Isabella snuggles with Evie. "No problem. I'll just keep enjoying time with my twin grandbabies. We'll meet later. These two are just a little bit too young to hit the beach yet," she says. "Sally, will that be okay with you?"

Sally takes docile little Jacob from David. "I would love to have you spend the day with us, Mom. I can always use the help. These two are a handful, especially at mealtime.

"Robert, why don't you go with your dad?" she adds. "It might be fun—but you guys keep me up to date and include me if you can. I've felt like I'm living in a bubble since I had the twins."

Robert kisses Sally on the cheek. "Okay, Momma. No problem."

He looks down lovingly at his little family and smooches each of the babies on their cheeks. "I love you guys. I'll touch base with you later, Sally. Maybe we can go down to the beach with Dad and Isabella and have a late lunch. Georgia said earlier today that she'd be happy to watch the twins if we wanted to go to the beach."

Robert told me the other day that sometimes when he goes upstairs to check on his little brood he feels as if his heart will burst with love and pride. He can't believe his luck when he gazes down at his two miracle babies. He is already such a good father to my niece and nephew, and he's always been a wonderful husband to my sister. One day I hope I can be as fortunate as them.

Emily turns to me and Sarah. "Do you girls feel like going for a walk down on the point? It's such a pretty day. Sally, you said earlier you can't get away this morning."

Sarah and I answer in unison. "You don't have to ask us twice!" We both laugh because it seems like we planned it.

We all set off in different directions. Emily and I must go work in a while, so we can't join the others for lunch. But we'll see them when they come to the pub for dinner later.

Sarah, Emily, and I walk to the point, down the well-worn beach path. The silky sand is warm on our bare feet. A strong salty breeze blows through our hair. I think to myself, thank goodness we aren't getting sandblasted.

Sarah is smiling. "I don't know if I need to pinch myself or not, but Matt is so different this year. I thought I was in love with him before, but now I'm head over heels," she confesses. "It's scary. I'm afraid I'm going to wake up and it will have all been just a lovely dream."

I squeeze her hand. "Just go with it. Don't fret, Sarah. I think you two were meant to be," I say. "And Matt looks as happy and ecstatic as you. He seems centered for the first time, at peace and no longer restless any longer—maybe because he's been fighting his feelings for you most of his life.

"I'm thrilled for you guys," I add.

We walk for an hour that morning and I breathe in the fresh ocean spray. "It looks like we may have storm coming in today," I note as the breeze picks up.

"I hope it holds off until later tonight. I enjoy doing my sets outside and working in the tiki bar."

Emily gives me a little wink. "I know, right? I love it when we can keep the tiki bar open in the summer. I think most of our customers enjoy it, too. And, speaking of customers, I think it's time for us to head back if we're going to open up at 1 p.m."

I stretch my arms over my head. "Yeah, it's almost noon already. We should take walks like this every day," I say. "Next time maybe Sally can come, too. She's feeling left out because she's so busy with the twins. A daily walk will be a good way to include her."

Emily brushes back her strawberry-blonde hair. "That's a great idea. We can all get a little exercise."

My evening at work is uneventful. Sarah comes out to the bar to tell me that the delivery company called. They'll be here by 11 tomorrow. "Guess tomorrow is moving day for you," she says.

I raise my eyebrows and smile. "Really, I can't wait to move. Not that I don't love my room at the inn, but you just don't know how perfect that cottage is for me. It felt like home when I was there yesterday."

"I'm so glad you like it," Sarah says. "Thomas and Matt really do great work. Matt says he and Thomas will help get the furniture arranged when it arrives."

I rub my hands over my cheeks. "It's like being in a dream. I can't believe how happy I am. I should have moved here years ago. I guess everything happens as it should," I say. "Thank you so much for letting me rent the cottage. Mom says David, Robert, and Sally's little family will be moving into Mom's house tomorrow, too."

"Hey, no problem," Sarah replies. "Having someone rent the cottage full time is good for business and having you here is great for the pub. Our profits since your arrival are already up big time. Chi-ching." She laughs.

"But seriously," she adds, "I will miss having you and your family at the inn. It's been fun with y'all there. Almost like a vacation. Luckily, we have other guests scheduled to come in this weekend."

Sarah comes around the bar to get a berry-flavored White Claw. She takes a long sip and sighs. "These are so refreshing. They don't even taste like alcohol. I have to be careful with them."

At the end of the evening, I go back to my room, but I'm restless tonight. I guess I am over-excited about moving tomorrow. I pace back and forth then decide that I need to get some fresh air. I say out loud to myself, "This is a great time to work on my new song."

I grab my guitar and slip out of the inn. I cross over the dirt and oyster shell path. The wind has picked up dramatically and dark clouds almost cover the full moon. The water is rough; white caps crash in the surf, eroding the shoreline. I don't care. I want to write my new song. I can see a transparent mist standing further down on one of the dunes—it's Evangeline watching me. I wave at her. She waves back but keeps watching. I feel protected, almost as if she is guarding me.

I sit down between two small dunes to get some shelter from the strong wind. I start to pluck at my guitar—then the lyrics and music flow out of me. It's a song about Evangeline, a young girl who turned into a woman. She longs for a love that can never be returned, a life with a man who is so far away. My heart melts around my words. I feel her pain and misery. My guitar strums out an eerie, haunted tune.

My senses perk up suddenly and my skin feels a chill. I feel Evangeline beside me, whispering in my ear. "Angie, you are in danger. You must hide quickly. They are coming, and they bring you harm."

I hear drunken laughter further down the lonely, foggy shoreline. I can barely make out the shadows of two figures. The obnoxious men stumble down the misty beach, passing a brown bag with a bottle between them. I can tell by their loud slurred speech that they are wasted.

I am scared. My heart is racing. It roars in my ears. My breathing quickens. I crawl behind the tall grass of the dunes and hold my breath. I want to close my eyes but I have to watch. It's Ricky and Rusty. They stumble past me. I feel the evil of their aura, like a dark, murky haze.

I wait until the two are mere spots down the gravel road before I come out from my hiding spot and run as fast as I can back to Shepard's Head Inn, up the stone stairs, and through the large wooden door. I don't stop until I have slammed my bedroom door behind me. I cover my face with my trembling hands, lean back against the closed door, and slide down to the floor. My breathing is ragged. I have never felt more afraid.

My body is shaking as I pull my teal-colored T-shirt over my windblown head, brush my teeth, and crawl into bed. It takes me a long time to drift off and, when I finally do, it is a restless sleep. I dream about Evangeline. She is locked in a windowless room on a pirate ship. There is a tiny black kitten with her. Tears run down her face onto the small furry creature. I can hear it meowing. The room is musky and airless. Evangeline is sitting on a smelly ragged quilt that covers a tan-colored cot. I feel a horrible fear emanating from her.

She gets up and walks over to a worn wash basin on a wooden bedstand. She peers at herself in a hazy looking glass. The face that stares back at her is frightened, bruised, and bloody. She takes a cotton cloth and dips it in the tepid water. She tries to wipe the blood from her battered face. Her tears mingle with the dirt and blood.

I watch her frantically search for a way to escape. There is a light tapping at the grubby narrow door into the room. She gasps in fear and hides in the dark brown wardrobe. She peeks through a crack to see her old friend, Roger Brown, and her fear turns into hope. He opens the door to her cubbyhole, and she falls into his arms. He puts his finger to her lips. "Hush, my dear friend. Daniel might not like me being here with you."

Uncontrollable tears stream down Evangeline's face. "Roger, please! You must help me escape. I can't stay locked in this room."

She is grasping at him in terror. Her bright blue eyes are swollen and bruised from the beating she received during her violent capture. He strokes her tangled black hair and wipes the tears from her blue-black cheeks. "Oh, my dear Evangeline, you must be patient. We will both be in danger if I help you get away now. I must wait until it is safe for us to escape. Daniel is a vicious man. I have watched him rip the throats from many a man just for talking when he was drunk. He is pure evil.

"I wish by God that I never joined his crew," Roger continues. "I must go now. He cannot see me here. I will return when I can. It breaks my heart to see you on this godforsaken sloop."

Evangeline pulls at Roger's tan camise and begs him not to go. "Roger, please do not leave me. I am fearful of what will become of me."

Roger takes her pale bruised hands gently into his. "I must, my dear one. It is not safe for me to be here with you. Daniel is a jealous man and believes you are his possession. I will return soon."

He hangs his head and his shoulders droop as he leaves. Evangeline gulps back terrified tears and leans her head on the cabin door.

Next I watch as Evangeline is being dragged by huge burly fellow with gentle brown eyes. He tells her, "My name is Jeffrey, and you must not struggle." He pulls her down a narrow pungent corridor and through a slim doorway into Daniel's quarters.

Daniel comes to her, and he pulls her up against his muscular frame. She struggles to escape his powerful, viselike grasp and bites one of his strong hands. Daniel backhands her and she falls, her lip swollen and bleeding. He throws her a vulgar revealing outfit. "You belong to me now. Put this on. I want to watch you undress and see your beautiful body."

Evangeline spits in his face. "I will never be yours!" she screams as she throws the indecent clothes back at him.

Daniel slams her down onto the bed and tears her already ripped clothes from her bruised body. "Fine. Have it your way. I will take you and make you mine. You are a feisty one. You're a beauty, though." Her clothes are thrown in a heap around her on the dirty quilt. She screams as his shaft enters her. "You belong to me now," he groans as he leaves his seed buried deep within her.

Evangeline loses consciousness momentarily and awakens to find Daniel wiping the tears from her cheeks. He strokes her hair and holds her in his arms. He gets up and he covers her with the tattered bed clothes. She watches him while he dresses, peeping through half-closed eyes at his powerful body.

I awaken from my dream. It is morning, and I am trembling and in tears. My stomach clenches. I run down the hallway to the bathroom and almost knock over my sister. Sally has just come back from the kitchen with bottles for the twins.

She follows me into the bathroom. I splash cold water on my face. Through wrenching sobs, I try to tell her about my horrible dream. She wraps her arms around me and pats my back. "Angie, it was only a dream. It's okay. You're here with me. It's alright. I have you."

I am still crying as she walks me back to my room. "It was awful. I saw poor Evangeline being captured and taken to Daniel's room. I felt like it was me being raped."

"You are safe, now. No one can hurt you," Sally says. She holds me in her arms and puts my head on her shoulder.

I look up into her cloudy blue eyes. "But you don't understand. Evangeline is right. We aren't safe. I went to the beach last night to write my song. I saw Rusty and Ricky. Evangeline came to me and told me to hide.

"I could feel the wickedness brimming out of those two. They were both stumbling down the beach, drinking from a whiskey bottle in a paper bag, drunk," I explain. "They had an evil aura, like a black cloud around them. I hid behind the dunes. As soon as they were far enough away, I ran back to my room. Sally, I have never been so afraid."

Sally takes my hands in hers and scolds me. "Angie, are you crazy? Didn't you hear what Grandad said about us girls staying in pairs? They could have hurt you—or worse. Promise me you won't do that again."

"But Sally, I've gone down to the beach alone lots of times. I didn't even think about it. I was anxious about moving today, and I wanted to work on my new song. I do my best work down there on the dunes."

I pick up my guitar and start to play the song I had been working on. "Listen. I was able to finish this last night." I play my song for her.

Loud cries erupt from down the hall. We both rush down the hall to Sally and Robert's room. Robert looks sleepy and frazzled as he tries to calm the twins. Sally picks up Jacob and hushes him. She hands Robert the lukewarm bottle for Evie. The two infants guzzle their bottles and quiet down.

Robert looks at me. "What's wrong, Angie? Did something happen? You look like you've been crying."

I rub my eyes and face. "I had another dream about Evangeline. It was terrible. I watched her being raped. I felt like I was there. Earlier in the night, I went to the beach and had a fright. Ricky and Rusty were there. I hid."

"Angie, you know better than that! Thomas warned everyone about how dangerous they are!"

Robert frowns then hands me Evie. "Here. She'll make you feel better. Please don't do that anymore. I don't want anything happening to you."

He pats me on my back, shaking his head. "I must go meet Thomas, Matt, and Dad. I'm going to go get some breakfast. I'll see you ladies downstairs."

Georgia has heard the commotion, and she comes to our rescue. She takes Jacob from Sally. "Don't worry. Before long, you won't need bottles. Your milk should start coming in any day now."

Sally laughs and pushes out her chest. "Yeah, then I can just pop one or two out and feed them both. Angie, I can take her if you want."

But I hold onto little Evie, keeping her close to me while I feed her. I start to feel calmer. My niece's eyes sparkle blue like the sapphires we found in Evangeline's box. "Evie, you are going to be a heartbreaker one day with those pretty blue eyes," I say. She coos back at me, blowing little milk bubbles.

Jacob is letting his frustration be known as he squeals when Georgia tries to burp him. Georgia laughs. "This tiny fella has quite the appetite. You don't need to worry about him. I think he's doubled his weight in the last two months." Then she turns to me and Sally. "Girls, I can handle these two. Why don't you two go down and get some breakfast."

I finish feeding Evie and burp her. Georgia settles Jacob into his car seat—Sally and Robert don't have anything else for the babies at this time. "I'll take her, Angie. We can sit her in the other seat," Georgia says. "We can bring the babies down after you two get ready for your day."

I join the others downstairs after I shower and dress in my favorite blue jean shorts and purple "Life is Good" T-shirt. By the time I get downstairs, Sally has already told everyone about my dream and what happened on the beach.

Mom takes me in her arms as big fat tears roll down my pink cheeks. She looks into my eyes. "Angie, please be careful. We have lost enough this year. We don't want anything to happen to you."

Sally and Jim nod in agreement. Jim shakes his head, "I am really worried about those two guys, especially if they are out there roaming the beach at night. I think it might be a good idea if you girls didn't live by yourselves for right now."

Thomas and George are both there, shaking their heads in agreement. "I can stay with you, Angie, if you want," Thomas says. "It's a two-bedroom house. I work a lot during the day. You work in the evenings, so we probably won't even see each other.

"George, same thing for you and Emily," Thomas continues. "At least we will be there at night, so we won't have to worry about those two breaking in while you sleep."

Jim pours himself another cup of coffee. "I spoke to Bobby the other day. You guys remember him, he's our local sheriff. He just couldn't fathom why they had released those two from prison so soon. Someone had their shed broken into and a weed whacker stolen. Bobby only has four deputies to patrol, and the return of those two to Ocracoke has everybody up in arms," Jim says. "Those two better watch whose houses they break into—they might find themselves having their heads blown off. Most islanders have firearms."

George turns to Emily. "What do you think, Emily? You're awful quiet. Do you want me to stay with you until things settle down?"

Emily shrugs. "I just can't believe that Betty Gamble has blinders on when it comes to those two. I know Rusty's her nephew, but she has spoiled him rotten since she adopted him when he was seven. She has never believed he's capable of all the things he's been accused of."

Emily looks back at George. "I'm just so used to being on my own, but I know you guys are right and it's only temporary," she says. "Yes, we can be roomies for a while. It will be weird, but I guess it's for the best."

George looks thrilled at the prospect. "I'll pick up my duffle bag after work today and bring it to your house."

Thomas ruffles Max's ears. "Angie, do you mind if Max comes with me? If it's a problem, I can get my mom to watch him for a while."

I rub Max on the head. "He's a good boy. I would love to have him come stay with me. Plus, he'll be a watchdog," I say. I wonder to myself how this is going to work out. I have already developed feelings for Thomas.

Paul looks worried. "Jim, do you think things are secure here at the inn?"

Jim walks over to a wall in the parlor. "Look here. It's a secret panel. You just push this latch. The safe is shrouded behind this wall. The girls and Sally are the only ones who know where the safe is—and now, of course, you guys.

"We also found a secret panic room up in Sarah's room. I guess it's been in the home since the original Whites bought the home," he says. "I never thought we would need to use the secluded room, but I still keep it stocked with enough food and supplies for a few days. I even added a two-way radio that is linked to the police department.

"I'll show you guys later where the room, if it's okay with you, Sarah?"

Sarah nods her head. "I think that's a great idea, Dad. And you've made me think: Did we ever look for more cryptic clues in that room? Maybe Evangeline or the old Emily hid something there."

Jim scratches the top of his head. "You know, I never really searched that room. Maybe we can go up later today and have a look."

Matt grins and puts his arm around Sarah's shoulders. "Good plan, but Thomas and I need to get over to David's and start the renovation. Text me when Angie's furniture gets here. We'll stop what we're doing and come help Angie move. Mom and Sally, do you need any help getting your things back over to Mom's house?"

Isabella stretches her arms over her head and flexes the muscles in her arm. "I think we're okay. David and Robert said they'd help get everything moved. Most of what we need to move belongs to the babies. You guys just give Angie a hand with her furniture."

Chapter 19

Moving Day

I can't believe the time has finally come for me to move into my new cottage. I have been looking forward to it ever since I arrived all those many weeks ago. It was just the start of summer then, and now I notice the days shortening and the nights starting to cool. Part of me feels a little sad to leave my room in the inn. I swear I see Evangeline sitting in the window seat, smiling at me as I pack up my things to leave. I swing my trusty guitar over one shoulder and my navy blue duffle bag over my other shoulder. I close the creamy white door to my room and walk down the stairs into another new chapter of my life.

My gold-colored keys jingle in my pocket as I fish them out to open the oak door to my cottage. This fresh beginning feels almost like returning home from a long journey, so many emotions wash over me. Thomas and Matt have remodeled the cozy cottage thoughtfully, adding so many special little touches that make it feel like it belongs to me.

I think how weird it is that Thomas has picked up on cues about me. He knows me better than my old boyfriend Larry, even though I lived with Larry for six years. The fact that Thomas has crafted a beautiful oak guitar stand is proof. My initials gleam off the heart that he carved into the case. Sunlight streams through the small windowpane, seeming to spotlight the new resting place where I set my guitar.

I try to shrug off my complicated feelings for Thomas. I have never felt happier than over this last month, and I don't want or need a new relationship at this point in my life. Sarah says that Thomas told her the other day that he is too busy to get involved with anyone right now. We'll just have to set that straight when he moves into the cottage later tonight. I am glad that I am off tonight so that I can get settled in my new home.

I hear a knock on my cabin door. I holler, "Come on in. I'm in here."

Emily carries in a huge basket and sets it on my marble counter. "Hey, lady. How's it going? Sarah put together this cute little crate of things you might need. I think she might have even added the kitchen sink."

I investigate the massive basket, amazed. "Wow, she's so sweet. Look at that—she even put in some cheese and crackers for us to snack on."

Emily grins and holds up a bottle of wine. "And don't forget you need wine with that cheese. I went into the wine cellar and found your favorite. I'll put it in the fridge to chill."

Putting my hands to my face, I sigh with contentment. "You guys are the best. You spoil me so much. I definitely have to stay here permanently."

I see Emily looking around the room. "Have you seen this place since the renovation was finished?" I ask. "I was just getting ready to put my bag into my new room. Let me give you a tour."

Emily nods in agreement. "I'd love a tour. What I see so far is gorgeous. Look at the shine on these floors. Thomas says this is the original flooring. I love the beautiful oak kitchen cabinets and marble counter tops."

She is amazed as I show her my cozy bedroom. I rub my hands over my new furniture. "I just love these magnificent oak nightstands and the dresser that Thomas and Matt made for me. Look, they even put a false bottom in the top drawer for me to hide things.

"It's crazy. I feel like my old life in D.C. has slipped away from me, old memories. It's like I've been here forever, even though it's only been two months. I can't thank you guys enough for letting me come live with you," I continue. "You know, Emily, I still have friends in Ripley, Maryland, but I never saw them because our schedules were just the opposite. I didn't realize how lonely I was until I moved here in June."

Emily hugs me. "I'm so glad you are here. I always miss you when you leave every summer after your vacation. It's also great having you working in the pub with me. Now, show me the rest of your place."

I take my toiletries out of my duffel bag and head into the small bathroom. "This is like a bathroom in a luxury suite!" I laugh. "The guys decorated it in a beach theme with seashells, fish, and sand dollars. I just love the seafoam green paint and the tan and coral tiles. Look at the medicine cabinet that Thomas built for me."

"It's lovely, so beautiful," Emily says. "Thomas and Matt do great work. I can't wait to see what they do when they renovate David's house." Emily rubs her hands over the bathroom counter, admiring their work.

There's another knock on the front door, and Matt comes in carrying the rest of my things from the inn. "Hey girls. Emily, how do you like Angie's new digs? Pretty sweet, huh?"

He looks around for a minute. "I see your guitar has found its spot on your new guitar stand. That thing is gorgeous."

He grins, taps me on the shoulder, and teases, "I think Thomas is quite smitten with you. He kept saying that he hoped you liked it. By the way, Sarah texted me and your furniture should be here any minute. Thomas and George are on their way over to help me with it."

We hear the beeping of a truck's back-up alarm. Thomas knocks and opens the door to the cottage. "Furniture's here. George is helping the guy unload it right now. You ready, Matt? It looks pretty heavy."

Matt heads out the door. "Sure thing. Let's get this party started."

The guys bring in two four-poster oak bed and mattress sets. They take one into my bedroom and the other into the spare bedroom. I watch as Matt and Thomas set up my bed frame and put the mattress in place.

"It's beautiful, Emily," I say. "It matches the nightstands and dresser perfectly. You guys are awesome. You make me feel special."

Sarah arrives carrying my new pale yellow and misty green bedroom quilt and curtains. "Wow, this place looks great. Really gorgeous!" she says. "I brought the quilt and curtains Emily and I made for your room. I made this blue-and-gray one last year. We can put it in the spare room for Thomas. How do you like the furniture, Angie?"

I hug Sarah and exclaim, "It's stunning. Everything is splendid. I am just speechless. Everything matches perfectly.

"The bedroom set and this comfy, tan leather sofa look like they are made for the place," I continue. "Did you see the guitar stand Thomas made for me? He even carved my initials on the top of the stand."

Thomas blushes, listening as I show Sarah my new guitar stand.

"I'm so glad you like it. I thought that you might need a place to put your guitar when you aren't playing it," Thomas says. Then he shifts the topic. "Are you sure you are alright with me staying here?"

I smile. "Everyone agrees that I shouldn't stay here alone for now. I think it's a good idea. Where's Max? I thought he'd be with you."

I point to the quilt. "Did you see the quilt that Emily and Sarah made for your room? It's so pretty." I know I am babbling but I can't help it. I am just so excited about my new place.

"I left Max at George's house for now. I was afraid he'd get trampled when we were moving the furniture," Thomas says. "I'm going now to get him and his bed and other pet items. I should be back within the hour."

Emily and Sarah both head toward the door. Emily looks back and grins. "We'll see you guys later. I need to go give George the keys to my cottage. It's going to be weird having him stay with me. I'm so used to staying on my own. I guess it's a good idea, though, under the circumstances."

Sarah hugs me goodbye and kisses Matt on his cheek. "Matt, I'll see you later at the pub," she says. "I need to take care of a few things at the inn before some new guests arrive. Angie, let me know if you need anything else."

Matt gives Sarah a proper good-bye kiss and waves to Emily as the girls walk out. Then he turns to me. "Angie, Sally told me about you going down to the beach alone. You know I don't like to be bossy, but you really worry me when you do stuff like that. It's just not safe right now. Those guys are really scary, and they might hurt you—or worse.

"You know I've never believed any of that supernatural crap, but Evangeline came to *me* and she warned me to be careful of the dangers. She said I must keep you girls safe. I don't want anything happening to any of you," Matt adds.

I can see that Matt is really concerned. I shake my head and tease him. "What has Sarah done with my little brother? You seem so different since the two of you hooked up, but happy."

Matt relaxes. "I know, right? I'm so head over heels in love with her. I think I'm going to propose to her. I know it seems awfully fast, but I think I've been in love with her forever. I just didn't want to admit it to myself," Matt says. "I'm going to ask her dad for her hand in marriage."

I squeal in delight and hug him. "I'm so happy for you! Sarah is perfect for you. And I don't think it is too soon—I always thought you two belonged together."

The spell is broken as the door busts open and Max bounds into the room. His tail wags and he jumps up on the two of us in greeting. Thomas grabs him by his collar. "Sorry about that. Hopefully with me living here, he will stop trying to knock you over. I have his bed and my things with me. I'll put them in your guest bedroom." He drags the doggie bed and his own duffel bag into the spare room.

Matt picks up his tools and heads towards the door. "I gotta' go. I'm heading over to the inn to help Mom, Sally, and the others get moved into Mom's house. You guys get settled. I'll see you later."

Max has his head resting on my lap. He gets up, trots to the door, and whines to go out. I pick up his leash. "Thomas, while get your things put away, I'll take Max for a walk on the beach."

Thomas looks uncertain. "Are you sure, Angie? He can be a handful." After a pause, he adds: "I can meet you over there later."

I attach Max's red and blue leash to his red collar. We head out the door and down to the beach. I sit on the sand and watch as Max races in and out of the surf, chasing sandpipers that deftly dart away from him. The waves crash over his paws, but he doesn't seem to mind.

I sense Thomas behind me before I see him. I look up into his forest green eyes. The golden flecks in his eyes sizzle like the sparklers on the Fourth of July. Max spots Thomas and runs up to him with a stick in his mouth. He drops it at his feet and the two play fetch for over an hour. Thomas laughs. "He loves this game. He'll play it until he wears you out."

I pet Max's sandy, wet fur. "I can't believe how big he's gotten. I swear, I think he has doubled in size in the last month."

Thomas laughs. "I know, Angie. I just went out the other day to buy him a new collar and leash. He'd outgrown his collar." Thomas holds up the lease and points to the collar.

Thomas sits down beside me. "I know it must be strange having me move in with you, but I think it might be fun. I've really enjoyed being around you the last two months. I hope it's okay—I plan to make us dinner tonight. I caught some fresh pompano and blues the other day. Do you like grilled fish?"

I put my hand on my stomach and laugh. "How could I turn that down? Did you hear my stomach growling?"

I continue, "It's just perfect—especially since I'm off tonight. My stomach is ready and waiting for your fresh fish dinner. Sarah put together a basket for us and it includes things to make a salad. Emily slipped a bottle of my favorite white wine in the fridge to chill."

Thomas nods. "Okay, so now I'm getting hungry. The salad will go well with the zucchini and yellow squash I bought at the farmers market today. Let's get Max back. I'm going to wash him down before he comes inside. He's been rolling in the wet sand and probably smells fishy."

We head back to my cottage, wash Max off, and towel him down. Thomas comes inside to prepare the fish. "I hope you like lemon and butter on your grilled fish. I lit the grill before I came in. It should be good and hot when I put the fish on."

"I put the vegetables in foil packets with a little butter, salt, and pepper to put on the grill," I say. "That's how we do it at home. I hope you like it. The salad is ready. I have some crackers and cheese. Do you like white wine?"

I uncork the wine and pour Thomas a glass. "Sarah is so sweet. Can you believe she stocked the fridge for us?" I walk toward the door. "How do you feel about eating on the porch? It's such a pretty night."

"Sounds great to me," Thomas answers. "I love eating outside." After he grills the meal, Thomas places the fish and freshly prepared vegetables on the small glass patio table on the screened-in porch. The rust-colored cushions have bright yellow daisies printed on them. I sit down, ready to eat.

I inhale and then taste the smoky flavored fish. I sip the crispy white wine. It tingles my tongue and the warmth of the wine embraces me. "Hmm, Thomas, you can cook for me any time. This dinner is awesome. Thanks so much for making my first night in the cottage a memorable one."

We finish our meal and Thomas pours us another glass of our chilled ambrosia. "Do you feel like sitting outside for a while longer? It's such a nice evening."

"Absolutely. This is wonderful. I love being outside on nights like tonight," I say. "This glider is so relaxing. Look at those fireflies starting to twinkle in the cedars. And those frogs—do you hear them croaking? I don't miss D.C. at all.

"How about you? Do you ever miss the city?" I ask him. "I still can't believe that I never met you before this summer." I'm enjoying myself. We sit on the glider and watch as the evening wears on.

Thomas points up at the golden sky. "No, I have always missed the island when I was away at school. Let's just sit for a while longer to see the sun set. Watch the horizon. It's always fun to watch what color it will be each night."

We watch the sun liquefy into spectacular hues of tangerine, lavender, gold, and rosy coral before it fades into the lapping water on the shoreline.

"Angie, look. Here come George and Emily. This should be really interesting. Maybe they will finally realize that they are crazy about one another. It's so obvious." Thomas waves to his brother and Emily.

"I don't know. The two of them are oblivious to the fact that they are in love." I also wave to Emily and George.

Emily jumps out of George's bright red 4x4 truck, sees us, and comes over to say hi. "Well, look at you two. Don't you look cozy."

George opens the screen door and joins us on the porch. "Wow, this place looks great. How was your fish dinner?"

Grinning, I give George and Emily a thumbs up. "It was fabulous. Everything was delicious. Thomas is a great chef. How was your dinner?"

George holds up a six pack and hands us each a bottle of Blue Moon. "I brought us brews. Want one? The pizza was good as usual. We got the white pizza with fresh spinach. Emily picked it. I was a little leery, but it was really delicious."

Thomas opens a beer and hands it to me. "That sounds good. I do like spinach. I'll have to try it one day."

We sit on my small screened-in porch savoring the peaceful Ocracoke Island atmosphere. George finishes his beer and turns to Emily. "I need to hit the hay. Emily, are you ready? I have an early service call on Hatteras Island."

Emily nods and takes one last sip of her beer. "Sure, I'm ready whenever you are." She turns to us. "Thanks for letting us join you on your first night in your new cottage, Angie. It's going to be so cool having you live right down the road from me. I can see us doing this on a regular basis."

I nod in agreement. "I know. I'm loving it already. It's like being on a permanent vacation," I say. "I'm so glad I decided to take you up on the offer to come play in your pub.

"Hey, what are your plans for the morning?" I add. "Do you want to see if the girls want to go for another walk on the beach?"

"Definitely. It's great exercise," Emily answers. "I'll text Sarah later and you can text Sally to see if she's interested. See you guys tomorrow." She gets up from the other glider she shared with George and walks toward the screen door.

George holds the door for her. "I'll see y'all tomorrow," he says to me and Thomas.

Max sees everyone getting up to leave and nudges Thomas with his cold wet nose. "Yeah, boy, I'm going to take you for a walk," Thomas says. Max, excited, starts barking when he hears the word "walk."

Thomas takes Max for his evening walk. When they return, I am coming out of the bathroom, ready for bed in my cute white-and-yellow shorts pajamas. I blush, feeling a little bit uncomfortable.

"Thomas, I want to thank you again for the wonderful meal. It was delicious. You made this night really special for me," I say as I head to my bedroom. "'Night. I'll see you in the morning."

Thomas nods and leads Max into his bedroom. “No problem. I enjoyed our first evening together. I’ll try to keep Max quiet in the morning, so we don’t wake you. He’s a little noisy when he gets up. ’Night.”

That night, I didn’t dream about Evangeline. I dreamt of Thomas and the evening we’d spent together. My dreams lately have been so vivid, just like I am there. I see Thomas’s broad tanned shoulders bending over the grill, cooking our fresh fish and vegetables. I hear his boisterous laughter as he watches Max run and chase the sandpipers on the shoreline. I feel the warmth arouse me when I taste the chilly white wine.

I am awakened to Max barking and hear Thomas telling him to settle down. I roll over in my soft bed and smile to myself. “Boy, am I in trouble,” I think to myself. “Thomas has already captured my heart.” I feel the protective ice melting around my soul.

That morning, Thomas heads over to David’s beach home to join Robert, David, and Matt. Thomas told me last night that today is demolition day. He laughed when he confessed that it was one of his favorite things to do.

“You just never know what you might find when you tear things down. It’s like a puzzle, almost like looking into a time capsule. It’s exciting,” he told me. “You know it was rumored that Blackbeard might have even stayed in that age-old dwelling.”

David’s home is one of the oldest on the island, dating back to the 1700s. It has belonged to the Brown family for generations. Evangeline’s friend, Roger Brown, owned the home after he helped Evangeline escape Daniel Teach’s grasp.

Thomas told me that they plan to start in the kitchen today. There is an ancient cooking fireplace that David wants to refurbish so that they can do some indoor grilling. David and Robert want to take down all the beautiful oak cabinets but reuse them. Thomas told me that they will need to be careful not to damage the cabinets when they remove them. David has shown him pictures of what they looked like in the past.

There is a lot that they plan to do to the old house. Thomas envisions the plans he and Matt have drawn up. For one thing, they want to take out the wall between the kitchen and living room.

Sally meets me at my cottage and we walk over to David's home. David is outside when we arrive, and he tells us an old story about the house.

"It was rumored that there were tunnels hidden somewhere in the house, but no one has been able to find them," David says. "You know, Roger was adopted by the Brown family. The dwelling was built fifty years before the family had arrived on the island. The legend said that Blackbeard and his cohorts hid out in the hidden passageways when the authorities were searching for them."

Matt greets us at the door, covered in plaster dust from gutting the kitchen. He hands Sally a broom. "Just in time, Sis, to help out. We just finished tearing down the walls. Nothing yet, but maybe we'll find something in the fireplace," he says. "Billy Alexander should be here shortly. Remember him? He is George and Thomas's cousin who does stone and brickwork. He's supposed to be really good."

Sally hands Matt the broom back. "Sorry, not today. Angie and I just stopped by to check things out. Plus, Robert and I have some news that might interest you."

I turn to Sally. "What? You and Robert are getting pretty good at keeping secrets."

As if on cue, Robert walks into the room and puts his arms around Sally. "Do you want to tell them, or do you want me to?"

"I'll do it!" she says. "I'm about to bust."

Sally grins, barely able to contain herself. "You know that the old PE teacher on the island hurt his back and Robert has been helping out this summer, right? Well, Robert has been offered a full-time teaching job at the island school. And I've been offered a part-time teaching job when Melody goes out on maternity leave. She's decided to cut her hours back to three days a week.

"So, guess what?" Sally adds. "We're moving to Ocracoke Island!"

I let out a big whoop and hug Sally and Robert. "That's so cool. I just love it. I'll get to see you guys all the time with you living right down the street from us. Did you tell Mom yet?"

The kitchen door opens and in walks Mom. "Did you tell me what? What did I miss?" she asks, looking from one of us to the other. "You all look like the cat that got the cream."

"It looks like we will be moving to Ocracoke Island, too." Sally puts her arms around Mom. "I hope you're not too disappointed, Mom. Robert and I were both offered teaching jobs at the little Ocracoke School. We couldn't pass it up, especially with David giving us the house. It just seemed like it was meant to be."

"Oh, honey. I'm so happy for you two," Mom says. "I guess this is the day of big news. David and I have something to share, too." She walks over to David. "Do you want to tell them your news first?"

David laughs. "I think I already told you guys that I put my house in Ripley up for sale before I left to come here in June. I have a contract on it. Your mom didn't tell you, but she put her house on the market, too, before she left for the island—and she has someone interested in it.

"So, guess what? We're moving here, too!" David says. "We both decided our Maryland houses are just too big for one person. Isabella offered to let me stay in her home until I can find a smaller place here on the island."

We all share a group hug, so happy over the news. I hug Mom a little longer. "I was so worried about us moving here with you being all the way in Maryland. This news is awesome—and now I can relax."

"Oh girls, nothing makes me happier than spending time with my family," Mom says. She hugs Robert and Sally, congratulating them on their new jobs.

Sally points up the stairs to the second floor and grabs my hand and Mom's hand. "Let me show you the room I want to use for the twins' nursery. It'll be great. It's right beside the master bedroom, and there is an adjoining door between the two rooms."

Sally opens the door to the master bedroom then leads us into the small bedroom. "Sally, it's perfect," Mom says. "When the babies get older, you can turn this into a study or sitting room. I am just so happy for you and Robert. And for me, too. I'm looking forward to being able to spend time with my family and the Whites."

Sally points to the built-ins in the room. "Don't you just love the way the rooms were constructed back in the day? These built-ins and the fireplaces are gorgeous. I can't wait to see Matt, Billy, and Thomas work their magic. Billy should be here anytime now to start work on the kitchen fireplace."

I shake my head with concern. "I'm worried about Billy finding out about our clues to Blackbeard's treasure. Do you know him very well?"

"Don't worry. I spoke to Thomas and he says that Billy is very trustworthy and reliable," Sally says. "You know he's Thomas and George's first cousin. They pretty much grew up together. They were like brothers. We were thinking it might even be a good idea to let him in on our secret, just in case we find any more clues."

"I suppose you're right," I respond. "It will probably be better to include him now than to wait until we find more clues. I remember him from the summers we spent here on the island. He is a little older than me."

"Stop worrying, Angie," my Mom says. Everything will be fine." She taps me on my shoulder as we head down the stairs to the first floor.

"I know, Mom, but I just keep thinking about what Evangeline has been telling us, that there could be danger if others were to find out about our discoveries."

I walk into the kitchen with the guys. Billy Alexander greets us with hugs. "Ladies, how are you doing? I can't wait to get started on this gem of a fireplace." He rubs his hands together. "Thomas just told me about all the clues you've found. This is exciting. And don't worry—I won't breathe a word of it to anyone." His smile beams at us.

He turns to Sally. "Congratulations on your twins. Robert was just showing me pictures of them on his phone. They are beautiful," Billy says. "I bet they are quite the handful. Hey, and I heard you and Robert are moving here permanently. That's just awesome."

Sally grins from ear to ear. "I know. I can't believe it's finally happening. Robert and I have always dreamed about living on the island but figured we'd have to wait until we both retired. Who would have thought we'd end up with jobs, a new home, and twins, all in one summer?"

Sally turns to squeeze David on his shoulder. "A lot of thanks goes to David for giving us his beach home. Everything has fallen into place splendidly. We even have someone who is planning to buy our home in Clements, Maryland. Can you believe our good luck?"

David hugs my sister. "It was my pleasure to give you two this home for your family, Sally. It's way too big for me. I want you guys to be able to enjoy it, just like Robert and Joseph did when they were growing up."

David reaches for one of the tools that Billy is holding in his hands. "Let's get started on the fireplace, Billy. Are you ready?"

"Yep, here goes nothing," Billy says. "I brought some extra tools with me if anyone wants to help." He hands David and Thomas each a chisel and a hammer.

Matt turns to Robert. "Robert, we can start demolishing the living room and the rest of the rooms downstairs while they work on the fireplace. Does that sound like a plan to you?"

Robert nods and heads toward the living room. "Sounds like a good idea. At this rate, we might be able to finish the house before we start the new school year."

"It will be close, but I think it may be possible with everyone helping out," Thomas agrees. "The hard part is the bathrooms and the kitchen. This is one of the biggest homes on the island. It has six bedrooms, three bathrooms, and an attic. And even a basement. But don't worry. We can finish some it even after you guys have moved in."

I look at my watch. "On that note, I need to head back to my cottage and get ready for work. I'll see whoever is there tonight."

Matt smiles at me. "Sarah and I should be at the pub around 5 p.m. George says he'll meet us there later once he returns from his job on Hatteras Island," Matt says. "Sally and Mom, are you going to walk Angie back? Remember, we want everyone to stay together or in pairs. It's just safer that way."

"Yes, they will walk me back and then head back to Mom's house," I answer. "We already discussed it. Geeze."

As we head toward my cottage, Mom turns to me. "You know Angie, Matt is right. Those two hoodlums are dangerous. You just never know what they might do."

Chapter 20

The Abduction

They leave me at my cottage. I walk in and immediately feel the calming vibe. I think to myself, "This is my new home. It's all mine ... well, for the most part, even if I do have to share it with Thomas for now." As I consider that, I realize that I like having Thomas in the bungalow. He's so sweet—and handsome.

Then I stop myself. "Whoa, girl. Enough. You do not need to get involved with anyone." I laugh out loud. I must be going crazy, talking to myself. I spritz on some of my summer cologne, grab my guitar, and run across the stone pathway leading to the pub.

When I walk in, George is already there, flirting with Emily. "How's it going? Did I miss anything?" I ask them. Emily hands me a club soda. "No, George was just telling me the news about Sally and Robert moving to the island. That's so cool. It makes me so happy to have your family here permanently. But what about your Mom?"

"Good news on that front, too!" I say. "David got a contract on his home. Mom, before she left this summer, put her house in Ripley on the market, too. She didn't tell us because she thought we might be upset. She already has someone interested in buying it."

I marvel at all the new developments in my family. "Can you believe that Sally and Robert were both able to get jobs at Ocracoke School?" I continue. "From what I understand it doesn't happen very often."

Emily wipes off the bar. "It really is amazing if you think about it. They even hired Georgia as a full-time nanny to watch the twins."

It's a good evening in the pub. A lot of the locals come into the pub daily and have dinner. I enjoy playing my soulful beach music for the crowd. Thomas has turned up and Max is with him. The sweet dog takes his usual place, laying on my feet while I play. I have started to carry doggy treats in a baggie in my pocket, and Max loves it. He always greets me enthusiastically and, for my part, I am happy having a puppy around me. I'd forgotten how much I miss my foster dogs.

The evening is a pleasant one and the balmy weather is perfect. The customers slowly head home. Thomas, before he leaves, comes up to take Max. "Bye, Angie. I'll see you at home."

When Thomas gets back to the beach cottage we're sharing, he breathes in my slightly floral perfume that still wafts in the air. He looks at his dog. "You know Max, I think I'm falling in love with our girl, Angie. What are we going to do?" He ruffles Max's head and heads for his bedroom.

At the pub, George is helping Emily and me clean up. Then he announces: "Girls, I am going to have to leave you. I have an early day. Will you two be okay walking back on your own to the cottages?"

Emily rolls her eyes. "What do you think, Angie? Are you ready to go now? I'm getting tired."

I pick up my guitar. "Do you guys mind going without me? I want to work on one of my songs. It's almost done."

George, being George, is always protective of us girls. "Angie, I don't think it's a good idea. You heard what everyone keeps saying about Rusty and Ricky lurking around."

I shrug. "Oh, come on. We haven't seen those two in days. Hopefully they crawled back into a hole somewhere or, better yet, left the island. My cottage is just down the path. I can see it from here. What's going to happen?"

George picks up his phone. "Okay, but if anything happens or you get spooked, you call me."

"Will do. Thanks, George. You're the best." I hug him and sit down on one of the outside lounge chairs.

George and Emily leave, and I lay back on the comfy vinyl lounger. I look up at the bright stars against the black night. A wayward cloud mists over the full moon and casts an eerie shadow over me. I have been playing for over an hour. I feel a chill run down my legs. I look around. I don't see anyone or hear anything but I decide I should head home. I sling my guitar over my shoulder and push my cell phone into the pocket of my faded blue jean shorts. My nerves are getting the better of me as I head across the dirt and oyster-shell driveway.

I hear gruff male voices come up behind me. One of the voices says, "Look at what we've found here, a foxy lady. And just the one we've been waiting for."

I freeze for a brief second and gasp. I start to run toward my house, but my flip flop buckles under my foot. I feel a dry chapped hand reach around my neck and a cloth slips over my nose and mouth. Fear grips me as I feel myself being lifted into someone's arms. My guitar crashes to the sandy ground. My world goes black.

I wake up with a splitting headache. I look around but do not recognize where I am. It looks like some type of musky, damp storm cellar. My body has been tossed onto an old army cot, and a dirty quilt is thrown over me. My hands and wrists are tied behind my back with a rough braided straw rope and they feel bruised. My fingertips tingle from being tied so tightly.

My lips are swollen, and I taste a mix of salty saliva and blood in my mouth. I am gagged with a grimy smelly bandana. My heart races, and a growing terror fills me as I try to remember what happened. I look around for a way to escape.

I hear a creaking noise over my head and watch as a rotten wooden hatch opens up above me. I am horrified when I see dirty, grungy Ricky climb down the ladder. I pretend to be passed out, but he isn't fooled. He tears the grimy quilt from my body, licks his lips. "Well, if it isn't sleeping beauty awakening from her slumber. Boy, I can't wait to get my hands on that lovely body of yours."

I frantically try to scoot away from his grip but to no avail. The cot creaks as he slithers down beside me. I try to scream but the gag on my mouth is tied too tightly. My chapped lips crack and bleed in the effort. I am terrified as Ricky pushes my tangled black hair out of my face. "Don't worry, sweetie," he says in a threatening tone. "I have to wait for Rusty to come back before we have our way with you."

He loosens the cruddy cloth from my mouth. My teeth bite down hard on his surprised finger. He pulls back his hand and looks at the bloody teeth marks on his finger. Then he backhands me, sending me smashing onto the rough cot. "You dirty whore! You just wait. You're going to regret that."

I scream at him. "You'll never get away with this. My friends and family will know you two are to blame for my disappearance!"

He howls with laughter. "Little lady, no one will ever find you in this abandoned storm cellar. Rusty has it so well hidden. You're going to tell us where we can find Blackbeard's treasure and then we're going to have our way with you. You just think you're so high and mighty."

I am both angry and afraid. Tears stream down my cheeks. "I don't know what you're talking about!" I scream. "You are crazy."

"Really? Do you think we're so stupid? We heard you talking at the pub the other day. And Rusty's Aunt Betty said your grandpa and Robert were researching Blackbeard at the library." He puts his hands around my neck and squeezes.

I struggle against his grip. He finally loosens his hold. I stutter, "My grandfather was just researching for his new book, that's all, nothing else."

Ricky raises his eyebrows, shakes his head, and sneers. "I don't know who you think you're talking to, but I told you, we overheard you tell that sweet little bartender, Emily, that you found another clue to Blackbeard's treasure."

He grabs a cloth from an old wooden night table and picks up a bottle marked chloroform. He pours some of the strong-smelling liquid onto the cloth and rapidly slaps it over my nose and mouth. "Enough of you. You're getting on my nerves. This will shut you up."

My head bursts, lights flicker. My panic evaporates as the pungent liquid overtakes me. I can't fight him and don't remember what has happened when my eyes close and everything goes dark.

Thomas, asleep in the cottage, is jolted awake by screams from Evangeline. "They've taken her! They have Angie! You have to help her, or she will suffer the same fate as mine."

Max barks frantically and jumps up and down on Thomas. Thomas rushes to get out of bed and runs to check on me in my room. He hopes he is just having a nightmare, but Evangeline follows him into my room. Evangeline is crying. "Thomas, you must find her. She has been captured." Evangeline vanishes.

Thomas runs out the front door through the screened porch and out onto the gravel driveway. He finds my beloved guitar abandoned on its side by the sandy path next to the cottage. He screams, "Angie, where are you?"

Max barks madly, looking around for me. He sniffs my guitar. He whines and tries to get Thomas's attention. "I know, boy. We'll find her. Maybe she's at the beach."

He is frantic with fear for me. His heart is beating wildly. He runs to Emily's cabin and pounds on the oak door. George and Emily both run to answer it. Thomas yells at the top of his lungs, "George, Emily, where's Angie? I just found her guitar by the side of the road. She's nowhere to be found. Didn't she come home with you guys? Evangeline woke me. She said Angie had been taken."

George's face turns ghostly pale. "Oh my God. No, this can't be happening." He runs his hands through his red hair. "She wanted to stay at the pub and work on her new song. She talked us into letting her stay. What have I done? I was supposed to keep you girls safe." He opens up his cell phone and calls the local sheriff.

Emily is hysterical. "George, it's my fault, too," she cries. "I let her talk us out of coming home with us."

Matt hears the commotion and comes out of his bungalow, his black hair all over the place. "Angie is missing," Emily cries. "Thomas found her guitar by the road. Evangeline came to him to warn him that Angie had been taken.

"It's just awful. I feel so guilty. We let her stay at the pub," Emily adds, shaking. "I hope she's alright. Maybe she just took a walk on the beach."

Matt takes the guitar from Thomas. "Angie loves this guitar. She would never leave it anywhere. It's like a part of her," he says. "George, what did the police say? It's almost four o'clock. How long ago did you see her?"

Emily is sobbing. She tries to answer through her guilt-stricken tears. "We left the pub around eleven last night. That was the last time we saw her. She was sitting on the lawn chair beside the tiki bar. She begged us to let her stay so she could finish writing her song."

Matt puts his arms around Emily. "It's alright. How could you have known? Besides, she is so stubborn when she gets something in her head. You can't stop her. We'll find her."

Police sirens wail and the red-and-blue lights are flashing as the patrol car comes to a screeching stop in front of our cottages. The sheriff, Bobby, jumps out of his vehicle. "Have you found her yet?" he asks. "I was afraid of this with those two nasty characters moving back to the island. We just don't have the staff to keep an eye on them. I called the other deputies. They are on their way. We'll do a search of the island."

Thomas yells. "This can't be happening. Not Angie. I am supposed to be protecting her."

Emily, crying, takes Thomas by the shoulders. "It's no one's fault. We just need to find her. I'm going to run over to the inn to get Sarah and my parents to come help us look for her. The more people we have, the better." As she starts to run across the street toward the inn, Matt calls after her. "Don't call Sally or Mom until we know something. I don't want to scare them. Maybe she did go for a walk on the beach."

Bobby and his deputies lead the search. "Sarah, Emily, and Jim, you folks take Will with you and go search the beach," Bobby instructs the group. "Everyone, keep your phones on you and call if there are any updates."

He turns to the guys. "Matt, Thomas, and George, you three come with me to Rusty's Aunt Betty's farm. I'll send the other officers to search around the island to see if anyone has seen anything suspicious.

"Normally, I don't like to involve people other than my deputies," he adds, "but these are desperate times. The faster we find Angie, the better her chances. I've called Hatteras Island Police and Rescue to come help us, but it will take a while for them to get here. It's already starting to get light out. That means she's probably been missing for five or six hours."

George interjects. "Robert and David are supposed to be at the house at 6 a.m. It's that time now. I'll go get them so they can help, too. Then I'll meet you at Betty's farm."

Thomas starts to lead Max by the collar toward the cottage, but Bobby stops him. "No, Thomas. Let's bring Max. I've seen Angie play at the tiki bar with Max at her feet. That dog loves Angie. He might be able to help us find her."

Thomas heads towards the cabin and calls back. "Okay but let me go throw on some clothes. I'm still in my pajamas."

In a flash, Thomas is in and out of the cottage. He has hurriedly thrown on a pair of his worn blue jeans and his beat-up black Nikes. He runs his fingers through his bedraggled blonde hair and scratches his day-old beard. He whispers a silent prayer, "Please, God, let her be alright. I love her." He rushes toward Matt's blue 4x4 truck.

Matt hits the gas as the truck follows Bobby down the dirt driveway, flinging dust and sand up into the air. Matt and Thomas blow past David's house. As they pass, they see George excitedly telling David and Robert about Angie being missing. David covers his face with his hands, and Robert is waving his arms wildly in the air, but Matt doesn't stop. He knows that they need to hurry to reach the farm where Rusty's been staying.

Matt hopes he is wrong and that his sister has just gone for a long walk on the beach. Nevertheless, a feeling of dread fills him.

Thomas squeezes Matt on the shoulder, even though he isn't feeling very confident himself. "We are going to find your sister. She's going to be alright. I just know it. She has to be. I don't know what I would do without her."

Matt pats Thomas on the hand. "Man, I hope you're right. I don't think I have ever been so afraid as I am right now. Look—Bobby is turning. We must be there."

Matt's dusty 4x4 and the white police 4x4 SUV slam to a halt. The sirens are blaring, and the lights are flashing. Startled by all the noise, Betty comes flying out her torn screen door in her pink cotton robe with her hair in blue spongy curlers. "What's going on, Bobby? You scared the daylights out of me. Has something happened?"

Bobby adjusts his gun belt. "Betty, we need to talk to your nephew, Rusty. We think he might have abducted one of the local girls."

Angered by the accusation, Betty stutters, "Now, Bobby why does everyone have to blame that boy. As far as I know, he's been home all night." She points to the tan mobile home beside her house. "You can go ask him for yourself. His truck is home. Just knock on the door."

Thomas, not wanting to wait, goes over to Rusty's rust-covered truck and opens its gray door. Max jumps up into the truck. When Thomas tries to pull Max out of the truck, the dog whines and comes to Thomas with one of Angie's hair scrunchies in his mouth. Her special guitar pick sits lost on the sandy floorboard. Thomas yells. "Bobby, he must have her here, somewhere! Look, here's her hair tie and her favorite guitar pick."

Rusty has come out of his mobile home. When Thomas spots him, he climbs out of the rusty truck and grabs Rusty by the throat. He threatens him, "Where is she, you bastard? We know you took her."

Thomas has a death grip on Rusty's throat. Bobby tries to pull him off Rusty. "Come on, man, or I'll have to put you in the squad car." He turns to Rusty. "Okay, where's the girl?"

Rusty massages his strangled throat. "I don't know what you're talking about. What girl? I've been here all night. You heard my aunt."

Betty stares at her nephew. "You did something to that girl, didn't you Rusty?" she says, accusingly. "I have always defended you, but never again." Betty points to Max. "It looks like that dog is tracking the girl's scent. She must be hidden in our abandoned storm cellar. Follow me."

Bobby handcuffs Rusty and puts him in the back of the squad car. The sheriff then follows an anxious Betty, who tries desperately to keep up with Max, with Thomas right on her heels and Matt not far behind. Max is excited, barking and sniffing the ground. He keeps his nose down toward the sandy ground, whining as he follows the scent. Thomas cheers Max on. "Go find her, boy. Find Angie. You can do it."

Matt and Thomas trail Max across the overgrown yard and down a long dirt driveway. The weeds spill over onto the driveway. Max keeps looking back at Thomas and Matt. He whines but continues searching. He finally reaches an old weed-covered door coming out of the ground. Betty points toward it. "That's it. That's the storm cellar."

"A storm cellar. Good boy, Max. Thanks, Betty," Thomas says. He ruffles Max's ears. He opens the corroded door and crawls down the rickety stairs with Max on his heels. Max's mournful barks vibrate against the corroding walls of the dirty dilapidated cellar.

Ricky heard them coming and he has a switchblade held to my neck. "Don't do it, man," Ricky warns. "Stay away. I'll slice her through if you get any closer."

I feel a sting on my neck as the knife penetrates the surface of my skin. I try to struggle against his blade. "Stop, you're hurting me!"

Max sees me being threatened and lurches at my captor. The shank draws a slender drop of blood from my neck. Max springs at Ricky and tears at his wrist with his sharp teeth, mangling bone and flesh. Ricky yowls out in agony. He tries to get away from Max. I collapse, falling back on to the cot. Thomas rushes over to me while Matt runs up and punches Ricky in the jaw, sending him flying backward.

Thomas sits beside me on the cot, unties my hands, and pulls my limp body into his muscular arms. "I've got you now, my love. I'm here. It's Thomas. Max and Matt are here. You're safe now. No one can harm you."

I am sobbing with relief. "The police are here. They arrested Rusty," Thomas continues. "Bobby will lock Ricky up, too."

Max jumps up onto the cot and licks my face, ecstatic to see me. Matt has tied Ricky up with rope he found.

I raise my head and look into Thomas' panic-stricken eyes. I whisper, "I knew you would come for me. I just knew it." I close my eyes and rest my head on Thomas's shoulder, into the crook of his neck. I must have gone unconscious again, because the next thing I remember is Thomas holding me in his arms in the backseat of my brother's truck with Max's head on my lap.

A siren wails as an ambulance arrives. They want to take me to the hospital, but I refuse. I just want to go home to sleep. "I am fine. I just have a little bit of a headache. I'm just really tired. Please can't I just go home and sleep?" I plead.

Frank, the bartender from SmacNally's, is also a volunteer EMS attendant with the local rescue squad. He checks my pulse, blood pressure, and my pupils. He holds up the dark brown bottle Bobby has handed him. "No wonder you have a headache. Looks like they gassed you with chloroform," Frank says. "Fortunately, your vitals are good. No bumps on your head that I can feel. I can't force you to go to the hospital. It's up to you. Just let me put a bandage on your neck where you were cut."

I lay my throbbing head back down on Thomas' shoulder. "Okay," I say. "Then I want to go home. Matt, drive me home."

Thomas strokes my tangled hair. He pushes a stray hair out of my teary eyes. "I'll stay with her. That way she won't be all alone. If I notice anything weird, I'll call you guys."

Frank shrugs. "Like I said, I can't make her go to the hospital. Call me if you have any concerns." He hands Thomas a card with his cell number on it.

Thomas caresses my face and looks into my eyes. "Angie, are you sure you don't want to go get checked out?" I vehemently shake my head. Thomas nods. "Okay, it's settled then. I'll keep an eye on you, but you have to promise me if you start to feel worse, you'll let me know."

It is agreed that I will go home under the watchful eyes of Thomas and, of course, Max.

I start to cry, still trembling in fear, unable to stop myself. "I'm sorry. I don't mean to blubber. I hate to cry. I just can't seem to help myself. I hate being weak. Must be a reaction from the chloroform."

Matt stops me. "Angie, you have every right to sob your eyes out after what you have been through. Do you remember anything that happened?"

I shake my head, my lips trembling. "Not a whole lot. Ricky kept putting that nasty cloth with the chloroform over my face. I was out of it most of the time," I say. "He said they were going to have their way with me when Rusty came back. He kept asking me where the clues were for Blackbeard's treasure. He said they overheard me talking to George and Emily. I lied and denied it.

"He said he didn't believe me, that Rusty's Aunt Betty saw Granddad and Robert researching Blackbeard. I told him that Grand Dad was writing a book on Blackbeard, that there were no treasure clues."

Thomas holds me tightly and shushes me. "It's alright now, Angie. You're safe. They can't hurt you anymore. After that stunt, they will both be going away for a long time."

Big, wet tears trickle down my cheeks. I sniffle and wipe my red nose with a tissue that Matt has given me. I close my eyes and rest my head on Thomas. It feels so safe, and I start to fall asleep in his arms. As I doze off, I think how I am going to miss Thomas when he moves out of my home. I sleep the rest of the way home.

Matt had called Sarah to let everyone know that they found me, and I'm okay. He tells them that Rusty and Ricky have been arrested for abducting me and are on their way to jail.

Sarah and Emily anxiously wait for me on the front porch of Shepard's Head B&B. They both race out to greet us as the truck pulls up. Emily hugs me so tightly that I can't breathe. "I'm so sorry. I shouldn't have left you at the pub. I feel so guilty," she says as tears stream down her cheeks. She is crying hysterically.

The Whites and Sarah hug me tightly, too. "We're so glad that you are home safe," they say in unison.

George comes over and pulls me into his arms. "Angie, you don't know how scared I was. I should never have left you in the pub."

I take his bearded face in my hands. "Look, you and Emily need to stop feeling guilty. It was my choice to stay at the pub. I thought I was safe. I guess I was just stupid thinking that way. Right now, I need to go find my bed. I'm exhausted and my head is pounding.

"Frank said the chloroform would give me a headache," I add. "He wasn't kidding."

I rub my face. Out of the corner of my eye, I see Evangeline smiling down at me from the porch stairs. She blows me a kiss and vanishes. I don't tell anyone. I just grin.

Chapter 21

Two Soulmates

Thomas walks me back to my cottage. He tenderly takes my slim hand in his big brawny one. Max nudges my other hand with his nose.

"Angie, I don't know what I would have done if anything had happened to you," Thomas says. He opens the door and holds it for me. "What I am trying to say is that you mean a lot to me, more than I can believe. I know that with Rusty and Ricky gone I could move back to George's house, but I want to stay here if that's okay with you." He is rambling on and it is so precious to me.

I raise my tear-stained face and gaze into his expressive deep green eyes. I reach out and tenderly take his stubbled face in my hands. Our lips meet and we melt together. It is such a tender kiss. Thomas holds me up against his warm, hard body. I quiver in his grasp as our passion ignites. He holds me away from him. "Angie, you just don't know how much I want you right now, but not after what you've been through. It wouldn't be right. I want our first time together to be perfect."

I hold him close to me. "Come lay with me Thomas. I just need to feel your body next to mine. You make me feel safe."

He caresses my bruised cheek with his finger. "Okay, I think that would be fine. Let me take Max out and I'll be right back."

Thomas grabs Max's lease and they go outside for his walk. I slip into the shower and wash off everything that has happened to me in the last hours. Then I head for my soft, cushy bed. I slide down under lovely handmade covers. I feel Thomas crawl into bed beside me. I pretend to be asleep. His hands softly caress my legs and hips. He rubs my back and nuzzles up next to me. "Oh Angie, I'm falling in love with you. I don't know what I'm going to do." I smile, not letting him know that I hear what he is saying.

I fall into a deep, dream-filled sleep about Evangeline and William. I dream about their adventures on a tropical island. She is living in a small house by the seaside. I hear the pirate Daniel Teach tell her, "You are mine. No one will ever find you in this place that is called Cat Island. You and my child, which you carry, will never leave me."

Later, I see her sitting all alone, rubbing her pregnant belly. "Oh Jacob, if you could only be here to save me," she says to herself. "Your child needs you. I will never let Daniel know that this is not his bairn."

I see Evangeline with a mist beside her. It is a vision that speaks to her. "My name is Virginia. I was captured myself. I was brought to this island when I was but just a babe." The woman in the vision is wearing clothes from the 1500s. I recognize the antiquated outfits from the research that my grandfather and father have done over the years. The ghost says, "You must never tell Daniel that your child is not his. It will put you both in grave danger."

Evangeline's friend Roger visits her frequently, pretending to stop by to see his cousin, Daniel. I hear Evangeline whisper to Roger when they are alone. "I long to be home but fear that will never happen. Daniel swore to me that I would never be allowed to visit my family. He said that I was his and that he would never share me with anyone."

Roger swears that he will not let that happen. "I promise to get you home safely when I am able." She feels protected with Roger nearby.

Time flashes forward. Evangeline's belly has grown large with child. She places her hand over her tummy. "I can't wait to meet you, my little one. I only wish that Jacob was here. I am so afraid that I will not be able to protect you."

I watch as the days roll into weeks, and the weeks into months. Finally, the day of William's birth arrives. Evangeline's friend, Lucy, and one of the local ladies on the island are there to help Evangeline deliver her wee one. I can feel her trembling in fear when the contractions wrack her petite body. Finally, the baby is born. William's blonde hair is curly and spiked up on his little head. His eyes shine like the green forest as the sun is setting. I sense Evangeline's heart melting when she gazes at the infant.

I wake up from my slumber. Max and Thomas are longer in the room with me. Thomas must have taken the dog out for his morning walk. I still feel the intensity of Evangeline's love for her little man. I wonder if I will ever know that kind of love. I am amazed at how much William looks like my nephew Jacob. I ponder whether Jacob will somehow be linked to William as I am to Evangeline.

There is a gentle tap and Thomas cracks open the bedroom door. "Angie, are you awake? I wanted to check on you before I leave to go to David's home."

Max nudges the door open with his nose and crawls into bed with me. He licks my face, whimpering with excitement at seeing me. Thomas grins and pulls Max off of me. "Sorry, this puppy really likes you, if you can't tell. How are you feeling?"

I push the hair out of my eyes and touch my temples. "I'm good, just a teeny bit of a headache. Frank said that I would probably have a headache for a day or two." I reach out to grasp Thomas's hand in mine and look up into his beautiful green eyes. "I just want to thank you again for taking care of me. Thomas, I don't understand what's happening between us but my feelings for you are strong. Do you think that it's the necklaces that are drawing us close together?" I pull him into the bed beside me.

He lays down beside me and takes my face gently in his hands. "I don't know, Angie. I just know that if anything would have happened to you ... well, I don't know what I would have done. I think I've fallen in love with you. I know it's so soon, but I can't seem to help myself. I felt like my heart had been ripped out of my chest when I realized that you were missing."

We are both quiet for a moment, then he adds: "Do you think it's possible for two past souls to cross over to create another soulmate in another lifetime?"

He strokes my hair and cups my chin. His tender lips brush mine and his eyes blaze into mine with a powerful passion. "I want you so much, Angie. I just don't want to take advantage of the situation."

I bring his lips down to mine, hungry for his kisses. "Oh, Thomas, I don't want to wait. I want to feel your body next to mine. I want to feel you inside me." A delicate teardrop rolls down my cheek. Thomas kisses the tear away. He kisses my earlobes, my neck, and caresses my nipples.

I wipe the tears from my face. "I don't mean to cry. I have never been an emotional person. My feelings for you are so strong."

I cling to him and feel his hard manhood against my thigh. Our clothes fall off and our souls erupt into an intoxicating passion that sweeps us both away. We lay spent in each other's arms, lingering in each other's pleasure.

Thomas kisses me on my forehead. "Maybe we'll just rest today and hold each other. My love for you is strong, too. I'll text Matt and tell him you're alright. He can let the others know you just want to sleep awhile longer. I'll tell him I'm taking the day off to stay with you."

He reaches down to get his cell phone from his faded blue jeans that lay in a heap beside the bed. He texts Matt to let him know I am fine but resting.

I put my head on Thomas' bare suntanned chest and breath in his earthy scent. We fall asleep and wake up later, still wrapped in each other's arms. Thomas caresses me, tingling, and arouses in me a passion that I have never known. Our bodies reignite in perfect unison when we climax. I feel like fireworks have exploded and sent us both into a world of titillation.

He reaches for his phone to check the time. "Wow, we slept for quite a while. It's almost one o'clock. I'm going to hit the shower. Want to come? It might be fun."

I watch his long muscular body get up from the bed. I hurl my tired body up out of bed, too. "Sounds like a good idea. I'm a tad bit sore this morning." I rub my hands over my bruised, raw wrists and arms and follow Thomas into the shower.

The shower proves invigorating. His hands gliding over my soapy nipples sends us both into another passionate embrace and climax. I laugh. "You were right, that *was* fun. I wonder how many other places we can find to do that?"

He playfully swats my bottom. "Well, if you'd like, I'm up for just about anywhere." I watch him towel off his sleek brawny body and dry his curly blonde hair. My heart melts just watching him. I slide out of the shower and get dressed.

I walk into the kitchen to find Thomas standing over my cast iron skillet making my favorite veggie scrambled eggs. "Mmm, that smells heavenly," I say. "How did I ever get so lucky?" I wrap my arms around his warm waist. I stand behind him and breath in his soft clean-smelling skin. The scrumptious aroma of the eggs makes my mouth water. "I am starving!" I announce. "I can't wait to try those heavenly smelling eggs."

We sit down on the soft brown leather sofa to have our brunch. I bite into the delectable eggs and their gooey cheese slides down my chin and onto my plate. "Yummy, these are really good."

There is a gentle knock at the door. Thomas gets up to answer it, still bare chested. Emily and George come in. Emily takes one look at me and asks, "Are you okay? We wanted to check on you." She looks at my flushed face and immediately knows. "Oh my God," she squeals. George looks at his brother in amazement.

Thomas shrugs and kisses me on my cheek. "What? We couldn't help ourselves. Oh, by the way, I'm taking the day off. Hope it's okay." Max is excited because everyone else is excited. He jumps between us and makes everyone laugh.

George just shakes his head and squeezes Thomas on the shoulder. "I guess under the circumstances that would be fine. Oh, and Angie, I wanted to let you know that Matt told your Mom and Sally what happened. I'm surprised that they haven't come over here yet.

"If you're up to it, they want everybody to meet at David's house to look for more clues," George continues. "The police called. Bobby said Rusty and Ricky were arrested and are being held on kidnapping and aggravated assault charges. Those two are going away for a long time."

"We'll let you two finish your meal and meet you over at David's house," Emily says, reaching to give Thomas and me a hug. She can barely contain herself. "Just wait until Sarah and Sally find out. They are going to be thrilled."

Chapter 22

More Clues

Not long after, we arrive at David's, where I am greeted with hugs from all. My Mom and Sally are upset that no one let them know sooner about my capture. Mom takes me in her arms. "Oh Angie, I don't know what I would do if anything happened to you. Thank heavens you're safe."

I look her into her teary pale-blue eyes. "Mom, I'm sorry, but I think it was for the best that they waited to tell you and Sally. I know they didn't want to worry you two."

Sally looks frustrated. "Now, this is exactly what I was talking about—about not being included. I could have helped look for you."

Robert steps over to hug Sally. "Honey, you know you've had trouble getting enough sleep. They didn't want to wake you. And I didn't find out until we got to Dad's house. By that time, search parties were already set up and Thomas and Matt were already on the way over to Rusty's house with the police."

Robert turns to me. "Next thing I knew, we were getting a call that they had found you."

Robert looks back at my sister. "It wasn't meant to exclude you, sweetheart. We just didn't want to worry you. Listen, Georgia is watching the twins. That means you can join the rest of us—you're not being left out—when we look for more clues at our house."

Sally nods and smiles through her misty tears. "Okay, that sounds good. I know I'm being silly, but I can't help it." Then Sally asks, "Thomas, tell me, is it true that Evangeline came to warn you that Angie had been taken?"

Thomas throws his arms up in the air and nods his head. "Yeah, it was crazy. I was sound asleep, and the room shook, or maybe it was just the bed. Max started barking his head off. Evangeline appeared and was flailing her arms, super excited, hollering that Angie had been abducted. She yelled that we had to hurry. I was trying to ask where she'd been taken, but Evangeline disappeared right after that.

"I ran outside with Max following me. I found Angie's guitar on the ground by the driveway," he continues. "I ran to wake up George and Emily and then Matt came out of his place. George called the police. Half of us went with officers searching on the beach and around the point. Matt and I followed Bobby to Aunt Betty's because we knew Rusty and Ricky had to be involved and they were staying there. Max found Angie's hair scrunchie and favorite guitar pick on the floor of Rusty's old truck. To her credit, Aunt Betty realized her nephew was lying and she guided us to her storm cellar, where we found that scumbag Ricky holding a knife to Angie's neck."

Thomas turns and looks at me tenderly. "I can tell you that I have never been so scared in my life," he adds, pulling me into his arms and kissing me on my forehead. There is a pause while everyone registers what has happened—and then Sally squeals.

"I knew it! I always thought you two belonged together. Well at least something good came of this," she says. "Why did they say that they kidnapped you?"

I raise my eyebrows. "Unfortunately, I guess I wasn't as careful as I thought I was. Ricky said he overheard me telling Emily and George about a clue we had found. And Aunt Betty happened to tell Rusty that she saw Grandad and Robert researching Blackbeard. I told Ricky that Paul was writing a book on Blackbeard, but he didn't seem to buy it. Anyway, it doesn't matter now because those two will be in jail for a long time.

"The police took my statement last night. I told them what I've just told you," I add. "I guess this really proves we have to be careful not to let anyone know about our findings."

Sally throws her arms around me and looks me over. She touches my swollen lip. "Whew, that must have been terrifying. They hurt you, didn't they?"

I gingerly touch my fingers to the black and blue bruising around my left eye. "They knocked me around a little bit and scared the devil out of me but, for the most part, I'm fine," I say. "Ricky kept saying, just wait until Rusty gets here and we'll have our way with you—the thought just sickens me—but Rusty was still at his house when I was rescued."

I pause, overwhelmed as I relived the nightmare.

"Thank God Max found my guitar pick and hair tie in Rusty's truck. Thomas tells me that Max followed my scent to lead them to the storm shelter. I remember Thomas and Matt flying down into the cellar to save me, but a lot of it feels just like a hazy nightmare, probably because they knocked me out with chloroform."

Mom and Sally are both trying to contain their tears. They hug me and say in unison, "We're so glad they found you."

Matt echoes them. "Angie, I'm so glad we figured out where you were when we did …"

I interrupt him, exasperated. "Enough. Enough. Can we please change the subject? Let's go search for more clues."

Thomas points to the kitchen. "Okay, we finished the demo in the kitchen, but we didn't find anything in there. Billy is going to get started on the stonework in the cooking fireplace with David's help while Matt and I start on the fireplace in the master bedroom. I hadn't planned to work today but why don't I lend a hand while you girls look in the other bedrooms to see if anything turns up? Angie, is that okay with you?"

I nod. "Absolutely, I need to take my mind off of that whole incident with Rusty and Ricky. Besides, I love looking for clues, so girls, let's go see what we can find."

Sarah, Emily, Mom, and I follow Sally into a spare bedroom. My sister has said she wants to clear this room out a bit.

"I think I'm just going to work on separating what David wants to keep here from what he wants to give to the Salvation Army or Goodwill. Will you guys help me put things in boxes? David told me the other day that he hasn't had a chance—or the heart—to do this since my mother-in-law, Samantha, died."

Emily lifts an old worn pillow from the bed. "We might need a throwaway pile, too. We can set things aside that might have sentimental value and have David help us go through them later."

Sally takes the old pillow and hugs it to her chest, laughing. "Believe it or not, according to Robert, he carried this pillow all over the house when he was a toddler."

"You know," Sarah says, "we can probably cover the pillow with a pretty beachy fabric that would look cute in this room."

Sally looks pleased by the idea. "You girls are so crafty," she says. "Hopefully, you'll wear off on me, too. I'd love to learn how to sew."

Thomas and Matt work on the fireplace for about an hour when Thomas notices a loose stone. He pushes the stone in, and the built-in bookcase creaks open to reveal a hidden passageway. We are still clearing out the spare bedroom when we hear Thomas yelling. "Hey everybody, come here! I think we've found something!"

We run down the long corridor to find a super-excited Matt. "Look! Look, it's a cloaked walkway," he says, pointing to the secret door. "I wonder where it will lead us. Let's see what we can find."

Thomas turns on his cell phone flashlight. "Let's go. Everyone, follow me—and be careful. These old wooden stairs look pretty rickety."

He starts into the passageway, then calls out. "Boy, you can tell no one has been down here for years. Look at all these creepy spiderwebs." I hear him exactly at the same time I swipe a spider web from my face. It gives me a chill because I hate spiders.

As we start down the stairs, I spot some old-fashioned lanterns sitting on a ledge. I pick up one. "Hey, does anyone have any matches? It feels like there is fluid in these two. Do you think they will still work?"

Matt takes one of the lanterns from me and pulls a box of matches from his jeans pocket. "I guess we'll find out. Stand back just in case." He lights the straw-woven wick, and it sparks to life, illuminating the stairwell leading down into a long-forgotten hiding place.

Under the glow of the lantern, we make our way down the decrepit, creaky stairs. The air is stagnant and musty. A silvery spiderweb catches my forearm and I glance at it to see a large hairy spider looking back at me. "Yikes. I really don't like these spiders. They make me cringe," I say. "Do you think that this was one of Blackbeard's hiding places?"

David is enthralled by the secret hideaway. "Maybe so. It was rumored that he had to go into hiding when British soldiers were pursuing him. And this was supposedly his home—though it's not inconceivable that the house belonged to any of the other pirates who roamed the island at the time. Stephen Bonnet was another famous pirate of that time.

"Our family has owned this property since Roger Brown's family moved here in the 1700s," David continues. "It was built around the time that Blackbeard would have brought his ship, Queen Anne's Revenge, into Silver Lake. Or, as it was known at that time, Cockle Creek."

By the time we reach flat ground, Max has moved to the front of our search party, his nose sniffing at each step. Thomas laughs. "Go for it, boy. Let's see what we can find." We are walking on a packed dirt floor and the walls seem to be painted plaster. A few steps farther and Thomas exclaims, "Look, there is a door here on the right." He shines his cell phone flashlight ahead. "And doors to what looks like three more rooms. Look at these antique glass doorknobs," he says.

Matt reaches the room first and swings it open. "Hey, there's an old cot in here. Maybe Blackbeard and his crew did hide here. Or maybe even Calico Jack or Stephen Bonnet."

We all squeeze into the damp cubbyhole. Dust mites swirl in the dank space lit by the antiquated oil lantern. An old wooden wine barrel is set up in a corner of the room, clearly used long ago as a nightstand.

Emily picks up an old horsehair brush sitting on the old wine barrel, looking at it. "Wow, look at this old brush."

Sarah takes the brush from her. "Can you imagine using one of these? You must have gotten some of the horsehair in your hair when you used it."

Thomas reaches down to pick up a box from the nightstand. It looks like the other boxes we found earlier. He opens the lid. Evangeline appears before us.

"You are very close," she says. "Remember, 'You need only to look under the setting sun!'"

Emily points to a wall. A sunset picture hangs against its yellow plaster. "Do you think it's that simple? Try looking at the picture frame," she says. "Angie, remember in your dream how Roger gave Evangeline a picture frame where she could hide her journal? Maybe this is it. Look, I think this painting is signed."

Thomas lifts the picture from the wall and holds it in his tanned hands. "You might be right, Emily. It looks like there is a latch on the back of the frame," Thomas says. "If I press on this latch, maybe it will open. Bingo! Look at that."

We crowd around him to see what's inside. He pulls out a piece of paper.

"It's a piece of a treasure map on the back of another clue. And here's an old brass key." Thomas examines the key then reads the clue to us. "It says, 'Look under the anchor of the ship.' I can't believe we found a key to the treasure. But what ships are going to still be around now?" he says, disappointed. Thomas turns the key over in his palm and inspects it more closely. With that, Evangeline appears, grins, and winks at Thomas, and then evaporates before our eyes.

Paul, Isabella, and Mary smile at the latest find. Paul examines the key and the parchment paper stating, "Wow, this is crazy. I feel like we are getting so close to finding the treasure map."

Mary and Isabella hug Paul laughing at his enthusiasm. Isabella says, "I know what you mean, Dad. This is so exciting."

David reaches out and takes the drawing of the map and the key from Thomas. "What do you think, Paul? I'm going to put these back in the frame for safe keeping. This parchment paper looks very delicate. It could be damaged if we aren't careful," he says. "Do you think there are pieces of the map on the back of the other clues? Maybe we just didn't see them. We'll have to look when we get these back to the B&B."

Matt pulls out his cell phone. "I'll give the Whites a heads up that we are all coming over. That way Jim will have time to get the other clues out of the safe.

In the meantime, let's split up into groups of four and look for the next clue. We need to watch for an anchor."

Thomas pats his brother on the shoulder. "Why don't you and Emily come with Angie and me to search the room at the end of the hall."

Matt puts his arm around Sarah. "Yeah, that sounds good to me," he says. "Sarah, Robert, Sally, and I can look in the room next to this one. And Mom, David, Grandmom and Grandad can look in the room across from us. It's crazy that there are four bedrooms down here. Blackbeard must have had his whole crew hiding underground."

Mom grins and takes David by the hand, pulling him down the narrow passageway. "Here goes nothing. Wish you all luck. Maybe we'll find all the pieces of the map or, at least, another clue to toward solving this puzzle."

I follow Thomas into the last bedroom on the right. Emily and George are right behind me. "It's set up just like the first room," I say. "Hey, but this room has pictures of pirate ships. Sneaky, huh? Do you think Evangeline and Roger were the ones who hid the clues down here?"

George erupts into his hearty laugh, his blue eyes sparkling. "I'm thinking so. You know the two of them really did do a good job hiding all these clues. No wonder no one has ever found them."

We each take down from the wall one of the four framed paintings of pirate sloops. I spot a model of a pirate ship sitting on top of the old whiskey barrel. "You guys look at the frames. I'm going to check out this replica of a pirate ship."

I pick up the ship and search the area around the anchor. "Check this out, guys. This ship has two tiny anchors on it, one on the mast of the sloop and one on the hull. It can't be that easy."

I push on the mast but no hidden compartments open. I push and pull on the anchor on the mast without success. But as I trace my fingers along the other petite brass anchor, the bottom of the hull pops open. I squeal. "Look! It's another piece of parchment paper. Maybe another portion of the map."

I unroll the paper, being careful not to tear it. "It *is* a clue," I say, triumphantly. "Listen to this: 'Look to where the spirits flowed freely.'"

Emily laughs out loud. "Wouldn't it be funny if the last clue is right in our little pub? We will have to ask Paul what other bars were around during the time frame we focused on," she says. Emily looks toward the passageway. "I wonder what the others have found. We need to let them know about this clue," she says.

Thomas heads for the door with the clue and pirate ship in his muscular hands. "Sounds good to me. It's really dusty and moldy smelling down here. It's a little oppressive," he says. "Can you imagine having to hide down here for any length of time? It would have been miserable."

As we slip into the passageway, we meet up with my mom, David, Grandad, and Grandmom. Mom, eyes opened wide, clutches a pine frame holding a sketch. She holds the picture up to my face. "Oh my God, Angie. Everyone always said that you resembled Evangeline, but this is incredible. You two could be identical twins."

I take the sketch from her and look at it. "You aren't kidding. It's like looking in the mirror, except for the clothes and hairstyle. Look, this one was signed by Roger Brown, too."

Sarah opens her cell phone. "I'll call Mom and Dad to let them know we are coming over. Matt, I know you already called but I need to let Mom know that I had dinner sent over for us from SmacNally's. I hope seafood is okay with everyone. I just ordered a bunch of different appetizers and that steamed, spicy shrimp you all like."

She speaks with her father and hangs up her phone. "Dad says he'll get out the rest of the clues so we can take a look at them. And by the way, Paul, he loves the little cedar chest you bought to keep the clues in. He thought it was a hoot—and so appropriate."

Chapter 23

The Cellar

By the time we all head back to the Shepard's Head B&B, it is getting late in the day. I hear my stomach grumble. I haven't eaten since the breakfast Thomas made for me.

Georgia is at the inn when we arrive. Sally White is holding wiggling little Evie, who coos in her arms. Evie is alert to everything around her, and her bright blue eyes are diligently watching Sally White. Jacob sits in Jim's lap, also taking everything in. The babies both spot their parents, and their little lips quiver. They seem to be trying to say 'Mama' and 'Dada,' even though they are only three months old.

My sister reaches down to pick up sweet-tempered Jacob. "How's my little man doing? Are you being spoiled rotten?" His small head rests on Sally's chest, and he begins rooting for his next meal. Sally laughs. "I know, little fella. I bet you and your sister are getting hungry. That's why I pump all those bottles of milk for you two angels. I want you to be happy when I start back teaching.

"Georgia, is it time to feed them yet?" Sally asks.

Georgia holds up two empty bottles. "Not any time soon. They both just finished eating about a half an hour ago. Jim and Sally gave me a hand with the feeding after I changed the twins. So, you are all set to relax for a little while.

"Since you're back, though, I'm going to head over to the house and clean the twin's room," she adds. "If it's okay with you two, I was wondering if I might go see my niece tonight?"

Sally picks up her feisty, little fiery-headed Evie. Jim hands gentle blonde-haired Jacob to Robert. "Sure, thanks so much," Sally says to Georgia. "We're good here if you want to take the night off."

Georgia smiles. "That would be great. I should be back around 10 o'clock tonight."

Sally pats squirming Evie on the back. "Sounds good to me. Have fun and tell Rosie 'hello' from us. Tell her to stop by sometime. We would love to see her."

Jim has spread the clues across the parlor table. "I laid them out in the order that we found them, just in case that might help," he explains.

We gather around the table and turn each of the clues over. Thomas takes out the last clue we found—the piece from the model of the pirate ship—and holds it while he looks at the tabletop. "Well, look at that. The clues all have drawings on the back of them," he says. "Let's see if we can put them together like a puzzle. Maybe it will form a map."

As we work, a bigger picture does start to take shape. Paul places the last piece down to almost complete the map. "Look at that," my grandfather says. "It looks like an island of some sort."

He studies the sketch for a minute. "I wonder if we use Google Lens, if it will tell us what island this is?" he asks.

I scratch my head. "I think I know. Last night I dreamed of Evangeline and William. Daniel said that they were on Cat Island. Could the map be Cat Island?"

Paul snaps a picture with his cell phone and laughs with delight. "These cell phones are great. I'll just Google Lens it and see what we come up with."

I watch over his shoulder. "That's it! It is Cat Island," I say. "The Bahamas, that makes sense. You know they were famous for pirates. But we still need to figure out the latest clue to finish the map."

Emily winks at me. "I think it's hidden in our bar somewhere, maybe the wine cellar. Wouldn't that be cool if it has been right under our noses all this time?" Emily looks at her watch and then at me. "But right now, we need to eat before we go get ready for work, Angie. Are you feeling up to it today?"

I hold my head. "I'm fine. My head stopped hurting hours ago. And it'll be good to be up on the stage. I'm going to sing the new song about Evangeline and Jacob that I finished the other night."

Out on the veranda, Sarah has had the staff from SmacNally's set up a seafood feast. The spicy aroma of steamed shrimp wafts through the air and makes my mouth water. "Thanks, Sarah. This looks great," I tell her. "I can't wait to try those red drum fish bites or the calamari."

I pick up a fish bite and pop it into my mouth. "Yum, this is heavenly. Apparently, there is nothing wrong with my appetite."

We polish off our early dinner, and I tell everyone that I need to get changed for work.

Thomas takes my hand in his. "I'll walk you back to the cottage," he says. "George and Matt, are you coming too? If Angie's going to work, Matt, maybe you and I can go back over to David's and get moving on the renovation. George, I know you have to go back to Hatteras to finish that job."

George looks at Emily. "Yeah, and I guess I need to get my stuff and take it back home," he tells her. "This has been so weird, but it's even weirder going back home. "Guess you'll get your house all back to yourself again, lady."

Emily grins and pats George on the shoulder. "I really appreciated you staying with me. It was kind of nice having you around all the time."

George shrugs his shoulders, blushing. "I know, right? I guess I'll see you guys later tonight at the pub."

As we walk back to our cottage, Thomas gets a sheepish look on his face then asks me: "Do you really want me to stay? I don't want you to feel pressured or anything. I know things are moving pretty fast."

I turn, take his face in my hands, and look into those brilliant green eyes of his. "I know it seems crazy, but I can't imagine my life without you in it. I want you here with me."

Thomas brushes his lips gently on mine. "Me too." He pushes a piece of my curly black hair behind my ear. "Angie, you just don't know how scared I was when you went missing. I was so afraid you were lost to me forever. It ripped my heart into shreds when I realized you had been taken."

I stroke his cheek, his chin, and hungrily pull his lips toward mine again. "Well, you saved me and I'm safe. I'm not going anywhere. My heart belongs to you." I drag him toward the door, grinning. "I have an hour before I need to go get ready to play in the pub."

He swats me on my bottom as we walk through the screen door, and then he wraps his arms around me. Suddenly he picks me up and carries me into the bedroom. He reaches down and takes each of my fingers up to his lips. He suckles them, making me squirm in delight. His mouth makes its way up my arm, finally reaching my neck. His strong hands caress me, and his lips move away to tantalize my nipples. Passion erupts between us, and I wrap my legs around his tanned muscular waist. I melt into his arms. We linger in each other's arms for a short while, not wanting to end this special moment.

I slide out of bed. "I guess I better get a shower and dress for work. Care to join me?"

He laughs. "Now that's an invitation I can't turn down." The water bubbles in the shower make our skin slick and reignite our rapture. Moaning in delight, we hold on to each other, letting the warm water roll off our bodies. We finish our shower not wanting to leave each other's arms.

As he finishes dressing, Thomas sits to tie his white Nike tennis shoes. He looks up at me and then stands and kisses me tenderly on my lips. "See you tonight. I'll stop by the tavern when I get off later."

Thomas puts the leash on an excited Max. "Come on, boy. Time to go to work." I reach down to pet the dog's fluffy ears and receive wet kisses from him in return.

I close the door behind them and gaze around at the new home that I already cherish. I touch the heart-shaped pendant on my silver necklace. Evangeline and Jacob appear with arms wrapped around each other. "Fear not, Angie. Thomas will make you happy. You have truly found true love."

They fade from my vision, leaving me awestruck. I grab my bag, guitar, and phone. I head out the door. How lucky I am to have such a wonderful life and to have met Thomas. I can't help but smile when I think about him. I make my way over to the pub just as Emily is arriving.

Emily takes one look at me and laughs. "You look like you're floating on air. You look so happy."

I hug myself. "I don't remember ever being this happy, Emily. I've fallen head-over-heels in love. It's so weird—to think that I only met him three months ago, and yet I feel like I've known him forever."

Emily just grins at me. "I knew it. I always knew in my heart that you would hit it off with Thomas. I'm so happy for you guys."

I rest my guitar against my trusty guitar stand on the little wooden stage. "What time do you want me to start playing?" I ask. "It looks pretty empty right now. Do you need help setting up the bar?"

Emily wipes down the bar counter. "Sure, I can always use help. Why don't you make some more Oxford Brew? Everyone loves the way you make it, and it's such a big hit this time of year. Probably you can start playing around 4:30 or 5 p.m. That's when the dinner crowd starts coming in."

"Sounds good to me." I walk behind the bar and grab the coconut rum. "Are the juices still in the fridge in the kitchen?"

Emily nods. "Yeah. I haven't had a chance to get anything out yet. If you don't mind, can you bring the lemons, limes, and juices when you come back?"

George shows up a little while later after finishing his job on Hatteras Island. "Hey girls. How are you doing?"

Emily smiles up at him. "Doing good. How's my favorite old roommate doing?"

George looks sad. He sits down on one of the bar stools. "I'm good, too. I guess this time tomorrow I won't be your roommate any longer."

Emily turns her back to him to hide a tear that has welled up in her eye. "I know you weren't at my house that long, but I kind of liked having you around. I'm going to miss you."

George perks up. "Aw, that's so sweet, Emily."

Thomas also arrives. "Hey George, girls. How's it going around here?"

George shrugs. "We were just talking about me moving out of Emily's place."

Thomas squeezes George on the shoulder and grins at me. "Angie, did you tell them yet or should I?"

I blush. "No, I hadn't gotten around to it yet. I wanted to wait for you first. Thomas is going to stay with me. We decided to make it permanent. I know it's early, but we just thought it felt right."

Emily squeals and comes around the bar to give Thomas and me a big hug. "How exciting. I'm so happy for the two of you."

Thomas turns to George. "Hey brother, I know it's short notice. I hope it's good with you. Maybe you can change my room into your home office like you've always wanted to do. I even know a good contractor who can give you a hand with that."

George swats Thomas on the back. "Congratulations, brother. And a home office to boot, who could complain about that?" And then he hugs me. "Angie, I'm so happy that you two got together. You've always been just like family to me."

Matt and Sarah arrive in the midst of the congratulations. Matt raises his hands. "Hey, what's going on? Did I miss something?"

I drape my arms around Matt and Sarah. "Thomas and I decided that he will keep living with me. He's not moving back to George's house."

Matt laughs. "That's awesome. I was wondering about that myself." Sarah looks straight into my bright blue eyes. "I knew it. I just knew you two would make a great couple."

Yellow specks sparkle in Thomas's forest green eyes. He wraps his arm around me. "I know it's fast, but it just feels right," he tells me. "I hope your Mom will be okay with it," he adds.

Matt laughs. "Are you kidding me, Thomas? I think she likes you better than me."

George teases Emily. "I asked Emily to come live with me but she's way too independent," he says. "Still, we should probably stay vigilant about the girls' safety. You never know if there are others out there like Rusty and Ricky."

Sarah turns around and sees Sally and Robert coming into the pub with the twins. She says in a low voice, "I can't wait to hear what your sister will say about you two. She's going to be thrilled."

The twins are growing so fast, and their individual personalities are already emerging. It is fun to watch them interact with others and each other. Labor Day has come and gone, and autumn weather has brought chilly air in the evenings. I watch baby Jacob reach his chubby little arms out and follow his gaze. In the corner of the pub, I see Evangeline with Jacob's arm around her. They are watching us and smiling at the twins.

Sally follows her son's line of vision and sees the same vision. "You just don't know how comforting it is to have those two guarding us. Almost like guardian angels, especially for the twins. Who would have thought it?"

She looks at us and can tell something is up. Sarah and Emily are grinning like the cat that swallowed the canary. "So, what's going on around here?" Sally demands.

Emily can't contain herself. "Tell them, Angie."

I put my hands over my face, blushing. "Well, I'm just going to spit it out. Thomas isn't going to move out. He's going to stay with me permanently," I say. "We know it's really early in our relationship, but we decided it just feels right." I know I am babbling but can't help myself.

Sally shifts sweet little Evie in her arms and looks at the baby. "Can you believe your aunt was worried about what I would think?" She leans over to put an arm around me. "Angie, I couldn't be happier for you guys. Under the circumstances and with everything you have been through, it makes so much sense. I wonder what Mom will say?"

"I really don't think we need to worry about it," Matt replies. "She loves Thomas like a son. I think she just wants Angie to be happy. I am ecstatic that all of our family will be living on the island. Whoever could have thought that would happen?"

"Landing jobs—for the both of us—and getting a contract on our house at the same time?" Sally says. "What are the odds?"

Robert perks up. "Well, what about Isabella and my dad getting contracts on their homes, too? It's as if fate had a hand in bringing us back to the island. It's always been a dream of Sally and mine to move here. And now it's happening."

I nod in agreement. "Well, like Evangeline said, 'The time is right.' Maybe this is what she was talking about when she came to Dad last summer. Maybe we were all meant to move here and make Ocracoke Island our home. Maybe the twins were meant to be born here and I was meant to meet Thomas. Who knows what she meant by it? I guess everything had to align so that we could find all these clues that will lead us to Blackbeard's treasure."

I look at my watch and step up on the little stage. "This song goes out to my new niece and nephew," I tell the crowd. "I hope you all like it. I sent it to my agent in Maryland back in July. She loves my songs."

I pick up my guitar and the music flows out of me. I look up and see that Sally has tears in her eyes when I sing the song about their twins. When I finish, I announce that my next song is a brand new one I just finished. It's about Evangeline and Jacob. I give the crowd an abbreviated version of their tragic love story before I start to sing.

When I go on break, my sister comes up to me. "Oh, Angie, I just love it when you sing that song about the twins. It's perfect. I can't wait for them to grow up so that they can listen to it themselves."

"And don't forget that the royalties will go into a trust for them for their college funds or whatever," I point out. "My agent said that the song has made its way up the ladder. It is already in the Top Five."

"Really? That's so cool. How many aunts can do that? Thanks so much." Sally kisses little Evie on her belly making her coo in delight. "We need to get these two little angels' home to their cribs. It's getting past their bedtime. Robert and I need to get a good night's sleep, too. We have to go to school tomorrow!"

She turns to all of us. "It will be so good to start teaching again. I always miss it when I am off for the summer," Sally says. "We'll see you all tomorrow."

Robert helps Sally pack up the twins, holding Jacob, who is looking around in wonder. Little Evie squirms in Sally's arms. The babies have such different dispositions. I love watching them grow.

Matt grabs Sarah by the hand. "Let's go for a walk. It's such a pretty night. The beach should be nice tonight."

Chapter 24

The Proposal

The moon shines brightly over Silver Lake. A gentle warm breeze blows over the dunes as Sarah and Matt walk down the beach. Matt points to a spot between the dunes. "Let's play a game," he says. "Do you remember when we were kids how we used to search for buried treasure?"

Sarah grins. "Of course, I remember. How could I forget? Those were such fun and happy times."

Matt looks nervous. "I hid something for you up there," he says. "See that conch shell? Go over and pick it up." Inside the shell, Matt has hidden a beautiful diamond solitaire ring.

Sarah reaches down to pick up the shell and spots a sparkling flash in the moonlight. She pulls the diamond out of its hiding spot, at first puzzled and then overwhelmed.

"Matt, what's this?" Her hand covers her mouth not believing her eyes. She turns around to see Matt kneeling on one knee.

Matt takes the ring from Sarah's hand and places it on her ring finger. "Sarah, I love you. I have always loved you ever since we were children racing up and down the beach with the wind in our hair. Will you be mine, forever?"

Before Matt can finish, Sarah kneels down in the sand, taking him into her arms. She knocks him over backwards in the sand and laughs. "Oh Matt, yes! Yes! I love you, too. I have always loved you. It has been my dream to be your wife."

Sarah kisses Matt while tears of joy roll down her cheeks.

Matt kisses Sarah with a passion that overwhelms the two of them. His finger gently wipes the tears from her face. "Sarah, I remember the first time I saw you on the beach. I was only six years old. You were chasing a seagull down on the shore. Your hair was shining in the sunlight, and you turned around and smiled at me.

"I knew then that one day I would be your husband," he says. "I know how crazy that sounds but it's true."

Sarah looks down at the dazzling diamond ring and then up into Matt's glistening cobalt blue eyes. "Matt, you have no idea how many times that I have dreamed about us getting married. It's surreal. You've made me so happy."

They hold hands as they walk a bit further, and Matt lays out a blanket for them in a little cove between the dunes. "Let's sit here and watch for falling stars," he says. "Remember that night when I first kissed you? That was my wish that night. To make you mine."

Sarah passionately moves her lips to Matt's. "That's so romantic. That's what I wished for, too," she says. "I never knew you were so sentimental. You have always been so aloof. I'm seeing a whole new side of you."

Sarah wraps her arms around Matt, sliding her sundress off her shoulders. "Make love to me, Matt. I don't want to wait any longer. I want to be yours."

Matt rolls over and takes Sarah in his arms. His hands caress her slender frame. He rolls on top of her, and they become one. "I love you, Sarah. We have such an amazing future ahead of us."

They linger in each other's arms, savoring the moment as a cool breeze caresses their warm bodies. Sarah loves the feel of Matt's strong arms around her body. She leans back against his muscular frame, happier than she has ever felt, and looks up into the starry sky and points. "Look, it's another falling star. Make a wish."

She smiles to herself, thinking that her wish has already been granted.

Matt kisses her earlobes and neck. It makes her shiver. "My first wish was to make you mine," he says. "I wish now to grow old with you and watch our children grow up. I can't wait to see what our babies will look like."

Sarah feels like she had gone to heaven. She turns in Matt's arms with her breasts touching his body, moving on top of him to make him hers once more. Later, laying together, she says, "Nothing could make me happier than I am now. I can't wait to tell the others that we are getting married."

Matt pulls a blanket around them and, snuggling up, he wraps his arms around Sarah. "Speaking of getting married, when do you want to plan our wedding?" he asks. "Let's not wait too long. I'd marry you tomorrow if I could, but when I asked your dad and mom for permission to marry you, your mom said she couldn't wait to see you as a bride."

Sarah laughs. "You asked my parents for my hand in marriage? That's so sweet. Were they caught off guard?"

Matt shakes his head. "Surprisingly, not. I think that they knew as soon as we got together that it would only be a matter of time," he says. "I didn't say anything to the girls, but I did tell Thomas and George. I wanted to know if they thought it was too soon. They were so keen on the idea that I was afraid they'd let it slip."

Sarah looks at her watch. "I don't want this night to end, but I have an early start tomorrow. One of the girls asked for tomorrow off and I told her I would take her shift. What type of day do you guys have tomorrow?"

Matt pulls on his jeans. "We have some things to do in David's home. We are supposed to meet up at around 6."

Sarah and Matt walk back to the inn, hand-in-hand, not wanting the night to end. He gives her a passionate kiss. "Just think, soon I won't have to kiss you goodbye. I can just roll over with you in my arms and kiss you goodnight."

Sarah smiles. "What about a Valentine's Day wedding—or even sooner? Think about it." Sarah blows Matt a kiss, then moves—as if floating—through the front door of the inn and up the winding staircase. Evangeline and Jacob look down at her from the top of the staircase, smiling, then turn and disappear into a mist. Sarah waves at them and whispers. "Thank you for sending Matt back to me."

Down in the pub, Emily, George, Thomas, and I are wrapping up the night. Matt arrives just as we are getting done. Thomas beams and says, "I think we need to celebrate. How often do I move in with a beautiful, accomplished musician who has swept me away? How about a bonfire on the beach?"

"I think that's a great idea!" Emily says. "I think wine is in order. What do you guys think about a little chardonnay? I can go down in the wine cellar and pick us out a bottle or two."

I go around the bar and grab some wine glasses. "Sounds like a great idea to me. A bonfire, great friends, and wine on a warm night. What a way to celebrate.

"Did you guys see that moon tonight?" I continue. "I hear it's supposed to get colder tomorrow. A cold front is coming."

George comes around to the wine cellar door and opens it for Emily. "I can give you a hand if you want. After you, my dear."

Emily's laughter rings out as they start down the stairs into the vault. "Maybe we'll find the other clue. We haven't had a chance to look yet." George grins back at her. "You never know what's going to happen."

Emily turns to George. "Well for now let's find a nice crisp white wine to celebrate Thomas and Angie's good news."

As Emily walks down into the cellar, she feels a chill against her ear. She recognizes Evangeline's voice whispering in her ear. "Look to where the spirits flowed freely," Evangeline says.

George is surprised to see Evangeline materialize before them briefly—then evaporate.

"Did you hear that? She wants us to look here," Emily says.

"You were right," George says. "Maybe we should get the others to help us. I'll go get them. You start looking."

Emily hands George the wine to take upstairs. Then she does a 360-degree turn. "Now, where should I look?" she wonders. "I've been down here a thousand times. Whatever we're searching for has to be somewhere that would have been around two hundred years ago."

Emily looks over and around where the kegs and the wine larders are kept. She moves her hands across the old wooden beams that hold the wine bottles. Then she notices a latch that she has never seen before. Her hand slides under the fastening and the wine rack creaks open to reveal a hidden passageway.

She squeals in delight and hollers up the stairs. "You aren't going to believe this, but I found another hidden passageway to an underground room!"

We fly down the stairs just as Emily opens wide the door into the hidden space. Thomas grabs one of the flashlights hanging on the wine cellar wall and moves into the passageway. We follow him down the musky steps under the pub. When we reach the bottom, we are in a vestibule with a wooden door at its end. Behind the old door, we find a tiny bed and a barrel holding a candle. Beside the candle is a small cedar box just like the others we have found.

Thomas opens the wooden coffer and shines the flashlight at its contents. It holds a beautiful diamond ring, a large ruby, and a sparkly red garnet. Evangeline's presence fills the tiny room. "You are close to finding the final piece of the treasure map," we hear her say before she laughs. "The final piece has been under your noses all these years. You have only to look on the walls in the parlor."

Evangeline disappears as her laughter rings through the stale, airless room.

I look at the others. "You've got to be kidding me. There is a clue hidden on the walls of the B&B? We've got to go look right now! The bonfire will have to wait."

We race up the stairs from the wine cellar, through the door, and into the B&B. My grandparents and the Whites are startled when we come running in. Jim hollers, "Where's the fire? What's happening?"

As we scatter to examine different areas of the room, Emily explains: "We found the other clue. It was in the wine cellar all along. Evangeline came to us and told us the last piece of the treasure map was here in the parlor, right under our noses. She says to look on the walls of the parlor."

Emily glances up over the fireplace and points to a picture that has been hanging over the mantel for as many years as anyone can remember. "Hey, that picture is a map. That's it! Can you believe it?"

George and Thomas reach up to lift the painting down. I look at the signature. "Did you realize this was signed by Roger Brown?" I ask. "It definitely looks like the pieces of the map of Cat Island in the Bahamas. It was named after

Arthur Cat, who was said to be a friend of Blackbeard. I read that other pirates used to take up refuge on the island when they were hiding from the authorities."

Emily points to details in the painting. "Look at these landmarks. There is even a waterfall like you had in your dream, Angie."

"I know," I reply. "Do you think that mark there by the waterfall is where the treasure will be hidden?" I point to an X on the map.

Sarah has heard all the commotion and she comes rushing into the parlor. "What's going on? I was getting ready for bed, and it sounded like a herd of elephants were running around down here. I thought I heard someone screaming." She looks at the painting laid out on the table.

"Is that what I think it is?" she continues. "I walk by that picture every day. I have dusted it so many times." Sarah points to the different landmarks and her dazzling new diamond ring captures the light.

Emily and I wail out in delight as Matt put his arm around Sarah. "Surprise, girls. Sarah and I are getting married."

We gather around the happy couple to congratulate them. It is a joyous gathering, and Sarah's parents beam at the two lovebirds. Tears well up in the eyes of Sarah's mother, Sally, as she sees how happy her daughter is about being engaged to Matt. "I'm so happy for the two of you," she says.

Sarah holds up her hand to show the girls her new ring.

"He surprised me on our walk tonight. Isn't it gorgeous? Can you believe it?" she says. "We're getting married! But first there is a treasure to find—or maybe we should combine both."

We all laugh.

"I guess we'll be planning a trip to Cat Island," I say. "Weddings and treasure hunting sound great to me."

Acknowledgments

I would like to take this opportunity to express my heartful gratitude to the following people who encouraged me to continue writing my novel. Many thanks to my friends Wendy Schofield, Kelly Foster, Peggy Durney, Joanne Crowley, Margaret Hayes, Patty Miller, and Teresa Simpson-Garriott, who have supported me and offered many welcome helpful suggestions.

I can't say thank you enough to my mom and dad, Doris and Dave Pipes, who encouraged me to continue working toward my dream of becoming an author. And on that note, a grand thanks to my father-in-law, Harvey Gagne, who also supported me and encouraged me to continue to keep working on this long project.

Also special thanks to my Uncle Con, Harry Knott, for always asking me when the next novel was coming out because he wanted to read it. You helped to prompt me to continue to pursue my dream of completing the sequel.

I would like to thank my siblings, Theresa Ferree, Debbie Herman, and Jason Long for encouraging me to finish writing this book and its sequel, *Cat Island: The Search for Blackbeard's Treasure,* which is part of The Pirate Series.

Warm and sincere thanks to my niece, Katie Ferree, for doing the beautiful illustrations, family tree, my logo, and book cover. You do extraordinary work and are extremely talented. I look forward to your help in the upcoming books.

I can't forget about my editor, Mary Dempsey, who took the time to guide and support me on this journey to becoming, hopefully, a successful author. Thank you so much for all your encouragement and guidance.

Last, but not least, a special thanks to my husband, Matt Gagne, who encouraged me to continue writing and pursuing my dream of becoming an author.

About the Author

After forty years of nursing, with more than thirty of them as a dialysis nurse, I retired in May 2023 to pursue my dream of being an author. *Evangeline Shores of Forever* is the first book of The Pirates Series. I started writing this novel six years ago, and the first edition came out in 2018 to coincide with the 300th anniversary of Blackbeard's execution. I decided to revise the first edition after suggestions from friends and family who have supported me over the years. I completed a sequel last summer and its editing will be wrapped up later this year. I hope you enjoy my novel as much as I have enjoyed writing it.

Made in the USA
Middletown, DE
21 July 2023